DETERMINED RIDERS

As soon as she found out that the Bitter Creek Jake Tulley gang was hanging out with her uncles in Jury Wells, Rebecca knew what she had to do.

"Sam," she urged, "we're going to Jury Wells."

"That makes three of us," Lone Wolf put in. He turned the head of his war pony. "Why don't you two ride along the main road. I'll keep off to the side in case somethin' happens."

"What could happen?" Sam asked in innocence.

"Anything," Rebecca quickly interjected. "If you knew Tulley like we do, Sam, you'd know." She glanced at the white warrior. "We'll see you outside of Jury Wells."

Half an hour from Jury Wells, Rebecca glanced at the side of the road and tried to spot Lone Wolf in the underbrush. There. She saw him instantly, like any proper Oglala woman. She turned away and continued to ride.

"We're almost there," Sam told her.

Without warning, two drifters burst from the cover of some nearby bushes, edging up to Rebecca and Sam before they had time to react.

"Oh, Christ!" Sam stammered. "Do what they tell you, Rebecca."

Like hell, she thought.

"Hold it right there!" snapped a lean, scruffy road agent. He gripped a four-and-three-quarter-inch Peacemaker, leveled at the young couple. "One move and you're both dead."

THE CONTINUING **SHELTER** SERIES
BY PAUL LEDD

#10: MASSACRE MOUNTAIN   (972, $2.25)
A pistol-packin' lady suspects Shell is her enemy—and her gun isn't the only thing that goes off!

#11: RIO RAMPAGE   (1141, $2.25)
Someone's put out a ten grand bounty on Shell's head. And it takes a wild ride down the raging rapids of the Rio Grande before Shell finds his man—and finds two songbirds in the bush as well!

#12: BLOOD MESA   (1181, $2.25)
When Apaches close in around him, Shell thinks his vengeance trail is finally over. But he wakes up in the midst of a peaceful tribe so inclined toward sharing—that he sees no reason to decline the leader's daughter when she offers her bed!

#13: COMANCHERO BLOOD   (1208, $2.25)
Shelter is heading straight into a Comanchero camp, where the meanest hombres in the West are waiting for him—with guns drawn. The only soft spot is Lita, a warm senorita whose brother is the leader of the Comanchero outlaws!

WHITE SQUAW
#1
SIOUX WILDFIRE
BY E. J. HUNTER

ZEBRA BOOKS
KENSINGTON PUBLISHING CORP.

ZEBRA BOOKS

are published by

KENSINGTON PUBLISHING CORP.
475 Park Avenue South
New York, N.Y. 10016

Printed in the United States of America

This one is for Dick House, who knows what the West was all about.

It is better to die on the battlefield
than to live to be old.
                    — Traditional maxim of Sioux existence.

Oglala squaws consider their life a servitude,
and being beaten at times like animals and
receiving no sort of sympathy, it acts upon them
accordingly.
                    — From: *MY CAPTIVITY AMONG THE SIOUX
                            INDIANS*, by Fanny Kelly, 1864.

ONE

Rebecca Caldwell clung to the afternoon shadows and listened to the voices in the stables. Her heart pounded in anticipation of what she knew would come.

She checked her surroundings then dashed from the alley. She reached the outer wall of the livery and pressed her back against the rough-hewn timber. The voices grew clearer.

"Come on, Shannon," wheedled a woman inside the livery. "How 'bout a little romp in the hay?"

"I wish I had time, sweetheart," a man returned. "But that's been the story of my life. Beautiful women and no time to enjoy 'em."

With a steady hand Rebecca reached into the beaded pouch belted at the waist of her elkskin squaw's dress and extracted a Smith and Wesson "Little Russian" .38 revolver from within. The short-barreled, double-action six-shooter had been her first acquisition after her escape.

Rebecca took a deep breath. She was about to kill a man, by no means her first, and her stomach knotted in anticipation. She'd killed twice before, both times in self-defense, while living with the Oglala Sioux. This time it would be for sweet revenge.

Nineteen-year-old Rebecca Caldwell was a half-breed, the product of her mother's rape by an Oglala warrior. Her lustrous black hair and high cheekbones radiantly emphasized her mixed bloodline. Only her sparkling blue eyes hinted at her Caldwell lineage.

A week after her fourteenth birthday, Rebecca and her mother had been traded to the Oglala by her two rapacious uncles and a gang of outlaws. They'd been given away as an afterthought, along with half a dozen repeating rifles and two kegs of whiskey. Five years of captivity and her mother's death in the Oglala camp had left the half-breed burning with a desire for vengeance.

After her escape a month ago, Rebecca's search for the vile men responsible for her half-decade of living hell had taken her across miles of treacherous prairie and to some of northern Nebraska's shadiest dives. But now, learning that one of the owlhoots was in Bazile Mills, Rebecca was on the prowl near the stables.

She could almost taste her revenge!

Rebecca edged closer to the livery's big double doors. Her fingers tightened around the rounded butt of the Little Russian. She padded toward her prey with practiced stealth.

"Oooh, stop that, Ed!" moaned the giggling girl inside the stables.

"Hummm. Just a preview of what's in store for ya, honey, after I finish off this here clodhopper. Shouldn't take me more'n a minute or two."

"Please be careful."

Shannon gave a sardonic laugh. "My shotgun takes care of me, honey."

Ed Shannon! Rebecca knew the name well. The familiar, hated voice left no doubt of his identity.

Five years ago, Shannon, the rest of the Tulley gang and her uncles, Ezekial and Virgil, had dragged Rebecca and her screaming mother from their modest sod house into the light of a hopeless future. They'd given Rebecca to the Oglala and consigned her to a life as a slave.

Ed Shannon. The name was like poison on Rebecca's lips.

Before that awful day, she wouldn't have recognized Shannon if she had bumped into him on the street. Now, the pretty half-breed knew the raw killer's face like every ridge of work-hardened callus that scarred her hands. He had robbed, raped and murdered across Nebraska and the Dakota Territory for nine years. She had learned that the vicious bandit's cold, evil eyes and his sawed-off Parker shotgun sent shivers down the spines of settlers from Omaha to Denver. And now the stocky badman's face had become etched forever in her mind. *Hollow cheeks, yellowed teeth, cold gray eyes* and *stringy brown hair that touched the shoulders of his white linen duster.*

Ed Shannon She'd finally caught up with him.

Rebecca gripped her .38 Smith and Wesson and prepared to burst into the livery. Then she heard footsteps from the alley behind her. She ducked back into the shadows formed by a tacked-on room and held her breath.

"Hey, Ed!" cried a lean scarecrow of a man.

Rebecca watched the drifter pound on the livery's double doors. "Come on, Shannon! That there plowboy's out there just beggin' to get sieved."

Rebecca heard a commotion from inside the stable. She watched the doors swing open and saw a slender, red-headed woman step daintily from the odorous barn. The gaudily dressed carrot-top swivel-hipped toward main street.

"Hold on, Jed," Ed Shannon called from inside. A moment later the notorious outlaw stepped from the livery.

Rebecca peered cautiously through the brightness at the

short-barreled Parker in Shannon's hands. In mounting fury she looked upon his hollow cheeks, bloodshot eyes and greasy shoulder-length hair. She flattened her body against the wall to avoid detection.

"That sodbuster's waitin' for you on main street."

"The boy's that anxious to die, eh, Jed?"

Jed emitted a low chuckle. "Hell, when are them sodbusters gonna learn not to mess with ya, Shannon? Seems like every punk in Nebraska is just achin' to go up against your scattergun."

"Yeah." Shannon gusted out a heavy sigh. "I'm gettin' too old for this, Jed."

"Naw! You just get better."

Rebecca watched Ed Shannon flex his shoulders and take a deep breath. Then the stocky outlaw headed toward the dusty main street of Bazile Mills.

Tentatively she raised her six-shooter and aimed at a spot between the departing killer's shoulder blades. A cold smile turned up the corners of her full, lush lips. Then the former Sioux squaw lowered her pistol.

She told herself that the range was wrong for her little pistol. But she knew she couldn't shoot a man in the back. Especially Ed Shannon. No. Rebecca wanted to look into the eyes of the man who had sent her into captivity. She wanted to see his reaction when she told him who she was . . . then kill him.

Rebecca watched Shannon disappear around the corner. Then the dark-haired girl pushed away from the livery wall and followed in his wake. Apparently Shannon was about to engage in a shootout. She hoped he survived.

She wanted him all for herself.

The silent-moving white squaw reached the mouth of the alley and peeked at Bazile Mills' suddenly quiet main street. She saw a nervous young farmboy who was standing fifty feet away. Nearer, his back to her, Ed Shannon lounged against a tie-rail, his shotgun at his side. All of the farm

10

town's five or six high-fronted buildings poised in the quiet of a church before a funeral.

Rebecca glided out of the alley and pressed against the shingled front of the Bazile Mills General Mercantile. Still gripping her revolver, she listened to some idlers from inside the shop.

"Hell, a shotgun against a six-shooter," deprecated one man. "Why, that Denison kid ain't got a chance!"

"Not the way Shannon handles that scattergun," a companion agreed. "And I reckon the boy ain't never seen him use it. He'd sure light a shuck iffin he had."

Rebecca noticed a man watching her, his lips curled in distaste. "Get off the street, squaw!" he yelled.

"Why, look at that!" a woman inside the store exclaimed. "A white squaw all dolled up in her best elkskin dress. Who does she think she is?"

"Wonder where her buck is?" the elegantly dressed man next to her rumbled. "Shameless woman, livin' with a stinkin' damn redstick."

"Git, Injun, before Shannon kills you instead!" Jed yelled at her.

The townspeople laughed.

Rebecca strode purposefully to the corner of the next building. Inwardly she seethed with suppressed anger. Since her escape from the Sioux she'd never become used to the jeers of white folk. In fact, at times she felt like a woman without a race—the Oglala had treated her like worthless property and the whites scorned her. And it had been white people who had given her away. For a moment, anger flared at this spate of unwarranted insults. It threatened to shatter the calm coolness in which she had wrapped herself to face Ed Shannon and kill him.

"Y—you . . . you killed my Paw!" cried the farmboy. Rebecca figured the boy was no more than in his mid-teens. "Now . . . Now I'm gonna make you pay for it."

"You'd best be headin' on home, kid," Shannon warned.

He still held the shotgun casually at his side.

"Like hell!" snapped the teenager.

The gunfight ended with startling quickness.

The youthful farm lad reached for his aged Le Mat 9mm pin-fire revolver. Before his hand touched the butt, Shannon arced his shotgun upward and tripped both triggers.

Rebecca winced as a handful of marble-sized shot slammed into the teenager's chest and face. The impact of the double-oh buckshot blasts lifted the youngster off his feet. He landed in a dusty heap, his bloodied face a mass of shredded flesh.

Shannon's gunshots echoed from building fronts.

While the sulphurous stench of spent gunpowder filled the air, a man standing in the parted batwings of a nearby saloon applauded. "Good shootin', Ed!" he cried.

"Yeah. Nice shot," Jed agreed.

Rebecca remained in the shadows and watched Ed Shannon stroll over to the dead lad's body. He bent and removed a five dollar gold piece from the boy's vest pocket. Rebecca compressed her lips into a grim line of determination and slipped her finger onto the trigger of the Little Russian.

Shannon turned on his heel and headed toward the livery stable. Rebecca saw a dozen chattering townsfolk pour out of the buildings and flock around the dead youngster's crumpled corpse.

Rebecca began to stalk her prey.

Halfway to the stables, Rebecca watched Shannon enter an alley. The outlaw paused and fed brass shells into the chambers of his scattergun.

Rebecca entered the narrow passage and stopped twenty feet behind him.

"*Mister* Shannon!" she cried. Her words had the effect of pistol shots.

Ed Shannon whirled around, his double-barreled Parker

arched upward in readiness, pointed at Rebecca's pretty face.

A tense moment passed between them.

"Don't you recognize me, Mr. Shannon?"

Shannon's stubbled face brightened and he lowered his shotgun. "Uh, I ain't been called Mr. Shannon since the last time I faced a judge." He produced a lascivious grin. "But I do declare, sweetheart, you're a helluva lot purtier than that old gavel pounder."

Shannon walked closer. Rebecca's pulse quickened.

"I'm disappointed," she told him. "Have I changed that much in five years?" She held her hands at her sides. Relentlessly her blue eyes bored into Shannon's ugly face.

Rebecca could almost hear the killer's brain working behind his puzzled expression. "I don't rightly recall when we met, sweetheart." He stood only an arm's length away now.

"Think on it," she taunted. "Five years ago. On the old Caldwell ranch. You, Jake Tulley and the others gave a teenaged half-breed and her mother to the Sioux."

A flicker of recognition passed over Shannon's face. "Yeah. I remember now. Injuns had us penned up in the house. Was them folks your kin?" Shannon eyed her costume, already suspecting the truth.

Rebecca glared at him and, after a few seconds the gun-hawk produced a wicked grin.

"You mean you're . . ."

". . . the half-breed," Rebecca completed for him.

They stared at each other for a long moment. Rebecca's deep blue eyes studied Shannon's hollow cheeks, yellowed teeth and cold gray eyes. She felt a tremor of excitement ripple through her stomach as Shannon scanned her tight-fitting elkskin dress.

"You sure have changed!" he opined.

"You haven't," Rebecca spat.

"Somehow, sweetheart, I get the feelin' this ain't no social call."

Rebecca's voice turned to ice. "I'm here to give you what you deserve for handing my mother and me over to the Oglala. And when I finish with you, I'm going to find Jake Tulley and all the others."

A nervous tic displayed itself at the corner of Shannon's mouth. "When you finish?" he repeated, breaking into a fit of laughter.

Rebecca stifled a tremor of rage as the shotgun-toting killer's harsh laughter bounced off the alley walls. Her hand began to rise, the muzzle of her revolver steady on Shannon's chest.

Shannon suddenly sobered.

"Why, you little bitch!" he grated. "It wasn't just me who done give you to them Injuns. It was your own damn uncles, too! Your own flesh and blood."

"They'll get theirs," she assured him.

"You're full of piss and vinegar, ain't ya?"

With surprising quickness, which caught Rebecca off guard, Ed Shannon slapped her gunhand with a trail-hardened fist. The small .38 went flying. His paw then reached down and grabbed her breast through the material of her dress. Roughly he pulled her close. She winced with pain.

"Yeah, five years is a helluva long time," growled Shannon. The killer's soiled linen duster smelled of sweat and horse manure. "Now let's get a good look at your purty body. For old time's sake, let's say."

Shannon began to tear off her dress.

Spurred by consuming rage, Rebecca smashed her right knee up into the startled bandit's crotch. Shannon let out a shriek of pain and tossed her aside.

The slightly-built young woman landed on the ground. Shannon recovered with amazing speed. He reached out and grabbed her slender ankle.

"You bastard!" she cried.

"No bitch hits me in the balls and gets away with it!"

Rebecca threw dust into his eyes. Shannon swore and brought his free hand to his dirtied face.

Suddenly free, Rebecca shot to her feet and stumbled toward the fallen revolver. Her quest for revenge had become a mad dash for survival. Behind her she heard two metallic clicks as Shannon cocked his shotgun.

She dove behind a nearby water barrel. The Parker roared in the confines of the darkened alley. A hail of hot pellets smashed into the staves of the filled container. Wooden splinters and miniature geysers of rainwater leaped into the air. Streams formed at the pellet holes and hissed against the hard clay soil while the barrel drained. Another shot would kill her. Rebecca ducked lower, unhurt but shaken by the close call.

"Bitch!" Shannon screamed, coming after her.

Rebecca heard the rasping of metal on metal that told of him reloading the shotgun. Quickly she began to crawl backward toward the mouth of the alley, keeping the barrel between her and the advancing gunman.

Shannon grew closer, his Parker shotgun leading the way. Rebecca reached her goal and rounded a building onto a side street. She figured surprise was on her side. The moment Shannon made the corner, she reached out and plucked the scattergun from his hands.

"What the . . . ?" blurted the startled killer.

Rebecca pivoted and smashed the heavy sawed-off shotgun into his stomach.

Shannon doubled over, his weight rocked back on his heels, nearly shoved off his feet. Then he jerked rapidly upright, his scream of agony lost in the bellow of the Parker.

His body slammed off the sidewall of the barber shop and danced a grotesque jig before volition left him in a red puddle on the dusty ground. Rebecca's eyes burned from the gunpowder. Her breath escaped in gasps.

"That's for my mother," she said calmly. Her ears rang from the gunshot.

"Shannon?" called Jed, the other outlaw.

Rebecca flew into action. She had little time to savor her moment of revenge. The victory-charged girl retrieved her revolver and sprinted from the alley the same moment Jed burst onto the scene.

"Hey, stop!" cried Jed.

Two gunshots from Rebecca's Little Russian pierced the air.

Bullets chipped the wood near Jed's head and he dove for the ground. Before he could bring his converted Remington to bear, the soil around him turned to pillars of dust and he felt a hot sting of a double-ought pellet enter his left shoulder.

Rebecca kept hold of the Parker, now empty and useless, as she started to trot down the street. Curious townspeople gawked after her. When she reached Main Street, she headed for a spreading cottonwood on the edge of town where she had tethered her pony.

As she ran, she began to smile. Revenge was sweet!

His name was Lone Wolf. A tall, muscular white man who, like Rebecca, had been a long-time captive of Indians. Known as Brett Baylor before his capture, he's spent ten years with the Crow until his escape with Rebecca a month ago.

Since then he'd sworn himself to a quest on the Spirit Path in order to exact revenge for the death of his pretty bride. She had been butchered by the same Indians who had taken him captive. Now the tall white warrior, who still preferred to dress like an Indian, was waiting for Rebecca on his pony on the outskirts of Bazile Mills. She came trotting up to him.

"So many gunshots," Lone Wolf observed.

"So many close calls," replied Rebecca. She reined in her snorting mount and glanced at her companion. Her face glowed with triumph. "But I was successful."

Lone Wolf, who still wore a narrow ridge of blond hair down the middle of his shaven pate in the traditional manner of the Crow Strong Heart warrior society, nodded his understanding.

Rebecca frowned and looked at her ripped elkskin dress. "I need some white woman's clothes," she remarked. "I attract too much attention in this."

Lone Wolf clucked in mild exasperation. "You are turning into a white-eye. If that's the case, what you need to do is go home."

"Home." She said the word wistfully, as though it was a foreign word whose meaning she did not know. "I never thought I'd see the homestead again. I don't know if I want to after what happened there five years ago."

"It's only a day's ride away."

She nodded. "Maybe you're right. After a month on the trail it's about time. Perhaps we'll even learn something about my uncles."

Two riders came helling out of the little town. When they rode close enough to recognize Rebecca's slender form atop her prancing Indian pony, they filled their hands and their six-guns blazed.

"Shannon's friends," the girl announced while she drew her Smith and Wesson.

Lone Wolf launched a single arrow that pegged into the ground a few feet in front of the charging men. It slowed them some and, when Rebecca returned their fire, they swung away and made haste back toward Bazile Mills.

Rebecca fired twice more for effect and gigged her mount into motion. When she and Lone Wolf had put three miles between them and town, Rebecca reined in. She turned a wry expression to her companion.

"You know, visiting the old homestead seems like a better idea right now. There's no going back . . . starting over, I can only go forward . . . for revenge. Even so, a stop-off there will give us a breathing spell. I'll race you to that old cottonwood on the ridge," she challenged.

Although unsettling, her encounter with Ed Shannon had shown her how much she did like a challenge.

TWO

A sea of buffalo flowed out of Dakota Territory, across the border into Nebraska.

Bitter Creek Jake Tulley pushed his black bowler hat away from his eyes and whistled softly. The mounted outlaw leader and his men rested on a treeless rise overlooking the endless mass of black, furry-humped beasts.

"Would ya look at all them animals!" he shouted. "Why there must be a hunnerd thousand bucks worth of skins waitin' to be harvested."

"Sorta makes you want to jump right down there and start shootin', eh, Jake?" tall, angular Luke Wellington enthused. Wellington was Tulley's right hand man, a dedicated road agent always looking for new ways for the gang to enhance its evil reputation.

"You do an' we'll all be up to our ass in angry Sioux." Tulley nodded to emphasize the finality of his statement. "But our day will come, Luke."

"What's a buffalo hide go for back East?"

"Around five dollars, cleaned, cured and delivered to the tannery."

"That ain't much," Wellington complained. " 'Cept there's millions of them."

"That's why we're gonna be in the buffalo hide business within the next few weeks," added Tulley. "First we make us a pile tradin' whiskey and guns to the Sioux. Then them red niggers get riled up on rotgut, go take a few white scalps an' the army runs them the hell outta here. That leaves the buffalo to us. So we make a second, bigger fortune in hides and smoked tongues." He thought for a moment, proud of his strategy. His partner, he knew, had bigger plans. Wanted to control the gold that glittered not far away in the Black Hills. Let him own all the gold. Tulley would be satisfied to steal it from shipments to the mint.

"That means I can get me some white pussy, instead of stray Injun gals," remarked three-hundred-pound Bobby O'Toole. The massive gunman's big right hand was wrapped around a whiskey bottle. The other gang members knew all about O'Toole's strange sexual habits.

"You'll have plenty of time for that, too," Tulley agreed. "With all the money we're gonna make on this here buffalo huntin' deal, you'll all be rich enough to retire."

Bobby O'Toole took another swig of whiskey. "Yeah, but I ain't gonna retire my pecker. I can't wait to sample some of them purty little girls."

Jake Tulley didn't try to hide his disgust. When O'Toole said a little, he meant *little*. The bandit chief's steely gaze caused Bobby to glance away.

"Hell, O'Toole," Luke Wellington growled, stroking the saber scar on his face, "by the time you get through with 'em there's nothing left to grow up and be women."

Jake Tulley held up his hand. "All right. We ain't gonna get nothin' done 'till we get some tradin' goods."

"Don't worry, boss," Wellington told him. "Some of the boys done scouted the general store in Eagle Butte. It's plumb full of flour, coffee, sugar an' shootin' irons."

"The Sioux'll go for that in a big way," Tulley agreed. "We're all set, but where's Shannon and the others?"

"They'll meet us at the campsite. Shannon had some unfinished business with some wise-ass clodhopper."

Tulley nodded. "Okay, boys, let's ride."

Cantering at the head of his gang of killers, Jake Tulley smiled to himself. Ever since that day when he'd been forced to save his life by trading that half-breed girl and her blonde mother to the Sioux, he had been waiting for the time he could get even with Iron Calf and his Oglala. Now, by trading rotgut and rifles for gold, then setting the army on the redskins, he stood to make a fortune . ... and get revenge at the same time. It would be his biggest score in a career filled with more failures than successes.

Bitter Creek Jake Tulley was a quick-draw artist with over thirty-six kills to his credit. Raiding with Quantrell in the War Between the States, Tulley had drifted west after the conflict like many legitimate rebel ex-soldiers and found easy pickings in Nebraska and the vast Dakota Territory. It didn't take him long to form a gang and build an evil reputation across the land.

Tulley, who got his colorful nickname after he'd robbed the Bitter Creek bank and killed six men in the process, was of medium build with short-cropped black hair, bushy black eyebrows and a neatly trimmed, pencil-thin moustache. Tulley's hate-filled gray eyes were known to narrow with satisfaction as he gunned down his victims with a lightning draw of his hair-trigger Peacemaker .45. As a memento of that bloody day in Bitter Creek, Tulley wore a black English bowler he'd taken from the town's plump banker just before he blew the man's head off.

"Hey Jake!" yelled Luke Wellington. "Lookee there."

Tulley halted the gang and peered through the afternoon brightness at a small wagon train in the grassy swale below them.

"Looks like them settlers are splittin' up," Bobby O'Toole

observed. "If they put down roots here-abouts, they could be easy pickin's for us."

Tulley watched the covered wagons rumble off in different directions. "Some other day perhaps," he replied. He tipped his bowler at the conestogas. "But now we got other plans."

"Awh, Jake," O'Toole protested. "Let us have a crack at 'em." He rubbed at a growing bulge at his crotch. "I saw a right cute li'll thing on one of them wagons an' I'm achin' to wet my wick."

"You're a fucking animal, O'Toole," the gang leader growled.

"Hell," cracked Wellington, "he's the size of one, only thing is to decide what kind."

The gang started to laugh, then stopped abruptly at the evil glint in Bobby O'Toole's reptillian green eyes.

"Let's head on," Tulley interjected, defusing the situation. "We got us some Indian tradin' to do."

The gang spurred their mounts and headed for Eagle Butte.

While leading his band of gunslingers across rolling hills and past blossoming fields of multi-colored prairie flowers, Tulley glanced at Luke Wellington. Along with Ed Shannon, the veteran killer was his most trusted gunhand.

Luke Wellington had several dozen kills to his credit, excluding Indians and Mexicans, whom he said didn't count. Tall and angular, with long black sideburns, curly black hair and chiseled facial features, Wellington's quick-moving brown eyes always seemed to be checking the terrain for signs of trouble. A veteran of the Union Army, Wellington had a long purple scar down the left side of his face, courtesy of a Confederate officer's sword. One of the few arguments he had ever lost had been to one of Jeb Stewart's lieutenants.

Then Tulley glanced at O'Toole and shuddered.

Only the mammoth killer's evil reputation as a rapist and

cold-blooded murderer could match his blubbery, three-hundred-pound body for grotesqueness. A pervert who preferred young girls, whom he sliced to pieces once he'd finished with them, O'Toole was also a bloodthirsty killer who was equally adept with a short-barrelled Peacemaker or a twenty inch skinning knife.

Bobby O'Toole's physical appearance was enough to turn away most would-be attackers. Although he had layers of fat rippling under his buckskin clothing and several chins on his fleshy neck, solid slabs of muscle rested just below. He had been known, in a free-for-all, to crush his opponent in his powerful arms, splintering ribs and driving the ends through lungs and heart. His deep-set, green eyes seemed to glare with maniacal glee at the prospect of another chance to kill or rape. His unkempt mop of greasy black hair fell to his massive shoulders and his ham-sized hands were usually wrapped around a bottle of rotgut whiskey. During a typical Saturday night drinking binge, he could down half a case of booze and still walk away. O'Toole's only vulnerability was the angry red and blue scar whose edges peeked above his bandana a few inches below his left ear.

Following his ravishment of a small girl in a Kansas cowtown, the local citizens had seized the fat murderer and tried to lynch him. Only the sudden appearance of the rustlers he rode with saved his miserable life. Even then, they had chased off the townies before they released the strangulation noose. It was said that a question about his scar could cost a man his life. Tulley knew that if the fat gunman wasn't needed so badly to carry off his schemes, he would dump the evil pervert without a second thought.

"Eagle Butte, Jake," yelled Luke Wellington. The lean gunhawk's voice brought Tulley out of his reverie. "Looks nice and peaceful, don't it?"

"Maybe they're waitin' for us with open arms," Tulley replied sarcastically.

"See any lawmen?" Tulley inquired of the gang while he

pulled his bowler hat down on his head. He peered through the shimmering waves of summer heat and scanned the little farm town ahead. Several clapboarded buildings and a tiny hotel seemed dwarfed by the vastness of the surrounding plains.

"Not a one."

"Anybody movin' near the general store?" Tulley's myopic eyes strained at the distance.

"Naw. But there's a buckboard we can use."

"All right, boys, check your irons," Tulley instructed.

After a moment of clicking and snicking, while the nine veteran killers pored over their weapons, Jake Tulley looked up and nodded. A malicious smile twisted his lips.

"Give 'em hell!" he yelled.

The Bitter Creek Jake Tulley gang galloped out of the prairie like a horde of charging Cheyenne braves. The outlaws screamed at the top of their lungs. Soon the afternoon air came alive with bullets. Tulley led the way, followed by Wellington and O'Toole.

Startled townsmen ran for cover. Women screamed and grabbed their children. Horses neighed and stamped at the tie-rails and sawed at their reins.

Within a few minutes the gang reined in their snorting mounts in a shower of rich Nebraska gumbo. Tulley wielded his seven and a half inch .45 Peacemaker while his men gathered around him in front of the small general store.

"There she is, boys. Let's clean 'er out."

While Tulley and a couple of his gunmen stood guard outside, Luke Wellington and Bobby O'Toole led a laughing party of outlaws into the shop. Soon they emerged with sacks of supplies and boxes of ammunition.

Suddenly an old woman stepped out of the mercantile onto the boardwalk. She clutched an ancient squirrel gun. "Get away from my goods, you varmints!" she shouted at the surprised gunmen. The craggy-faced woman's snowy white hair ruffled in the breeze.

"Oh-oh, boys, looks like we're goners," O'Toole drawled.

Two men rolled their eyes in mock horror, snickered and continued to work.

"I said git!" cried the woman. She poked air with the muzzle of her .31 caliber rifle.

Bobby O'Toole turned from the tailgate of the buckboard and took two panter-quick steps toward the plankwalk. The movement was surprisingly fluid in a form so gross. Suddenly he froze. The old bitch had ratcheted the hammer back and now the .31 caliber hole was centered smack on his forehead.

O'Toole felt the blood rush from his face. Christ! That thing could take off the back of his head. Seconds ticked by. Then, he suddenly realized Tulley was laughing at him. The chuckles turned to a deep-bellied guffaw. O'Toole forced his eyes away from the deadly black hole and up along the barrel so neatly bedded in curly maple, to the hammer. Poised like a deadly snake above the bare nipple, it . . . *Bare nipple!*

Blood raged back into the face of O'Toole, even as his mighty hand flickered out and snatched the rifle from the tenacious granny's hands. He stepped into the move and swung his other fist at the old woman's head with enough force to shatter it. Fortunately the woman's fingers were ensnared by the trigger guard and the pain of their breaking jerked her forward and to one side. O'Tooles massive wrist slammed into her shoulder and tumbled her into the street.

"Enough!" barked Tulley, tilting the muzzle of his Peacemaker to center O'Toole. He leaned toward the woman. "Ma'am, if you know what's good for ya, you'll get the hell away from here right now while the gettin's good."

The elderly shopkeeper scrambled to her feet and stumbled back a pace, eyes flicking between the hardcases.

"Ma!" cried a female voice.

Tulley looked up to see a lithe, young blonde girl burst from the hotel. She raced toward the trembling, pain-wracked woman. The girl's fully developed breasts bounced beneath the cotton blouse she wore. Her long, golden tresses glistened in the sunshine. Tulley noticed that O'Toole had seen her, too.

"Ma, are you all right?"

"I . . . I think so, Millie," the shaken woman replied.

"My, my," O'Toole purred. "What have we here?"

In sudden fury, the good-looker rounded on the gang. "Leave my ma alone!" she snapped.

O'Toole stepped forward. "It wasn't your ma I was talkin' about sweets."

With incredible quickness for such a big man, O'Toole reached out and grabbed the wide-eyed blonde by her slender arms.

"Let me go. You're hurtin' me."

Tulley saw O'Toole glance at him, a maniacal glint in his green eyes. "Jake, let me take this here fancy piece around back."

"No!" shrieked the white-haired woman.

O'Toole slapped her aside as though she were a doll.

The other gang members stopped their work and looked at the blonde. Tulley knew they'd all heard of the way O'Toole preferred to take his women. Maybe it would be best to kill the fat slug now, before he brought the whole countryside down on them. So thinking, Tulley eared back the Colt's hammer, liking the sudden blanch and shocked eyes O'Toole turned on him.

In the alley by the store, Constable Hank Greene cocked the left hammer of his old 10 bore scattergun, knowing he had to make the shot good, rehearsing in his mind the moves he must make. Step around the corner and fire the first round at the gunman on the horse, cock the right barrel and nail the animal holding Millie, step back and reload. Hank wished he could take the animal first, but with his back turned he was no immediate threat while the lean gunhawk need only flick his Colt up. He also wished he had half a dozen deputies.

Awh . . . shit, he sealed his decision. Go!

At the first hint of motion, Tulley rocked the Colt to his left and tripped the shot, the revolver's roar instantly drowned in the thunder of the old Belgian ten bore. A handful of buckshot arced up and out of town while Hank kicked his life out on the boardwalk, desperately trying to stem the rushing death of a gaping throat wound.

"Oh . . . my . . . God!" gasped the old woman. She regained her feet and staggered to the safety of the nearby hotel.

In the same instant, O'Toole let go of the screaming blonde and tardily spun to face this new danger, hand darting to leather.

Tulley glanced at O'Toole and shook his head.

"All right," he commanded. "Let's finish up."

Within half an hour the outlaws had taken a mound of supplies from the shop. They piled the bags and cloth sacks onto the buckboard in front of the store. Luke Wellington added four Sharps buffalo guns to the pile.

"Roll that wagon down to the saloon, load up all the whiskey you can stack on. Then let's see if these pilgrims has any more shootin' irons," Tulley ordered. "O'Toole, you go with them."

Three bandits quickly emptied the saloon of all the whiskey they could find. The gang clustered around the buckboard like eager kids on Christmas morning.

"Drive the buckboard, O'Toole," Tulley directed. "You're probably too tired to ride after all the excitement ya just got."

Grim-faced, the rest of the outlaws mounted their horses and trotted out of Eagle Butte into the prairie. Jake Tulley tugged on the brim of his English bowler and dug spurs into his gelding's flanks. Visions of Sioux gold and eastern greenbacks danced in his head.

Bobby O'Toole saw the covered wagon first.

"Why look at that!" the fat man exclaimed. He pointed at one of the settler wagons they'd noticed before in the valley. "Looks like we got us a straggler."

Tulley halted the gang and peered through the late afternoon sunshine. They'd stopped on a boulder-strewn ridge overlooking a narrow trail. Tulley noticed a wobbly mule-drawn conestoga about fifty yards ahead, having difficulty negotiating the rocky track.

"Let's take 'em, Jake," Luke Wellington urged.

Tulley could sense the excitement bubbling among his mounted gunmen. He knew once they began their campaign of ridding the area of Indians, then stripping the prairie of buffalo, life might be kind of dull for most of the thrill-seeking killers he kept around him. Maybe he ought to let the boys blow off a little steam.

Tulley took off his dust-coated derby and wiped his brow with his sleeve. He peered at the inside of the bowler for a moment, as though inspecting the leather sweatband.

"All right, boys," he drawled a bit reluctantly. "Have some fun." He turned to Bobby O'Toole. "You stay here with me, O'Toole. No sense bringing that wagon down off this trail."

"Gimme a break!" O'Toole whined.

"I did . . . back at the general store." Tulley's dangerous gray eyes bored into O'Toole's. The blubbery killer's face glistened with perspiration and his unkempt mop of black hair blew in the wind.

Tulley watched O'Toole's fat fingers twitch in readiness. The bandit leader's hand slid toward his own hogleg. The tension nearly crackled in the air, projected from the hard, intense faces of the other highwaymen.

"Do what the boss says, O'Toole," Luke snapped, siding his leader. "Hell, if he'd let you take that girl back of the store, we'd have heat on us from all points of the compass. Why, we'd be strung up on sight."

O'Toole paled at the reference to hanging, but the green, cunning madness crept into his eyes and flowed out at Luke Wellington. He'd live to rue this day. Bobby swung back to Tulley, extending his hands palm up.

"Sure, Boss, just a passing thought."

Someone snorted in derisive laughter.

Tulley released the breath he had been holding. "Take 'em down after them pilgrims, Luke."

The gang leaped their horses forward.

As the marauders approached the creaking conestoga, Tulley watched several frightened settlers peer from within. The driver began to lash his tired mules, cursing with inspiration. All to no avail.

Luke Wellington and the other outlaws overtook the fleeing wagon within a hundred yards. Immediately gunshots echoed across the prairie. Only one settler returned fire, a middle-aged man with an old Model '63 Remington percussion rifle. The fat bullet cracked through the air, struck a rock near Luke Wellington's head and moaned off into the distance. Before he could reload, the outlaws swarmed around the frightened immigrants.

A woman screamed, threw up her hands, then flopped backward off the wagon box, her heart shattered by a .45 slug, fired at point-blank range. The man beside her cried out in anguish and lashed at one outlaw with his bullwhip.

Luke shot him, then ducked when he realized he had let his attention stray from the sharpshooter with the Remington. The big muzzle-loader boomed near Luke's head and hot powder kernels speckled his face.

"Yeow!" the gunman cried, then whipped his Frontier '72 Colt toward the defender and blasted a .44 slug into the courageous settler's gut.

With a grunt, the fighting farmer doubled over and the Tulley gang swarmed over the beleaguered wagon.

A few quick shots sounded, a frightened scream came from inside and Luke ducked under the canvas cover.

When he emerged from the back of the covered wagon pushing two wide-eyed teenaged girls ahead of him, Jake Tulley glanced at Bobby O'Toole, who sat on the spring seat of the buckboard. The fat outlaw's hand tightened on the reins and he sucked in a deep breath. Tulley could picture precisely what thoughts were going through O'Toole's pea-sized brain.

Tulley turned his attention to the mini-massacre below. He watched his boys finish off a couple of wounded settlers with quick shots to the head. Luke gave one of the struggling blondes to another gang member and tossed the other one across his saddle. Bobby O'Toole snorted in anticipation.

"Control yourself, O'Toole," Tulley informed the three hundred pound road agent. "I've got a job for you that's sure to make you happy. We want to make this look like the Sioux did it. So, get down there and cut them throats, take the scalps.

Bobby licked his lips, an eager light flickering in his glazed green eyes. He drew his big skinning knife and advanced on the dead, walking with a rolling gait. Luke Wellington, who had ridden up during Tulley's instructions, exchanged a glance with another man and both quickly looked away, uncomfortable in the presence of the grisly deed.

Down below, Bobby O'Toole went gleefully about his task. Ragged slashes crossed already dead throats with macabre precision. When one cut elicited a moan from trapped air in the victim's lungs, Bobby jumped backward, his mind made jittery by superstitious ignorance. He bent again and slipped the point of his skinner under the loose skin of a settler's scalp and made a swift, circular incision. The small patch made a sharp, zippery tearing sound when he jerked it free. In ten minutes the grim business ended.

Then the gang set fire to the wagon.

As the murderers trotted back toward Tulley, the gang leader pulled on the brim of his bowler and examined their captives. "Well, looks like we got us some fancy goods to liven up the camp tonight."

"Yeah, an' me first!" Bobby O'Toole enthused.

"Shut up, O'Toole," Tulley commanded. He swept the others with his gaze. "All right, boys. Let's ride. We've got us a wagonload of tradin' goods to get to ol' Running Snake and some purty fluff to haul our ashes."

Stringing out into a long single file, the gang responded to their orders with alacrity.

Tulley led his band of killers and the two teenaged captives to a semi-permanent campsite three hours ride north, across the line in Dakota Territory. A massive herd of buffalo grazed nearby. Hunted by the Cheyenne and Sioux, not to mention illegal hiders, they represented the last large gathering of the precious beasts. Tulley appraised the undulating grass that extended for miles in every direction. The spot, he knew, was considered sacred by the Oglala. The place where he would soon pay them back for humiliating him.

The gang reined in their horses and dismounted. They quickly erected Tulley's big, white Silby tent, which was kept safe in a hidden caché between visits.

"Can't wait to get me some of them buffalo," Luke Wellington enthused. He walked to where Tulley stood beside the two frightened white girls, huddled in the grass.

Tulley looked away from the whimpering teenagers, toward his number one man. "First things first. I'll send a man to contact Running Snake about delivering the goods."

A hard-faced gunslinger reached down toward the younger, wide-eyed girl at Tulley's feet. Tulley nudged him away with a riding crop, then reached down and pinched

31

both girls on their buttocks. He felt his cock stiffen in his tight whipcord trousers. Desire rose demandingly. But, naw, he could wait until he got back to that redhead waitin' in Buffalo Gap. Let the boys have what fun they could.

"W-What's going to happen to us?" the elder girl inquired in a small, frightened voice.

"Well, missy, I think I'll let my boys decide that," Tulley replied with a lurid smirk. He turned back to the gang. "Time to get your asses hauled, fellers. Enjoy it while you can."

Five men, led by Bobby O'Toole, rushed toward the women.

"No, Bobby. You wait. You'll get your turn last."

"The way I *like* it, Jake?"

The outlaw leader nodded, regretting his decision already. When he had taken O'Toole on, he had no idea of the mountain-sized gunhawk's insatiable lust for young girls—the younger the better—nor his grisly practices after he had used them. O'Toole's bizarre sexual proclivities could get them all on everyone's lynch list. Behind him, one of the girls screamed.

"Make all the noise you want, honey," one hardcase gloated. "Ain't nobody gonna hear you out here, 'cept them buffala." He undid his gunbelt and lowered his trousers. His fat, reddened penis swung upward, alert and ready to do service.

"No! Oh, no!" the immigrant girl begged at the sight of the offensive shaft. The bandit lowered himself between her legs and shoved mightily. The helpless girl, her legs held apart by strong, rough hands, shrieked in a special agony when her maidenhead ripped asunder under the insistent pressure of the huge phallus.

The gap-toothed gunslinger, known as Shorty not for his size but for his quick fuse, ground his hips half a dozen times, made five quick, deep thrusts into her struggling body and then cried out in completion, spasmed mightily

32

and went slack.

He pulled out and made way for another. A glance at the young girl's nearly hairless mound revealed blood. "Hey!" Shorty exulted. "I got me a virgin!"

"Me, too," another bandit yelled gleefully while the throbbing tip of his distended penis probed against the fragile obstruction in the younger girl's dry, fevered passage.

"Some fellers have all the luck," Bobby O'Toole grumbled from nearby.

New cries of pain and horror rose from the abused girls. They tried to struggle against the greater strength of their captors, only to go slack with shamed submission as one after another, a parade of reddened, swollen organs bobbed before their eyes and plunged into their most secret depths. Agony of mind, coupled with that of the body, threatened to drive them from reason. Their only respite came while the outlaws changed places. Every member of the gang took his turn with the sobbing, anguished sisters, relishing the younger, tighter one the most. Then it came to be Bobby O'Toole's turn.

He grabbed the older girl first, taking her by the hair and dragging her some distance away to where the high buffalo grass hid his actions from the other gang members. His victim sobbed and pleaded until his massive weight crushed the breath from her lungs. His engorged penis, small for so large a man, probed and shoved to force entry. Not in her savaged vagina, but the small, puckered button of her anus.

New shrieks of outrage and pain came from her raw throat when O'Toole achieved his purpose and penetrated her. He grunted like an animal until an early climax ended his enjoyment.

Then he began to work with his knife.

A final coughing gurgle of pink-bubbled breath and a last convulsion told him when he should quit. With a maniacal glint in his eyes and a new erection, Bobby started back for the other one.

None of the gang would meet his eye when he entered the camp and few would look each other in the face. Sickened by the sub-human noises that came from the bloody site of O'Toole's pleasure, the men isolated themselves within the prisons of their minds and wondered how long they could endure Bobby O'Toole.

The younger girl took longer to satisfy O'Toole. When her moans and shrieks ended and he returned to camp, hands and arms blood-soaked, clothes splattered, a happy smile on his thick lips, Tulley spoke sharply to him.

"Make sure it looks like the Sioux did it. Then get washed up and change those clothes," he snapped. Tulley, too, would not look at O'Toole. From a distance he heard the drumming of hooves.

"Somebody's comin', Jake," yelled a gunman.

"It's Jed and the others," cried another.

Jake Tulley smiled and walked over to greet his returning gang members. The riders came into view and Tulley saw they were a man short. The newcomers reined in in a shower of dirt. Tulley's face slackened and he frowned.

"Where's Shannon?" he demanded, glancing at the three gunmen who were dismounting. "That there sodbuster didn't finish him off did he?"

The gang gathered around, anxious for news.

The lean outlaw named Jed stepped up to Tulley, licked his lips, then glanced at the ground. "I . . . I got some bad news for ya, Jake," he began.

Tulley's eyes narrowed. "Give it to me."

"Shannon's dead. Got his guts blown apart."

Incredulous, the gang members murmured. Tulley couldn't believe it.

"That plowboy killed Shannon?" he asked, his voice rising an octave. "Why, I seen Ed Shannon outdraw three cowboys outta Texas at once! Shannon's the best there is

34

with a scattergun. I don't believe it."

Jed licked his lips again. "It weren't that kid that shot Shannon. It . . . it was some . . . squaw. Shot him dead in an alley."

Tulley blinked in astonishment.

"Damn!" breathed Luke Wellington.

"What do you mean, a 'squaw'?" Tulley demanded in a cold, deadly voice.

Jed shrugged his slender shoulders. "All I know is we was gettin' our horses after Shannon done shot that farmer's kid. Then we heard a bunch of shootin' an' saw this purty little Injun gal run out of the alley. She'd finished Shannon off with his own shotgun," Jed ended in a tone of awe.

Silence hung like a sodden poncho upon the clearing.

Bitter Creek Jake turned and glanced out at the grazing buffalo. One of his best men dead at the hands of the damned Injuns. Would they never stop getting one up on Jake Tulley? He felt his anger beginning to boil up inside of him. The bad news soured what had been a rather nice day.

"Who is this *squaw?*" he asked Jed, still looking away. The outlaw leader spat out the word "squaw" as though it were a curse.

Jed shrugged. "Just some Injun bitch."

Tulley clenched his teeth. Ed Shannon had been like a brother to him. They'd ridden together for ten years. His sudden loss came as a shock. At last he turned and glanced at the faces of his men.

"All right, boys," he began in a cold, hard voice. His gray eyes narrowed and he tipped his bowler at a jaunty angle. "I'll give a bonus of five hunnerd dollars to the man who brings me that damn squaw. Or her head!"

"The outlaws exchanged glances.

"We'll teach folks that they can't mess with the Jake Tulley gang and get away with it. Five hun-dred dollars to the man who finds that squaw."

Luke Wellington nodded. "She's as good as dead now, Jake."

Jake Tulley took a deep breath. "Good!" Jake knew money talked. "Now let's secure the camp. Running Snake will have word to us soon."

THREE

After a night in a cold camp on the vast Nebraska prairie, Rebecca and Lone Wolf took to the trail at first light. Meadow larks called their haunting melody over the vast stretches of waving buffalo grass, much of which stood chest-high to their horses. In the orange glow of the ascending sun, it appeared a yellow green sea in restless, unending motion. The peaceful scene did little to ease the discomfort of Rebecca's thoughts.

"Squaw" and "White squaw," the *good* people of Bazile Mills had called her. How strange their customs seemed to her now. They gathered like vultures, to watch a hardened killer like Ed Shannon gun down a frightened, inexperienced boy, yet had howled in lynch-mad fury when she had defended herself against the same murderer. Through the night, she had awakened frequently, the image of Shannon's shotgun-blasted body burning in her mind. Killing him had been harder than she had expected. Not just the physical task of defeating him, but the emotional burden it had placed, unasked, upon her. The revenge had been sweet, yet with it had come the realization that she had committed herself to repeating the same scene over and over until she had avenged herself on all those responsible. Would she find it worthwhile? Now they rode toward the site of the old Caldwell farm. What challenge to her determination would she find there?

"Do you think the old place is still standing?" Rebecca gave voice to her troublesome thoughts. The spirited war pony she'd taken during her escape from the Oglala camp continued to eat up the miles.

Lone Wolf turned his head toward her. "Most likely," he opined. "Unless, of course, the Sioux or the Cheyenne burned it down during the past five years."

"That's encouraging."

"Only tellin' it like it is," replied the white Indian.

"Your honesty overwhelms me."

Rebecca smiled and relaxed for a moment. Her horse's motion, combined with the warm sun and spicy scent of sage was sybaritic. She was glad to have Lone Wolf along for a couple of reasons. First, getting across the treacherous plains was difficult for a woman under any circumstances. Second, she needed someone who understood her long ordeal with the Sioux.

"Keep your eyes peeled for hunting parties," Lone Wolf cautioned.

Rebecca felt a chill in her stomach. The Sioux still loomed large in her life. Then, as she continued to canter along the dusty trail, Rebecca glanced at the familiar landmarks all around her. She felt as though she was going back in time. Unbidden, the years slipped away. The brutal Sioux attack on the Caldwell farm and its horrible aftermath came rushing back to her in a series of vivid mental images . . .

. . . Rebecca and her mother, Hannah, had shared the Caldwell's small sod house with her grandfather, Jeremiah, and her two wise-cracking uncles, Ezekial and Virgil. Life in those days had been simple and happy. Rebecca and her mother kept house while Grandpa Jeremiah and her uncles tended to opening fields from the thick prairie sod and husbanded their few head of cattle.

Then Jeremiah suffered a heart attack in 1870 and became bedridden. Her lazy uncles turned away from farming and drifted into banditry as their livelihood. The uncles soon became members in good standing of the feared Jake Tulley outlaw gang and invited the bandits to use the Caldwell place as their permanent hideout.

For most of 1870, Rebecca and her mother stayed away from the many gunmen around the farm. The women remained like prisoners inside the house and cared for Rebecca's ailing grandfather. Then, in July 1870, when Rebecca turned fourteen, the warlike Oglala went on the warpath. Settlers were scalped, women raped and babies slaughtered. The army tried to patrol the prairie, but for the most part the settlers were on their own. Finally, on a muggy morning while Rebecca pulled on a blue cotton dress, about two hundred Sioux warriors attacked the Caldwell spread.

The first warning came when gunshots pierced the morning stillness. One of Tulley's bandit crew cried out in pain.

Blood-curdling war cries began to fill the air and painted war ponies thundered through the bare patch outside the house. The evil hum of arrows chilled the women's hearts.

"Oh, my God!" gasped Rebecca's mother.

"What is it, Mother?"

"Indians!"

Feeling a sudden jab of anxiety in her stomach, Rebecca rushed to the window of the embattled soddy. The horrified teenager spotted dozens of paint-streaked, war hatchet-toting braves leaping from their mounts and rushing the barn and outbuildings. Three of Tulley's men lay dead in the yard.

"Oh, no, Mother. Look!"

"I'm afraid to."

"What are we going to do?"

When Rebecca turned sharply from the window, she saw her ashen-faced mother backing against the far wall. She noticed the fear rising in Hannah's blue eyes.

"Mother?"

"I . . . I don't think I could face another savage! Pray that they kill us, Becky. Pray that it is all they do . . . *kill us,*" she repeated vehemently.

Rebecca thought of her grandfather's shotgun hanging over the fireplace and started that way. Then she heard a noise from the bedroom. Both she and her mother turned toward the sound.

"It's . . . an . . . attack," gasped Jeremiah Caldwell, leaning in the doorway. "Get . . . me . . . my shotgun." The old man's haggard face was lined with strain and his wasted body trembled with weakness.

An instant later, Rebecca's grandfather tumbled to the floor.

"Papa!" cried Hannah, rushing to the body.

Rebecca also knelt next to her emaciated grandfather. She saw immediately that it was too late. Jeremiah Caldwell had suffered a fatal heart seizure. Rebecca stood and began to quickly close the wooden shutters.

Suddenly the front door burst open. Rebecca's two uncles, Jake Tulley and three members of the bandit gang whom Rebecca recognized as Ed Shannon, Bobby O'Toole and Luke Wellington, rushed into the house. They slammed the pine door behind them. Rebecca watched several arrows whoosh through the sod dwelling's open windows and thud harmlessly into the back walls.

"Goddamned Injuns!" snarled Jake Tulley. The outlaw leader removed his bowler hat and wiped his brow. "Hell, that there is Iron Calf. We've been sellin' whiskey to the bastard for years and look how he treats us."

"We can fight 'em off from in here," said Rebecca's lean uncle Ezekial, stroking his bushy mustache. "Maybe them red bastards'll get tired and move on."

"I hope so," Tulley returned. "An' damnit, them 'skins done killed off all the other boys before they could even get outta bed." Bitter Creek Jake glanced at Jeremiah Caldwell's dead body on the floor of the house's main room. "I see the old man finally croaked," he observed in an off-hand manner, feeding cartridges into his revolver. "You two can stop moonin' over him and start reloadin' for us," he told Rebecca and her mother.

Ezekial and Virgil looked quickly at their dead father and then returned their attention to the Indians. Rebecca didn't notice the slightest bit of sorrow on either of their faces. She controlled her rising anger and glanced at thirty-four year old Ezekial.

The older of the two Caldwell boys was built like his father; lean, bony with deep-set brown eyes. Ezekial sported a bushy brown moustache which he stroked when he became nervous. His shaggy brown hair fell to his shoulders in a style popular among plainsmen and mountain men more than twenty years ago. His wide-brimmed hat seemed always dusty and his dirty clothes smelled nearly as bad as the untended cattle in their father's dilapidated wooden corral.

Family loyalty aside, both of her uncles disgusted her.

Thirty year old Virgil, with his round pudgy face and big, blue eyes that danced with mischief, was built more like his late mother. Despite his gentle nature, the stubby Caldwell brother's high-pitched cackle was a familiar sound in many of Nebraska's more disreputable drinking establishments and bawdyhouses.

Rebecca ignored Tulley's order and turned to comfort her mother. "It'll be all right, Mother," she said with more conviction than she actually felt. She knelt beside Hannah

41

Caldwell. "The Sioux won't harm you."

Returning the Indians' fire, Ezekial, Virgil and the outlaws knelt quickly beside the open windows and began to shoot at the passing warriors. Soon the shadowed interior of the Caldwell's little sod farmhouse was filled with acrid, greasy-gray clouds of spent gunpowder.

Rebecca's eyes burned with smoke and grief. She slumped on the hard-packed dirt floor beside her whimpering mother. The pretty fourteen year old's hands trembled and her mouth grew dry. Fear spiraled in her when she heard a warrior's ear-splitting cry at the front door.

"Reload this thing, damnit," Tulley snapped at her. "Or do you want them Sioux inside here with us?"

Rebecca broke away from her mother and forced herself to obey.

The battle raged into the early afternoon with half a dozen braves falling dead in front of the farmhouse. So far, none of the defenders had been wounded. Rebecca and her mother remained huddled in a corner near Jeremiah Caldwell's corpse. They numbly reloaded weapons, Hannah's fumbling fingers frequently dropping several rounds in a row. Another hour passed and the bandit's cartridges ran low, along with their morale.

"We can't hold out much longer," Uncle Ezekial observed. "We ain't got much ammunition left and there must be a hundred of them Sioux left."

Stricken, Rebecca watched Jake Tulley nod his head.

"Hold your fire a minute, boys," he ordered.

A nearly palpable silence filled the room. The Sioux warriors, possibly expecting the white men to surrender, responded in kind. Rebecca's ears rang in the sudden quiet.

"What's up?" asked Uncle Virgil.

"Maybe we can buy our way out of this mess," replied Tulley. He removed his bowler hat and ran a hand through his close-cropped black hair. Rebecca saw the gang leader study her and her mother closely.

"Whatcha got in mind, Jake?" asked fat Bobby O'Toole. His green eyes seemed lost in the swollen fat on his glistening face.

With a growing sense of revulsion, Rebecca watched Jake Tulley get to his feet and step over to where her late grandmother's Sheffield china tea set rested in a cupboard. The delicate china had been carried in padded leather trunks all the way from Ohio. Tulley fingered the cups and saucers and the nearby white linen tablecloth.

"We might be able to persuade Iron Calf an' his bucks to take these here goodies in exchange for lettin' us go. We got two kegs of whiskey besides."

"Not the china!" cried Rebecca.

"Shut up, girl," snapped Uncle Ezekial.

"Yeah, Becky," added Virgil. "Keep outta this. Besides, them Injuns are kinda your kin anyway. You should be lookin' forward to seein' 'em."

Tulley smiled and Rebecca thought she saw a sudden gleam of madness in the gang leader's eyes. "Just a minute, boys. I think Virgil just gave me a better idea how we might get outta here."

Then Tulley drew back his arm and, with a quick, vicious swipe, sent the delicate Sheffield cups and saucers flying off the cupboard and onto the hard-packed floor. Grandma Caldwell's china smashed into dozens of tinkling pieces.

Hannah seemed to snap out of her grief-stricken lethargy. "How dare you!" she shouted. "That was my mother's tea set."

"What's your plan, Jake?" Uncle Ezekial inquired, ignoring the destruction of beauty.

"Well, much as them Injuns like fancy geegaws and likker, there's something else makes 'em feel a raid was a real success."

Fascinated, Rebecca watched Tulley put on his bowler

hat and step over to where she huddled on the floor with her sobbing mother. The black-haired girl's pulse quickened and she heard her mother suck in her breath.

Tulley grabbed Rebecca by her hair and jerked her painfully to her feet. The gang leader thrust her toward the door. All of a sudden the realization of what he had in mind struck her like a slap in the face.

"Oh, my God!" she cried, eyes wild with dismay.

"You mean give the women to the Injuns?" wondered Ezekial.

Tulley's grip strengthened on Rebecca's hair. She grimaced with pain and watched her mother stagger to her feet. Tulley's voice came hard as rock.

"It's either these here womenfolk or your goddamned scalps," Tulley snarled. "I for one ain't much for settin' around this here sod house waitin' for the ammo to run out."

An ominous silence filled the house.

Virgil cleared his throat.

"You . . . can't . . . be serious!" Rebecca's mother uttered in a strangled voice.

"But they're my family," protested Virgil.

"Shut up, Virgil," Tulley snapped. "Well, boys, what'll it be? All I gotta do is open the door with little missy alongside me and talk to ol' Chief Iron Calf. Whiskey and cunt's two things that'll turn any man's mind from fightin'."

Tulley's men gave instant, noisy approval of the idea.

Rebecca couldn't believe what she had heard. But when she saw the indecision playing on her Uncle Virgil's pudgy face, the awful truth sent a wave of nausea washing up from her stomach. She struggled to keep from throwing up.

"Mother, tell them they can't do this!" she cried.

"Ezekial? Virgil?" sobbed Hannah Caldwell. Her blue eyes pleaded for mercy. "How can you even consider handing your own family to the Sioux?"

"Hell," Tulley grunted. He pulled Rebecca's hair a little

more. "This one here's a half-breed slut anyhow. Iron Calf'll probably take her for a wife. An' you've been had by the redsticks, so you'll be ready for some more."

Swallowing her fear, Rebecca watched Ezekial and Virgil exchange uncertain glances. Slowly they nodded at Tulley. "All right," Ezekial reluctantly announced. "Let's do it."

"No! You can't!" screamed Hannah Caldwell. "Don't do this to us."

A few minutes later, while Rebecca and her trembling mother clung to each other near the back wall, Tulley held a brief pow wow in front of the house with the Oglala Sioux leader, Iron Calf. The Indians had already been given a quick look at Rebecca and her mother at the open doorway and two spare bottles of whiskey broken out. Now came the negotiations.

Her uncles, both of whom understood sign language and spoke a bit of the Lakota language, took part in the parlay. The outlaws—O'Toole, Shannon and Wellington—remained near the windows, guns at the ready, just in case.

Rebecca couldn't see what went on, though deep down in her soul she knew it was only a matter of minutes before they would be given to the Indians. What happened after that was anybody's guess. From the gruesome tales she'd heard about white women living with the Sioux she expected the worst. The whole incident seemed like a horrible dream complete with ruthless villains and bloodthirsty savages.

The nightmare began to come true while voices floated in through the window on the hot summer air.

"We did not know it was you, Tul-ley," Iron Calf said for the fourth time in a mixture of English and Lakota.

"Then . . . then you'll be willin' to call off your braves? Let us go?"

"You have more whiskey?"

"Sure. Two kegs of it, Iron Calf. It's yours."

"Wašté! Waštéšte!" the chief enthused.

"You bet it's good," Tulley returned. "Damned good. An' we got the women. White women for your men to enjoy."

Iron Calf frowned slightly. "What good are white women? They lack the skills of good camp keeping. It takes many beatings to impress on them what Dakota girls seem to know from birth." Still, until they had come onto the Caldwell farm, the raid had been disappointing. The diversion might do the warriors good. He returned his level gaze to Jake Tulley's anxious face.

"Do you have guns for us?"

"Christ," Bobby O'Toole breathed in awe a few minutes later. "They've done it. Now we can get the hell outta here."

"Oh, no. Oooh, no-no-no," Rebecca's mother moaned.

"Mother, what are we going to do?"

Rebecca watched the three outlaws holster their weapons and walk cautiously from the house. They headed for the liquor cache. Bitter Creek Jake poked his head in the house, a wicked smile creasing his face.

"Good day, ladies," he said jauntily, tipping his bowler hat. "I'm sure you'll be in good hands from now on." Laughing, he headed for the corral.

Rebecca turned a cold gaze on her two uncles. They seemed ill at ease, embarrassed.

"We, uh, we'll be ridin' with Bitter Creek, Hannah," Virgil told his sister in a murmur.

"Ezekial! Virgil!" cried Hannah. "Please don't leave us to the savages! For the love of God, don't let me go through that kind of hell again!"

Rebecca's heart fell when the shamefaced uncles paused for only a moment in the doorway. Then they strode toward their horses. Immediately her mother shrieked horribly and buried her face in Rebecca's shoulder.

Suddenly Rebecca felt terribly alone.

Until a dozen chattering, half-naked Sioux warriors

sinewy Crow fighting men proved too much for the lone white man. One angled behind Brett and tackled him around the waist. Swiftly a pair of panting warriors grabbed his arms and lashed him to the top rail of his small corral fence. Helpless, he forced himself to watch without making an outcry while the brutish Crow warriors had their way with Mary Anne a second time, then began to slice the skin from her living body.

Mary Anne screamed with each touch of the knife. Her anguish became too much for Brett to bear. "Oh, God, have mercy!" he cried.

His prayers seemed to be answered almost immediately when Mary Anne slumped dead after five excruciating minutes of torture.

Expecting to be butchered himself, he was astonished when the Indians took him back to their village. After an hour in the skin-tented camp, Brett was told by an Indian who spoke some English that the Crows respected bravery in an enemy and that he had been spared to provide proof to the whole band of his strength.

Instantly he realized why he had been preserved. Images of tortured captives from the tales he had read rose behind his eyes. Many tribes, he recalled, turned particularly courageous captives over to the women and children to torment in an attempt to humble them and also to pay a twisted sort of homage. He shuddered at the thought.

Early the next morning, his fears proved justified. He was taken from the lodge where he had spent the night, lashed to a pole run under his shoulders. The fetters were removed and, with deft strokes of their knives, the Crow warriors cut his clothes away. Naked, they dragged Brett to where two poles had been driven into the ground. A wizened medicine man came forward, shuffling in a dance to the sound of a hidden drum, and shook his tortoise-shell rattle in Brett's face. Before the warriors could bind him, Brett made a desperate bid for freedom.

Swiftly he snatched a knife from the beaded leather sheath on one brave, seized the medicine man and held the blade to his throat.

"One move and your shaman gets his throat cut," Brett growled.

The quick-thinking medicine man wanted no part of a throat slitting . . . particularly his own. He began to harangue his people in a high, sing-song voice. The gist, Brett learned later from the English speaking Crow, was that Brett had proven himself worthy of being called a Crow Strong Heart. He, the old man declared, would adopt him to replace a long dead son and propose the white warrior's membership in the most respected Crow warrior society.

Over the next ten years, Brett led the life of a Crow warrior. He quickly became skilled in the use of bow, war club and lance. He learned hunting and tracking skills and earned the reputation of a ruthless Crow Strong Heart. He became known as Lone Wolf, the most ruthless fighter on the high plains and, in truth, he took pleasure in it.

Until he met Rebecca in the Oglala camp . . .

. . . Rebecca reined in her pony. She had fallen behind while daydreaming. She was surprised to find Lone Wolf perched in a cottonwood tree. His keen blue eyes scanned the prairie.

"See anything?" she inquired lightly. She shaded her eyes from the sun's glare.

"We've got company," murmured Lone Wolf.

Rebecca frowned and glanced at the prairie. "Who are they?"

"Crow, about six of 'em and they're pushin' hard."

FOUR

Lone Wolf jumped down from the tree and strode purposefully to his prancing pony. "Looks like the Crow want me back. Must've been trackin' us for a month now."

He took a coil of rawhide rope, his bow and a quiver of arrows from his pony's back.

"What are we going to do?" Rebecca inquired.

"Prepare some tricks for my former friends."

"Tricks?"

"A few things the Strong Hearts taught me along the way."

"Such as?"

Lone Wolf tethered both ponies and started to jog into the surrounding prairie. "Follow me and I'll show you," he instructed.

Rebecca shrugged and followed.

Watching Lone Wolf work rapidly, she appreciated his skill. He quickly took his braided rawhide lariat and stretched it across the trail in a slight dip, invisible until a rider came directly upon it. He secured one end to a thick sage bush trunk, then used his knife to dig loose dirt and cover the improvised snare.

"A trip-line," Rebecca enthused.

"Yeah. And no way for them to spot it."

Then he padded to a spot farther along, where the faint trace dropped once more and obscured the path. He cast around a fraction of a second until he found what he sought.

"Help me toss all the rocks we can onto the trail," he instructed Rebecca. "That'll cause any who get past the trip to break stride. You'll be right over there, crouched in those bushes. If you get a clear shot at a target, let 'em have it. I'll be back at the rope to pull it up. Then I'll stick them with a few arrows. They know there are two of us, so some will be bound to push on past the ambush to locate you."

Rebecca felt a twinge of anticipation in her stomach. Her years with the Oglala had taught her their hatred of the Crow. "You don't need to tell me more," she said through a grim smile.

The drumming hoofbeats grew louder in the still air.

Lone Wolf started back toward his chosen position. "In a few seconds they'll be right on top of us. Take care of yourself."

"Don't worry."

A second later, Lone Wolf disappeared into the tall, waving buffalo grass on the opposite side of the trail. Rebecca bit her lip and hunkered down in the sage clump. The Crow ponies plunged toward them in a steady rhythm. She glanced around to make certain their own horses had been well hidden in the grass; thrown, hobbled and muzzled. Satisfied she drew her Little Russian and eared back the hammer. She wanted her first shot to be a good one.

In the near distance, two Crow warriors topped the long swell of prairie and thundered down toward Lone Wolf's snare. Right at their heels came a second pair. A short distance behind, the remaining braves rushed toward their intended victims.

Looking between the leafy, pungent-smelling branches, Rebecca felt a sudden stab of excitement while she watched the six shaven-headed Strong Hearts riding toward the trip-line. The first team came right on top of it when Long Wolf yanked on the rawhide rope and it rose in a shower of dust. Braced against another sage bush on his side, it came rigid two feet above the trail.

The ponies squealed when their forelegs went out from under them. They plunged toward the earth, unseating their riders, who tumbled in the dirt with startled cries. Too close to avoid the collision, the second pair crashed into the elevated rumps of their brothers' mounts. They also flew from the crudely-made wooden saddles, one tumbling to his left, away from Lone Wolf, while the other cata-pulted over his animal's head and fell among thrashing hoofs.

Already Lone Wolf had an arrow in the air. It struck the nearest warrior full in the chest, with a meaty smack that Rebecca could hear from her hiding place. The white warrior launched another shaft while confusion slowed the actions of his enemy.

The last pair of Strong Hearts had swerved in time to avoid the pile-up, and whipped their mounts forward to locate the second party in the ambush. They bore down on Rebecca until they spotted the obstacle field of loose rocks. Quickly they knee-reined their well-trained ponies and split off the track into the tall grass to each side. Their battle-wise instincts told them the only logical position would be the clump of sage twenty yards ahead.

Over the heaving rumps of the charging Crow ponies, Rebecca saw Lone Wolf draw back the gut string of his powerful ash bow and let loose another missile. A Strong Heart screamed, a high, piercing sound, and clutched at his belly where only the fletchings protruded.

Transfixed, the blood-dripping flint point protruding from his back, he staggered in a small circle and dropped to the earth. Then Rebecca had no time for being a spectator. The Crow braves had closed the distance to fifty feet. Quickly she brought up her Smith and Wesson .38 and took aim on the nearest. At the last moment she leaped to her feet in the middle of the sage bush.

Only twenty feet away, the surprised Crow had time to blink before the .38 muzzle blossomed a pale orange-yellow. The bullet slammed into his broad, dark face and his eyes bulged from the force of impact. Rebecca fired again.

The Strong Heart's features went slack and a thin line of blood trickled from a hole in his left breast. He leaped backward with the slug's hammering force. Immediately Rebecca turned sharply, mindful of the second warrior. Her action came none too soon.

He careened directly at her with a heavy stone war club poised to smash her head into a bloody pulp.

Pulling through the long double-action trigger of the surprisingly accurate pistol, Rebecca sent a hot .38 round toward her enemy. The charging Crow brave cried out as the 148 grain soft lead bullet tore into his right shoulder. The wincing warrior dropped his club and reined in his mount.

Rebecca risked a quick glance over her shoulder. She saw Lone Wolf engaged with the last Strong Heart, who wielded a steel-bladed trade hatchet. While she watched, immobile for the instant, a knife flashed in the white warrior's left hand and he stooped in on his opponent. The Crow fell for this invitation and swung his sharp-edged weapon. A grunt from the enemy before her brought Rebecca's situation back to her very real danger.

The warrior jumped his pony toward her, a knife in his left hand. Rebecca fired the Little Russian again and the slug peeled hide from the right side of the Strong Heart's ribcage. He spun part way in the saddle, recovered and made a quick decision.

Rebecca watched with relief as the wounded Crow brave changed directions and swiftly galloped away from her. Then she looked toward Lone Wolf again.

Her companion still struggled with his formidable opponent. The steel axe whistled through the air and he lunged to one side, away from the assault. His big hunting knife flashed in the afternoon sun. The grinning Crow moved in a shuffling gait that subtly closed the distance between them. He feinted, then struck out with a round-house swing that, when it missed Lone Wolf, sent him stumbling.

Instantly Lone Wolf lunged forward and buried the tip of his blade between two ribs. With a grunt he forced it to the hilt. Then, with a mighty heave, he drew it toward him. A rush of rich red blood followed.

The Crow warrior shuddered, took two tottering steps forward and fell dead. He joined the corpses of his fellows, scattered in a ring around the wily white man.

Lone Wolf looked up and saw Rebecca standing on the rise above him, her Smith and Wesson hanging at her side, tightly gripped by her powder-smudged fingers. He trotted up to her.

"Are you all right?"

Rebecca nodded, trying to find her voice.

Then Lone Wolf looked beyond her to the body of the warrior she had shot. "Well, look what you did!" He grinned with satisfaction.

"Not bad for a woman with a pea-shooter," she said, a mischievous twinkle in her eyes. "But one got away. I wounded him, twice." She began to reload her Smith and Wesson.

Lone Wolf gave an approving chuckle. "You're right, you can take care of yourself," he observed. "I think those uncles of yours and the other owlhoots had better watch out."

"Well," she returned, placing her gun in her beaded pouch. "At least we ended this Indian threat."

"Not yet," he told her.

She looked up. "What do you mean?"

"This Crow war party must have been given orders to bring me back dead or alive. They wouldn't be able to return to Two Dog's village without me. That there wounded warrior ain't gonna quit 'till he gets me or we get him."

Rebecca smiled. She noted that he had said, 'we.'

Sudden laughter from over the next rise made Rebecca and Lone Wolf rein in their horses in the middle of the trail and listen intently. It was mid-afternoon and they had left the five dead Crow braves an hour behind.

"What is that?"

Again they heard laughter from the nearby swale.

"Sounds like a party," Rebecca added.

"It's a party all right," Lone Wolf drawled. "An Indian war party."

Straining her ears, Rebecca picked up a few words of guttural conversation that drifted to her from the stream bed ahead. Her blue eyes saucered and she glanced at Lone Wolf.

"It's Lakota. Those are Oglala braves."

He nodded. "Seems like we've stumbled upon some warriors and caught 'em off guard. Let's see what they're up to. Maybe it's a party sent after you."

She felt a slight tremor of anxiety ripple through her chest. "I suppose we ought to look, just in case."

They dismounted and eased forward on foot, leading their ponies behind. They entered a small stand of cottonwood and tied up the animals when the twinkling, pale green leaves closed around them. Then they advanced on the ridge like a couple of stalking warriors to a spot in the bushes that opened onto a clearing in the creek bed.

Rebecca's pulse quickened. "Why, they're only youngsters."

She swallowed hard and glanced at two young Oglala warriors who stood beside a scalped middle-aged settler couple. The laughing Indians were trying on some of the dead woman's dresses and seemed to be enjoying themselves while three others rummaged in the box of a partially burned wagon.

Rebecca clenched her fists. It was difficult to look at Oglala warriors so soon after her escape.

Suddenly dozens of bad memories surfaced and flooded her brain. She saw her dead mother, her once pretty face lying in a pool of blood. She felt the lash of willow branches stinging her back. She felt the humiliation of having to endure physical abuses for seemingly endless years.

Her hands began to tremble.

"I don't think they did the killing. That wagon's been hit a long time ago." When Rebecca did not reply he glanced hard at her. "You all right?"

"I don't know if I'll ever be all right," she replied in a hoarse whisper. She felt beads of cold sweat forming on her forehead. "All I know is I can't wait to see my uncles and the Tulley gang."

The Oglala youngsters laughter pierced her thoughts and she realized she'd been sizing up the situation, counting the young braves and developing a plan.

"I see some white woman's clothing for you," Lone Wolf pointed out. "Close to your size, I reckon."

Rebecca smiled. "Yeah," she returned. "Maybe I'll just walk in there and take it." She rose suddenly.

"Rebecca!" Lone Wolf hissed in an attempt to stop her.

"Watch this," she whispered.

"You tryin' to get yourself killed?"

Rebecca gritted her teeth and walked boldly downslope to the stream bed. The laughing young warriors grew silent and whirled to face her. They smiled when they recognized her.

59

"Ho! If it isn't pretty little *Śinaskawin* coming home to her people," greeted the youngest of the braves in Lakota. He stepped forward to welcome her.

"Maybe she misses good Oglala loving," snickered another.

"How would you know, with that *slukila* of yours," teased a third from the charred wagon box.

Rebecca reached into her belt pouch and drew her revolver. When she raised it at the nearest warrior, all their faces slackened in astonishment.

Youth and inexperience had betrayed them.

She squeezed the Little Russian's trigger. The .38 Smith belched fire and sent a hot slug slamming into the throat of the nearest youth. The bullet exited through the back of his head in a shower of blood and brains. The dead brave fell heavily to the ground.

As though in slow motion, another warrior reached for his knife.

Rebecca shot him in the stomach.

The startled Oglala brave clawed at the sledgehammer pain in his belly, opened his mouth in a silent scream and then tumbled dead next to his bleeding friend, his liver destroyed by Rebecca's bullet.

From behind her, Rebecca heard the haunting melody of an arrow in flight. The young Oglala who poised to leap on her from the wagon seat took the shaft in his chest. He made a graceful half-pirouette and toppled toward the prairie dust.

"Haun-nn, haun-nn," he moaned his surrender to darkness.

Rebecca centered the blade front sight of her Little Russian on one teenager, who ran toward where the ponies had been ground-tied. The little .38 cracked again.

Her first bullet entered through the youngster's armpit and burst his heart. He continued to run, a dead lump of flesh, for several steps, then pitched onto his face and curled into a fetal ball. Lone Wolf's bowstring twanged and a flint arrow point buried deep in wood where an instant before the remaining brave had been standing.

Rebecca turned slightly, squatted to get a clear line of fire under the wagon where the now frightened youth cowered. He made a fumbling effort to nock an arrow an instant before she squeezed the trigger.

Soft lead howled off the steel rim of a wagon wheel. The richochet struck the Oglala in his right eyesocket and pulped a large portion of his brain. He slumped into silent death while Rebecca took a step toward him, the Smith .38 held ready.

"Five years is a long time," her voice grated out.

Lone Wolf strode briskly down hill. "I wouldn't believe that if I didn't see it," he exclaimed, looking into her glowing eyes.

Rebecca merely nodded and licked dry lips. "Killing is easy, once you've started, isn't it?" she asked in a husky, awe-filled voice.

Lone Wolf put a long arm around her shoulders. "Yeah," he agreed softly. "And you've only begun."

"Let's have a look at those clothes," she said at last.

Riding along the little used trail once again, Rebecca felt a warmth of happiness spread through her chest. She's been able to select a corduroy riding suit from among the dead settler's woman's wardrobe and had decided to wait until shortly before they arrived at the farm to put it on. She tingled with anticipation as they neared the old homestead.

"I wonder what the old place looks like," she speculated aloud.

Lone Wolf, his narrow ridge of blond hair blowing in the wind, trotted alongside her. His eyes scanned the area for signs of trouble.

"Maybe it's not even there."

"What do you mean?"

"Fire, storms, who knows what could have happened to an abandoned farm in five years? Besides, we'll find out in less than half an hour. Your grandaddy's place should be right over this rise."

Rebecca gripped her pony's Indian-made reins and tried to control her rising excitement. She'd waited five years to return home, yet now her determination seemed to flag. She rode alongside Lone Wolf in brooding silence as they passed a small copse of cottonwoods.

Then came the sudden attack.

The final Crow warrior whom she had shot back on the trail leaped from the branches of a leafy tree. His painted body, slicked with streaks of blood, slammed into Lone Wolf and knocked him off his pony.

Rebecca expertly controlled her prancing horse. "Look out!" she belatedly cried.

The wounded Crow quickly rolled on top of Lone Wolf and raised a war hatchet. Screaming something in the Crow tongue, the brave slashed downward at the white warrior's head. Lone Wolf rolled to the side. The wild blow struck the ground.

Rebecca leaped from her painted pony and hauled out her revolver. Aiming the weapon at the struggling combatants, she realized she couldn't get a clear shot at the Crow brave.

She edged cautiously to within two feet of the flailing men, then raised her Smith and Wesson and extended her arm. She poked the muzzle against the side of the Crow's head.

"Lone Wolf," she snapped in English, "look out!"

He ducked. She squeezed the trigger.

Like a butcher's hammer striking a steer's head, the lead slug snapped into the Strong Heart's temple, blowing shards of bone into his brain. Flesh blackened and curled back from the entrance hole, burnt by the muzzle blast. Rebecca watched the shaven-headed brave's eyes roll as he slumped dead to the ground.

Lone Wolf rose upward, his knife ready for a finishing stroke.

"No need," Rebecca told him, confident of the effect of her shot.

FIVE

Half an hour later, Rebecca flattened some wrinkles in the corduroy riding habit and stepped out from behind some leafy bushes. Her lustrous black hair glistened in the late afternoon sunshine.

"What do you think?" she asked, modeling the new clothes in front of Lone Wolf. She whirled and her long hair and split skirt flew away from her body.

"Not bad."

"Not bad?" she returned archly, her eyebrows raised. She resented his casual remark, yet she felt uncomfortable, too tightly confined in the garments so different from the freedom of Sioux garb.

Lone Wolf pursed his lips, searching his memory for the proper "civilized" white compliment. "All right," he said with an easy smile. "It's beautiful . . . and so are you."

She curtsied. "Why thank you, sir," she murmured, then burst into a rich, throaty chuckle.

"How does it feel to be a white woman again?"

She shrugged. "I . . . uh . . . good . . . I don't know yet.

Uncomfortable if you want the truth. And just wait until I have to use a knife and fork and powder my nose with all the proper church ladies."

Lone Wolf laughed. "Well," he said, walking over to his pony. "The Caldwell farm can't be more than half a mile. Maybe there you'll get to try some of those 'civilized' things."

Rebecca's heart beat faster. What would she find when she reached home?

"You'd better bury that Indian dress," Lone Wolf advised.

"Bury it?"

"Wouldn't take a Sioux war party long to find it if you didn't."

Rebecca plucked at the tightness across her breasts. This sort of getup was a nuisance she decided. "I think I'll take it along. After all, it is my only change of clothes."

Lone Wolf cocked an eyebrow, intrigued by her decision. "Suit yourself."

Cantering up the gentle slope leading to the house where she'd spent her childhood, Rebecca found her mind filled with a strange mixture of emotions. She was glad to be back on the homestead, but saddened by thoughts of her murdered mother. She was happy to be on Caldwell land once again, yet for some reason she felt like a complete stranger. Even so, she thrilled to recognize the familiar terrain where she had romped as a child. Then her mind clouded again and she was filled with hard, cold fury when she recalled that day when she had been given away to save an outlaw's life.

They reined in on the crest of a grassy knoll.

Rebecca's heart pounded. She peered through the blinding late afternoon sunshine at the little sod house below and the sparkle of the pond beyond it where she used to go skinny dipping. The old Caldwell place looked in good condition. Except for the broken-down corrals, everything appeared the way she remembered it, including the fragrant, flower-filled meadows all around the house. The little soddy looked almost lived in. In fact, a tendril of white cooking smoke drifted lazily into the sky from the chimney.

Her eyes widened. "Somebody's living there."

"Looks that way."

"Why, of all the nerve!"

Lone Wolf chuckled at her indignation. "After all, it has been empty for five years. Maybe it's your uncle," he offered.

She felt a sudden spasm of hate grip her stomach. "I never thought about that."

"We'd better take things nice and easy," he suggested. Lone Wolf took up his bow and drew an arrow from his quiver.

"Surely Ezekial, Virgil and the Tulley gang wouldn't come back here when it's so vulnerable to attack?"

"There's only one way to find out."

Rebecca swallowed hard. "All right, let's head on down. At least I'll get to see the old homestead." Then she glanced at Lone Wolf's clothing.

"Think you ought to go down dressed like that? Or aren't you ever going to change out of your Crow duds?"

"Like I told you, I ain't a white man and I'm not an Indian. Though," he admitted ruefully, "after ten years with the Crow, I feel more like an Indian. I'll just keep these buckskins and this Strong Heart haircut for a while."

"Make you a mighty inviting target."

"I'll have to duck quickly, then," he returned with a smile.

Rebecca chuckled and headed toward the house.

As they trotted down on the place where Rebecca had dashed impatiently through stuffy rooms and peeked through the narrow rifle slits in the shutters at the wind-blown Nebraska snow, she felt a twinge of nostalgia. Approaching the squat house and looking around at the dusty front yard, she recalled her Grandpa Jeremiah's tender brown eyes and gentle demeanor.

Then Rebecca's brain flooded with furious thoughts about her rapacious uncles and the Tulley gang. Her grip tightened on the reins. All the happy images of her childhood evaporated to be replaced by a cold, hard resolve to find and punish the ones who sent her to the Sioux.

Suddenly a rifle cracked from the house.

"That's far enough!" a deep male voice called.

"Who are you?" Rebecca demanded as she reined in her mount.

"That's for me to know and for you never to find out," the man returned. "Now git before I improve my aim a little."

"Watch it," Lone Wolf cautioned. "He sounds scared."

"If it were my uncles, they would've recognized me by now."

"Not necessarily. Captivity changes a person."

She stroked her pretty face. "I think I'll take a chance."

"Like with those Oglala? But be ready to duck."

"My name is Rebecca Caldwell," she yelled. "I've . . . I've been away for a while. This homestead belonged to my late grandfather. I'm all that's left of the family, so it's mine now."

There followed a long, tense pause.

"No it ain't! This here is my place. Now git!" yelled the man.

"I don't mean to cause you any harm," she shouted. "All I'd like to do is look at the place where I grew up."

"What's that Injun doin' with ya? He looks like a damned renegade."

Rebecca smiled and glanced at Lone Wolf. "It's all right. He's a tame Indian."

Suddenly the flimsy front door jerked open and a middle-aged settler woman appeared with her hands on her hips.

"Why, child," she shouted, "you come on down here.

And bring your Injun friend with you if ya like."

"Molly!" cried the man in consternation. "Get back in here!"

"Oh, hush, Elroy," snapped the rosy-cheeked woman. "Can't you see that the poor child just wants to have a look at her old homestead?" She turned back and beckoned to Rebecca and Lone Wolf.

"Come on, child," she called. "We have some vittles on the table if you feel hungry."

Hungry? thought Rebecca. Her stomach growled in reply.

Rebecca and Lone Wolf trotted up to the house and dismounted near the doorway. For Rebecca, it meant she was all the way home.

"Don't believe I caught your name, young man," Molly directed to Lone Wolf as he and Rebecca stepped up onto the low stoop. Her head tilted at a pert angle and her eyes sparkled with curiosity.

The white Indian gave her a shy smile. "The name used to be Brett Baylor, though I've been called Lone Wolf for so long it's hard to answer to anything else. The, ah, Crow sorta took me in," he ended uneasily.

"Land sakes! What an awful ordeal. Now you two go on in there and take a seat. It's only plain fare, but tasty if I do say so myself. My goodness, I know folks back East who would give a year's pay for a set of purty buckskins like you're wearin'," she enthusiastically confided to Lone Wolf.

"They're comfortable," the taciturn young man returned. Deep within he felt embarrassed and confused. Then he caught scent of the cooking aromas from inside and his stomach lurched. In a second a warmth spread through him. He, too, had found a bit of home.

"Squatters?" Rebecca inquired as she finished the last of the thick venison stew.

"Well," the woman evaded, "we like to think of ourselves

as the second wave of pioneers. Now, have some of this apple pie. We found this here place abandoned," she returned to her explanation while Rebecca took a slab of the dried fruit confection. "And fixed it up a bit."

"A bit?" growled Elroy Jameson. Rebecca learned he was gruff, but tender-hearted. His blessing over the meal had brought tearful memories of her grandfather. "Why this here land was overgrown with weeds and the sod roof was about to fall into ruin. We done saved the house, that's what we did."

Rebecca smiled and stuffed another forkful of Mrs. Jameson's apple pie into her mouth. It was the first time she'd used a fork in five years and she felt as clumsy as a four year old. Yet, her white girl's memory hadn't forgotten how delicious stew, mashed potatoes and homemade apple pie tasted.

The Jamesons, a childless couple from Illinois, had allowed Rebecca and Lone Wolf to enter without further questions. For Rebecca the actual experience of walking into the sod house after leaving it under such savage conditions brought a lump to her throat. Beside her, Lone Wolf produced another of his fleeting, self-conscious smiles and accepted a second slice of pie. Rebecca finished her portion and began to pump the Jamesons for information about her uncles, the Tulley gang and general news about the area.

"Then you haven't heard anything about my uncles, Ezekial and Virgil?"

Mrs. Jameson shook her head. "Why, child, us bein' what some folks might consider squatters, we just don't socialize much. Your best bet for news would be in Jury Wells. Them townsfolk would know somethin', I'm sure."

Elroy Jameson, a short, stocky man with a full head of curly gray hair, cleared his throat. "As for them outlaws," he began, "everything I've got is second hand, so's to speak. I talked with some drifters the other day and they mentioned that the Tulley gang was raisin' hell up north a ways. Said they was shootin' up the prairie towns around Fort Robinson."

Rebecca sighed and put down her fork. "Well," she said, her voice weary, "I thank you for the meal and your hospitality. Perhaps we ought to be moving on."

"Nonsense, child!" Molly Jameson returned. "We have a big copper bath tub in the back room. If you want, I can heat some water for you."

"A bath! In a tub?" the words escaped Rebecca's lips before she had given full thought to the effect they might have on her hostess. All the same, the image of bathing in the tingling, fresh waters of a swift-moving stream, Sioux style, instantly compared itself with sitting in a confining tub with the soap scum, body oils and liberated dirt floating around, waiting to coat the skin again when getting out. The idea hardly appealed.

With only slight regret, she realized that her ways and those of the whites vastly differed since her captivity. Even so, the vestiges of her former "company" manners rose to chastize her and she made a new face, summoning words to moderate her first outbreak.

"Why . . . That would be lovely," she sighed. "It's been . . . well, it's been a while since I had a hot bath."

"Well, don't fret none," Molly Jameson comforted. She added wood to the Caldwell's heavy cast iron stove they'd claimed upon moving in. "I'll have your bath water ready in no time."

"Oh!" Rebecca squeaked. Her hands went to her mouth.

Lone Wolf's hand sought his hunting knife. His concerned eyes went from open doorway, to windows and back to Rebecca.

"What's wrong?" a suddenly worried Molly Jameson asked.

"Sheffield china!" Rebecca cried out. She pointed at two chipped saucers leaning against the top shelf of a nearby cupboard.

70

Mr. and Mrs. Jameson exchanged glances.

"Why, yes, child," Molly began gently. "I suppose you recognized them, eh?"

Rebecca nodded, tears welling in her eyes. "It used to belong to my grandmother. My—my grandfather was going to give the whole tea set to me when I got married."

"Well, we found two saucers on the floor when we moved in. The rest of the set, I'm sorry to say, was smashed to pieces."

Rebecca nodded, her brain filled with a vivid image of Jake Tulley tossing the china onto the tamped-earth floor. "I remember the day it happened."

"You're welcome to them," Molly Jameson offered. "They seem to mean more to you, child, than they ever could to me."

Rebecca wiped away a tear and shook her head. "No," she announced as she stood up. "That's part of my past now. All I'm thinking about is the future."

Her cold eyes met Lone Wolf's.

"Well," Molly began, then returned to the original subject. "I . . . I'll just heat up some water for you. It won't take long."

Rounding on her husband and Lone Wolf, Molly instructed them to fetch the tub into the bedroom while she gathered up her large pots and stoked the kitchen stove.

"Then you bring me the water, Elroy, ya hear?"

"Oh, no," Rebecca interjected. "I'll get it. I always used to enjoy drawing water from that old well." Rebecca went about her task and carried two bucketsful to the tub, while Molly heated the remainder.

In spite of open doors and windows, the soddy grew insufferably hot and the two men sweated over a smoke and sassafras tea. The women fussed around in the bedroom.

How odd it felt, Rebecca thought when she lowered herself into the steaming tub. The hot water turned her skin a glowing pink and her nose wrinkled at the unaccustomed scent of heavily perfumed soap, which Molly Jameson had provided.

"It's my last bar," the older woman confided. "Can't get the likes out here often and when you can it costs too much. I brought this all the way from Ohio. For special occasions, don't you know? I figure this is one. Enjoy your bath, dearie."

But could she enjoy it? Rebecca wondered when she thought again of the captured effluvium that would soon scum the surface. Never mind, her practical side admonished, feel how it's relaxing your tired muscles. Rebecca sighed and surrendered, still caught between the white world and the red.

The hot bath water had a strangely sensual effect on her. She felt a twinge of sexual desire in her loins. She'd missing growing up as a white girl and attending barn dances. She had never experienced a normal girl's sexual explorations. Now, lying back in the copper tub with her eyes shut, Rebecca suddenly recalled her emergence as a woman while still a captive slave . . .

. . . It happened one hot September evening in 1872, when Rebecca was sixteen. Feeling hot and sweaty, she had walked to her favorite swimming hole around a bend of the creek, beyond the Oglala village. She hauled her full-length elkskin dress over her head and stood completely naked at the water's edge.

Rebecca stared at her golden reflection in the shimmering water. She smiled and recalled when, as a twelve year old, she'd been studying her naked body at the Caldwell's farm's waterhole and been surprised by some peeping-Tom neighbor boys. Now she ignored the hustle and bustle of the nearby Indian camp and turned her attention to the present.

She gently ran her long, tapered fingers over her

curvaceous figure. She began at firm, round breasts with their taut, rose-colored nipples and wide, puffy aerolas. Then she closed her eyes and slid her hands across her flat, smooth stomach, thrilling to the delightful sensation it sent through her body. Slowly she advanced to the sparse, wispy triangle of pubic hair. She gasped as her fingers lingered for a long, luscious moment in the silky folds of flesh at her moistened vaginal opening.

Suddenly she heard a twig snap behind her.

Sucking in her breath, Rebecca whirled and found herself peering into a handsome Oglala youth's gleaming brown eyes. It was Four Horns, one of her admirers. She tried to cover her nakedness with her slender arms. Four Horns smiled broadly.

"I saw you leaving the camp," he informed her in Lakota. His eyes roamed over her body. "I'm glad I followed you."

Rebecca's heart pounded. "Go away!" she snapped in mock anger. "I'm . . . I'm not dressed."

Although the Sioux made little of nudity, children of both sexes often running through the camp naked until the age of eight or ten, it was traditional for males and females to bathe separately. This intense scrutiny by the lusty youth embarrassed Rebecca nearly to the extent it excited her.

Four Horns chuckled. "So I see."

"Somebody might come."

"I don't care."

"Well, *I* do."

"I've had my eyes on you for two summers now, *Śinaskawin.* And now I finally have a chance to look at all of you."

Then, while Rebecca felt her face flush and her shapely body tremble with a curious mixture of anxiety and sexual desire, Four Horns began to strip.

"What . . . What are you doing?" she demanded, taking a step backward.

"I'm taking advantage of the situation," the muscular youth told her blandly, a twinkle of mischief in his eyes.

"What if the *akacita* catch you?"

"It'll be worth it. Besides, who cares about the camp police?"

She saw Four Horns glance quickly at her loins. She shifted her feet nervously, yet made no attempt to escape. Then she watched, entranced, as the muscular brave peeled off his traditional hair shirt and step out of his bucksin loincloth. He was now completely naked.

Enraptured, her eyes scanned his body.

He chuckled again, a warm sound that thrilled her. "Do you like what you see?"

"I . . . I think we've gone too far," she offered, licking her lips. "I want to be your friend, Four Horns, but I'm not ready for lovemaking."

"When will you be ready, *Śinaśkawiṅ?*" He took a step toward her and smiled. "I'm ready now. Every man in the Oglala camp dreams of you. But it will be I who makes love with you."

"Please, don't talk like that."

"Surely you must want sex as much as I do."

"I . . . I don't know what I want," she wailed, her heart beating against her ribs. "Please leave me alone."

"Leave you alone? How can I do that?" He stepped closer, his long penis fully grown. Rebecca found herself scanning the copper-skinned youth's smooth chest, muscles arms and remarkably long organ.

Suddenly, pushed by her rising panic and teenage insecurity, she turned and splashed into the swimming hole. She dove head-first into the cool prairie water and came up sputtering in the middle of the stream.

With her long black hair matted against her head, Rebecca glanced at Four Horns on the bank. He laughed and slowly stroked his shaft. With a quickly intaken breath, he leaped toward her. Rebecca's face slackened when he entered the water.

"Don't!" she cried.

"Here I come!" Four Horns cried, diving under the surface.

Rebecca felt panic rising again. "Four Horns, where are you?" she shouted. She peered through the gathering dusk at the shimmering ripples on the water. Four Horns remained submerged.

Without warning the handsome boy surfaced with a watery gasp directly behind her. The wide-eyed girl whirled at the unexpected sound, her hands going to her mouth.

"My, you are skittish," he accused. "Like a newborn colt."

His long, unbraided hair lay plastered against his head and his naked body glistened with water.

"I . . . I . . .," Rebecca stammered.

"What's wrong? I'm here . . . you're here . . ."

"I . . . I don't think we should be doing this," she blurted. Despite her spoken protests, her loins began to quiver with desire. She couldn't keep her eyes off Four Horns' naked body. Suddenly she realized the reason she was afraid—she didn't trust her own feelings.

"You'll love it, believe me."

Before Rebecca could take any evasive action, he stepped forward and enveloped her in his muscled arms. When their naked bodies touched, she felt his long, hard penis against her abdomen and thrilled to the touch.

"Oh!" she squealed.

"That's just a sample of what's ahead," he promised.

"Four Horns, please don't!" she begged. Her full breasts ached for his touch and her loins pulsed with desire.

For the first time in her young life she was sexually aroused. She didn't know how to react—especially with one of the people she had silently sworn to hate. She'd led a sheltered life before becoming a captive and, because of her strict Christian upbringing, hadn't indulged in any of the mild sexual explorations common in the Oglala village. During her previous two years of captivity, under Iron Calf's supervision, Rebecca had remained completely innocent and celibate. Now her pent-up passion drove her wild.

Four Horns pressed his muscled body against her shapely frame. The pressure of his elongated penis against her body sent a delicious tremor of desire rippling through her loins.

"Oh, Four Horns!" she gasped, closing her eyes.

I can't let this happen, thought Rebecca. I can't let myself fall in love with an Indian!

"Four Horns, I . . ." she stammered.

By then it was too late.

She opened her eyes in time to watch him reach under the surface of the water. She felt his big hand groping near her fully aroused maidenhood. His seemingly educated fingers brushed against her silken mound before they gently entered her sensitive and already moist opening.

She sucked in her breath. Never had anything felt so good!

Four Horns let his fingers enter her fully. Pulses of pure joy surged through her.

"Oh . . . my . . . God!" she cried in English. Instantly her hungry body utterly betrayed her studied intentions. Her long, tapered fingers reached out of their own accord and wrapped tightly around his hardened penis.

"That's more like it!" he enthused.

She began to stroke him in the manner she had seen him do. "I . . . don't . . . think . . . we . . . should . . . be . . . doing . . . this," Rebecca stuttered. She writhed in delirious ecstasy. Four Horns' fingers expertly strummed her sensitive flesh. The present retreated and they became two gasping lovers standing waist deep in the middle of the swimming-hole.

Then she heard voices approaching. Four Horns stiffened at the sound.

"Somebody is coming," he cautioned.

"Oh, don't leave me now, Four Horns," she begged.

"I must, or we will both be in trouble."

"Stay with me!" Rebecca pleaded, her body atremble with need and desire.

"I can't," he replied. He removed his long fingers from her slippery channel. "But I will come to your lodge tonight and we will make love."

"But . . ."

"I'll see you after midnight. Loosen two ground stakes. I'll slip under the sidewall and enter the lodge that way."

Before Rebecca could protest any further, he climbed from the water, gathered his clothes and sprinted away, to be swallowed up by the growing darkness. She stood for a moment and tried to collect her thoughts. The intimate contact had been exhilarating. How she regretted its ending . . . and longed for more. She touched herself there in sweet remembrance, but no, it wasn't the same.

Then the approaching voices in the darkness spurred her into action. She leaped from the water and started to dress. All she could think about was Four Horns' gentle hands on her fully aroused body.

She could hardly wait for midnight.

As the summer night wore on, Rebecca lay under a buffalo robe inside the chief's teepee, where she lived, and waited for Four Horns. It was well past midnight by her reckoning and the sixteen-year-old had grown anxious.

The boisterous Oglala had spent the evening dancing to their drums, feasting on bowlsful of puppy stew and singing around crackling bonfires. Rebecca's mother had gone to sleep early on her own side of the lodge. Rebecca suspected the alacrity with which the chief's wives had provided the small lodge stemmed from fear of Hannah's mental state.

Now, wide awake, Rebecca lay naked under the robe and dreamed about Four Horn's touch on her velvety body.

She trembled and pulled the robe closer to her chin. Four Horns had stroked a simmering fire in her body. Now she longed to make love for the first time.

Glancing at her sleeping mother, she smiled and felt it strange that both Caldwell women had their first sexual experiences with Sioux men. Then she frowned. Although still a virgin, and presumably chaste and modest, she was beginning to fear her new lover wouldn't show.

Then Rebecca heard his voice.

"Šinaskawin?" came a loud whisper.

"Y-yes, I am here," she returned. She checked to see if Iron Calf and his wife remained asleep. "Don't make so much noise."

"Is the skirt unfastened?"

"Yes," she hissed, her desire building.

Then, while Rebecca pulled the buffalo robe tighter against her naked body, her heart began to pound with excitement. Four Horns slid under the bleached buffalo hides and entered the lodge.

The tall youth stood in the lodge's shadowy interior. His copper-skinned body reflected the last flickering flames of the cooking fire. Rebecca's widened eyes flitted from his broad, bare chest to the skimpy leather loincloth he wore.

"I was afraid you weren't going to come," she admitted in a hoarse whisper. Her heart thudded against her ribs. Her loins quivered and grew hot with desire. She felt her nipples harden and her velvet passage moisten even more.

"I wouldn't miss this for anything," whispered Four Horns. He glanced around the teepee's interior. "I've wanted to make love to you for a long time. I can't think of a better place than here in your own lodge."

"Oh, Four Horns," Rebecca cried. Her voice was heavy with desire. She threw aside the robe and knelt, naked, in front of him. She looked up into Four Horns' hungry brown eyes, then reached out and unfastened his loincloth. His long, fully distended penis bobbed free.

Without a wasted motion, she grasped the hard shaft of flesh and stroked it inexpertly. Slowly she rubbed the sensitive tip of his penis against her smooth, trembling abdomen, uncertain of what to do next. Her young lover stiffened at the silken contact, his back arched and he writhed with ecstasy.

Instinct took control of Rebecca's will. She drew fully back on his foreskin and directed his pulsing shaft downward, to the curly thatch that lightly covered her quivering mound.

"Aaah!" Four Horns gasped.

"Shhh!" Rebecca cautioned in a soft, trembling whisper. "You'll awaken Iron Calf."

Four Horns pressed against her and she felt his hugeness probe into the fleshy folds at the outer portals of her moist, eager chamber. A sudden, irrelevant thought caused her to giggle.

"This is not a *slukila*," she solemnly pronounced, using the Lakota word for a child's penis.

"Now who is making noise?" he snapped in feign crankiness. Then, when his throbbing maleness encountered the hot flow of her juices he murmured in her ear.

"No. That is surely a *sluka*, every bit of it."

Four Horns smiled and lay Rebecca on the fluffy buffalo robes. Her naked back snuggled against the downy hair. She watched the muscular youth lean forward and hover over her glistening body.

"Now," he whispered, "I will make you mine."

Rebecca swallowed hard. Her desire spiraled.

"Yes, Four Horns, oh, yes!"

He leaned forward and began to smother her golden-skinned body with passionate kisses. His full, sensuous lips lingered for a long, delicious moment on her tautly erect nipples, sucking them greedily like a baby might. She felt a cold tremor of desire ripple along her spine.

Reaching upward, she clung to Four Horns and brought

79

his head down to hers. She returned his kisses with a passion of her own, starting with his smiling face and working her way along his body.

Panting with desire, Four Horns buried his mouth in Rebecca's downy pubic bush, his firm tongue parting the silky folds of flesh at her sensitive opening. She writhed atop the robes. She felt him lapping at the lacy screens and she groaned with delight.

"Oh! Oh, Four Horns, take me now!" she pleaded.

Rebecca reached out and found his rod-stiff penis. She quickly guided it into her.

Four Horns came down gently on her virginal body, his hardened cock slicing slowly through her slippery channel until finally, after several attempts to penetrate, he thrust his shaft violently through her maidenhead. Swiftly he plunged into her innermost regions. Rebecca shrieked with pain and delight.

Iron Calf stirred in his sleep, grunted and resumed a sound snore.

"Aaaah, Four Horns!" she breathed. She wrapped her slender arms around his back as they lay coupled on top of the buffalo robes. Slowly he withdrew his massive, swollen member, only to thrust deeply once more. Rebecca gasped and clung to him. Pinpoints of colored light exploded behind her tightly closed eyes and she began to rock to the ageless rhythm of love.

Four Horns gathered his knees under him and drove his throbbing lance deeply, to the very mouth of her womb.

Rebecca's eyes popped open, her wildly stimulated body in the grip of incredible sensation. Her head thrashed from side to side and her mouth formed a soundless cry of pure animal delight.

Was it always like this? She wondered on it through a maze of splendor. If so, then why, oh why, had she waited so long? The swift, sharp pain of her deflowering had long since faded in memory and she strove with all her body and soul to match the delicious meter of Four Horns' love-making. *I'm alive . . . and . . . this is real,* she exulted, *and it's . . . it's wonderful!*

Then time lost all meaning for Rebecca while the healthy teenagers earnestly labored in the fields of Venus.

Finally Four Horns cried out softly, arched his back and exploded into her. His rich flood and final, spasmodic thrusts drove Rebecca over the edge into glorious completion.

Four Horns collapsed on top of her.

Rebecca's heart pounded like a runaway horse.

Lying clasped together inside her mother's small, conical lodge, the two perspiring lovers remained silent in their post-sexual bliss. No longer a virgin, Rebecca sighed and thought about her new dilemma.

When she glanced at Four Horns' athletic body she felt another tremor of desire. The fingers of one hand strayed to the moist, tingling mound at the juncture of her thighs. There she circled the flaccid shaft that still connected them. At her touch, Four Horns murmured softly and his relaxed manhood surged with new life. Rebecca thrilled at the hot mass that enlarged inside her.

"Oh, yes. I want you again," she whispered in her lover's ear. "I . . . I *need* you again," she concluded, almost pleading.

Four Horns ground his pelvis in a lazy, circular motion that brought new delights to Rebecca's young, vibrant body. She wanted it to never end. She grasped his churning buttocks and forced his great length deep within her, nature directing her to contract and expand the muscles that controlled the burning passage which he penetrated with a sweet violence that grew more dear to her with each stroke.

And, yes, oh yes, it was every bit as wondrous as the first time. Perhaps even better.

* * *

Early the next morning, while dropping hot stones into the buffalo-paunch kettle to heat Iron Calf's breakfast soup, Rebecca had misgivings about their passionate encounter of the previous night. Would he hate her now for surrendering so easily? Would he feel contempt for the white captive who had become a wanton with an insatiable desire for his maleness and the tremulous release the hot gush of his juices gave to her? A stab of fear drove through her breast when she saw Four Horns approaching. She lowered her eyes and turned partway away. In two strides he reached her side and caught her arm in his strong grasp.

"Tonight I will stand under the blanket with you."

"W-what?"

"I want the whole band to know that you are my girl and that some day we will become as one."

Marry? Rebecca found no words to make reply. Marry a . . . a savage? No! And yet . . . memories of their ecstasy flooded over her, "And afterward?" she inquired shamelessly. "When we have been under the blanket, will you come to my side of the lodge again in the night?"

September turned to October, the Moon of Falling Leaves, and the young couple stood or sat under a large, colorful trade blanket nearly every night. The Dakota courtship custom brought many giggles and stares from the people of Iron Calf's band. Yet, Rebecca saw a subtle change in her status. More often now she did the work of all women, not the dirty, unpleasant tasks of a slave. Whenever possible, she and Four Horns would slip away to make love along the creek bank or under the spreading branches of a venerable cottonwood that graced a low hill to the west of the encampment. After Four Horns' first proud announcement, they never discussed marriage again.

Then, in November, it became urgent to do so. Rebecca discovered that she was pregnant. Frightened of the implication, shamed in her white girl's soul, she said nothing of it, enduring morning sickness and hiding her secret from all eyes. For one wild, hopeless day she thought she would go mad, or kill herself, or do something else equally drastic. Then she shrugged off the mood. Oglala girls got pregnant all the time, had healthy, wrinkled-faced babies and went on with life in camp. Would she be any different? A week later, Four Horns came to Iron Calf's lodge with a string of ponies, a newly made, ash bow and a lynxskin quiver of exquisitely fashioned arrows.

"I come seeking a wife," he announced after politely scratching the doorflap to announce his presence.

To Rebecca's shock and growing anger, Iron Calf entered into the negotiations with high spirits. In the end, without even consulting or considering her wishes, a bargain was struck and Iron Calf announced to those nearby that Four Horns had a woman and he had a fine new buffalo pony and four other horses. The camp crier, the *eyanpaha*, took up the tale and carried the news throughout the rings of lodges. Two days later, Chief Iron Calf made the marriage official.

"This young man wanted this girl, my adopted daughter, so we gave her to him," Iron Calf said simply to the gathered Oglala. "This marriage is known as *iyotanyapi*, for it binds this *wicahca*, a true husband, with this *wankanyankahca*, his true wife."

Outside the teepee of Four Horns' parents, the gathered Oglala whooped with joy.

"So, therefore," concluded the chief, "go forth together and bring many boy children into our band."

Again the people cheered.

Rebecca didn't know whether to laugh or cry . . .

. . . Finally Rebecca stood, stepped from Mrs. Jameson's tub and began to dry herself. Suddenly the door swung open. Still jumpy after so many years living in constant danger, she reached for her small flencing knife—which wasn't there—then turned toward the door.

She saw Lone Wolf. Her face slackened with relief.

"I thought you might have drowned," he said by way of explanation. Then he began to leave.

"No!" she cried. "I mean, don't leave."

He hesitated for a moment in the doorway.

"Please . . . please come in, Lone Wolf," she invited.

He closed the door. "All I really wanted to say is it's about time we moved on," Lone Wolf offered. "Seems like your uncles headed north, as did Tulley's gang."

Rebecca nodded. She suddenly felt unbearably sexy.

She lowered the towel and revealed her naked body to Lone Wolf. She watched his icy blue eyes roam quickly over breasts, stomach, pubic mound and long legs. She shivered with desire under the glare of his scrutiny.

"Why do you do this?" he inquired coolly.

"I . . . wanted you to see all of me," she replied lamely.

"So, I have seen you now and I realize more than ever that you are exactly like my dead wife. She even had your firm breasts. But I let her down ten years ago. I can never love another woman."

"Don't you want my body?"

"Yes. Of course I do. Only . . ." he hesitated, shyly reluctant to discuss himself. "I have sworn a medicine oath, my feet do not stray from the path of Power." He smiled at her, relaxed by his revelation.

She nodded her understanding and covered herself with the towel. "Perhaps I have really discovered a man I can trust," she responded sincerely.

"I am at your service," he offered finally.

Rebecca smiled. "Then I'll get dressed so we can head after Tulley again. I've had enough of this old house for now."

Lone Wolf went out. Rebecca sighed and finished dressing.

SIX

Rebecca felt better, mentally, after visiting the old Caldwell homestead. She bid farewell to the Jamesons and told them they could continue to live on the property.

Now she rode beside Lone Wolf. The sunshine warmed her back through the corduroy riding suit. She felt distinctly uncomfortable and longed for the supple, luxuriant caress of her Sioux deerskin dress. For its freedom, too, she thought as the seams bit into her underarms. They headed north, toward the Nebraska state line and the Black Hills beyond. And, hopefully, the Jake Tulley gang.

"What do you know about Tulley?" she asked Lone Wolf.

"I heard some about him while I was with the Crow."

"And?"

"He's a bank robber, rapist and murderer who's wanted in several states and territories. Even the Crow don't like him. He's a good character to avoid."

She nodded. "I learned that five years ago."

"He also rides with some of the toughest, best shootin'

gunmen on the frontier. Fellas like Luke Wellington and Ed Shannon."

"We can forget about Shannon," Rebecca said with finality.

"Yeah, but you can bet Tulley and his boys won't forget about it. Them other gunhands got a good description of you in Bazile Mills."

She felt a chill in her stomach. "I'll just have to be ready, that's all."

"Let's hope we find 'em before they find you."

They rode along in silence for a few minutes. Then Lone Wolf glanced at Rebecca. "Havin' any second thoughts about goin' after the outlaws?"

"None whatsoever."

"That's good. You'll need that determination to carry you through. Tulley's got lots of owlhoot friends around."

"I'm ready."

"I think you really are."

"I can still picture Tulley and the others in my grandfather's house. I remember Tulley's twisted face when he smashed the china."

Lone Wolf looked at her. "Remember what I told you. Keep cool when you face these men. There's no such thing as careless heroes out here on the plains. Just lots of dead fools."

She nodded. "I'll remember that."

Rebecca gripped her reins and rode on. She knew her quest for vengeance wouldn't be easy. Her encounter with Ed Shannon and her talk with Lone Wolf confirmed her suspicions.

Traveling across undulating fields full of fragrant blossoms and past leafy cottonwoods laden with twittering birds, she became mesmerized by a giddy feeling of freedom. She'd often dreamed about such rides during her captivity. It was one of the things that helped her survive. It nurtured her, kept her sane until she escaped. Now she was in heaven and at peace with herself.

Until gunshots echoed from up ahead.

"Listen," Rebecca warned as another volley drifted their way.

"Rifles," estimated Lone Wolf. "Sounds like they came from just over that rocky ridge up ahead. Could be somebody huntin'."

"Or it could be something else," Rebecca speculated.

He nodded his shaven head. "Let's have a look."

Digging their heels into the flanks of their ponies, Rebecca and Lone Wolf galloped up the grassy hill until they reached the boulder-studded ridge. She studied the valley below. A dozen gunmen carried on an attack against a large sod house about a hundred yards away from where she sat with Lone Wolf.

White men! Her heart beat faster as she squinted through the sunshine and looked for familiar faces among the vermin below. Most of the gunslicks fired from behind rocks and trees, their faces turned away. Several rifles poked from the windows of the sturdy farm house. Suddenly she spotted a bowler hat.

She sucked in her breath.

"What is it?" Lone Wolf asked her.

"He's down there."

"Tulley?"

Rebecca nodded. "There, behind the big rock. I can even see his black moustache now."

Gunshots echoed all around her.

"Well, it's your choice," he offered. "What do you want to do?"

Her eyes remained fixed on the man with the bowler hat. "I really don't have a choice," she replied tightly. "I can only do one thing, and that's ride down there and confront Tulley."

Lone Wolf grabbed his bow and arrows. "All right, let's go. We've got surprise on our side. And since we're outnumbered, we'll need it."

She glanced at him. "Do you have a plan?"

"Let me sneak up a little closer on foot. I'll pick off as many of his men as I can before they realize what's happening. Then we'll ride together into the valley."

"Fine," she agreed. For once she had seen no sensible way to handle the situation. "But Tulley's mine."

"You got him." Lone Wolf nodded, dismounted and padded into the high, waving buffalo grass. His bow and quiver were gripped in his hands.

Rebecca dismounted and tethered both ponies to a nearby box elder. Then she darted behind a big rock and watched the action below. Her heart sank at what she saw.

The outlaws rode recklessly through the farmyard. Few shots sounded in defiance and it became obvious that the settlers in the house were losing heart . . . and the battle.

Soon she spotted three members of the Tulley gang at the side of the lumber and sod house. They attempted to drag a screaming teenaged girl through a narrow window. One of the bandits fired a pistol through the opening. She looked for Lone Wolf down on the hill.

Could he see the scene at the window?

Two arrows sped through the air in answer to her question. One of the gunmen screamed with pain and released the girl. The remaining outlaws' faces slackened. One's jaw dropped and he reeled drunkenly when a third shaft buried itself to the fletchings in his chest.

The third bandit started to run. A fourth arrow struck him in the back, the tip protruding out his gut. He clutched his belly and screamed like a demon released from hell. Lone Wolf shot him again, the shaft buried deep between his shoulder blades. Slowly he sank to his knees.

In another second, all three outlaws lay dead on the ground.

The teenager ducked back into the house and closed the wooden shutters.

Then Rebecca noticed the other gang members looking up at the rocky ridge. She saw Jake Tulley pointing at the hill where Lone Wolf lay in hiding.

Another arrow struck an outlaw in the chest. The man had been standing next to Tulley. The outlaw leader dashed toward his horse. Confused by this new element, the gang began to panic.

Rebecca's heart warmed when she saw the bandits leaping for their horses. At least Lone Wolf had interrupted their latest evil scheme. Then she spotted two more familiar faces from her past.

Fat Bobby O'Toole and scar-faced Luke Wellington. Vivid images of the two hardcases kneeling near the windows in the Caldwell house on that fateful day flashed before her mind's eye. She could see them cheering when the deal was made with the Oglala.

Rebecca stood, her hand reaching automatically for her Little Russian, as another of Lone Wolf's arrows struck a bandit, skewering him in the neck. It was time for her to get into the fight. She ran to the horses, mounted hers and pulled Lone Wolf's along by the halter.

"Let's get the hell outta here!" Jake Tulley roared.

"We're under attack!" cried a wide-eyed bandit.

"Goddamn Injuns!" shouted another owlhoot.

"Let's ride!"

The Tulley gang galloped toward the distant horizon on the far side of the house. Suddenly the reprieved settlers unleashed a volley of lead.

"Christ, I'm hit!" yelled an outlaw.

"Damn, we're surrounded!"

"Head for that ridge over there!" cried Tulley. "Follow me, boys!"

Rebecca's heart skipped a beat. She watched the remaining gunmen spur their horses and race up the side of the hill, right in her direction. Lone Wolf was too far away and out of bow range to help her. She slipped from her mount and crouched behind a big rock.

It reminded her of the times she'd hidden from enemy tribes while in captivity. She tightly clutched the grip of the S&W .38 and took careful aim. The words of Iron Calf came back to her.

"It is where you place the bullet that kills," he had instructed her. "You don't down a buffalo by shooting it in the tail."

Within seconds the gang had thundered past.

The short barreled .38 bucked in Rebecca's hand. One of Tulley's brigands yelled in surprised pain and the hat flew from his head a moment before a rich red stain spread on his back where a dime-sized hole let daylight through.

Rebecca's Smith and Wesson cracked again and a rider pitched forward over his saddle horn, then slid down his mount's churning front shoulder, leaving behind a wet, carmine smear. The Tulley gang lashed their horses to greater speed and disappeared over a tall grass-covered swell.

Rebecca glanced behind her and spotted Lone Wolf running toward her.

Suddenly Jake Tulley appeared near the big rock to make sure his men had escaped unharmed. He gripped his bowler hat with one hand and his reins with the other. Except for a little gray at his temples, she thought, he looked unchanged after five years.

Tulley glowered down at Rebecca.

She fired a quick shot that missed and his horse reared onto its hind legs.

Lone Wolf released an arrow.

The singing shaft zipped past Tulley's head. The outlaw leader's narrowed gray eyes locked with Rebecca's. A slight flicker of recognition passed over his face as he quickly studied her features. She felt a chill pass over her as she took aim once more.

Tulley looked down the black bore of the Little Russian,

cast a quick glance at Lone Wolf and dug his spurs into his horse's flanks. The Smith cracked behind him and his mount screamed at the bullet crease on its left haunch. Swiftly the bandit boss churned away in the dusty wake of his men.

Lone Wolf dashed up to Rebecca. "Tulley, huh?"

She nodded, her heart pounding. "I think he recognized me," she said reluctantly. "He stared at me like he knew who I am and why I am here. And he got away, damnit, he got away!"

"I doubt he remembered you. Besides, he's gone for now. There'll be other chances."

She stood dejectedly. "I know," she admitted. "But I doubt I'll have any closer chance than this. I could have reached out and touched him," she concluded in frustration over her poor marksmanship.

Her head hanging, she turned and walked to the ponies. Oh, how she wished she'd shot him!

"Thank you for helpin' us!" shouted a grateful farmer. He wore blue denim bib-overalls and a red-checkered work shirt. He looked to be about forty.

"Oh, yes, both of you!" added his faded, washed-out wife.

"You're lucky we came along when we did," Rebecca told them.

The rancher nodded. "They hit a neighbor 'bout half a day's ride east o' here last week and wiped 'em out. Folks thought it 'twas Injuns 'till we heered 'bout some others. Shoulda stocked more ammunition like I aimed to, but didn't."

Rebecca and Lone Wolf stood in front of the bullet-riddled sod house. The granger, his wife and their six children, hovered nearby. After briefly explaining Lone Wolf to the frightened settlers, Rebecca began to hear a tale of terror concerning Tulley and the local farmers.

"What kind of trouble have your neighbors had?" she had asked. It brought an instant response from the farmer. Now she glanced at the blonde teenager who'd been hauled from the house by the outlaws while he continued his tale of disaster. The girl appeared to be about fourteen, the same age as Rebecca when she was taken captive by the Sioux.

"It's been my suspicion," the farmer summed up, "that this gang's tryin' to run us farmers off. Some o' my neighbors think the same way. A few who've proved up on their homestead claim even they got offers to buy. When they turned that down, Tulley and his gang hit them. Oh, I know this is supposed to be free for homestead settling, but that sort of thing has happened before."

He exchanged an uncertain glance with his wife, who hugged their daughter closer. "It's either that," he went on, "or they're just plain poison mean."

"Knowing Bitter Creek Jake Tulley, I can assure you of the last," Rebecca told them. These settlers' problems concerned her little. She had one goal and would pursue it relentlessly. Still, some knowledge of Tulley's activities might help.

"Why would they make a grab at my girl here?" the farmer went on, confident enough now to ask what bothered him the most.

"One of Tulley's men, the fat one, has unnatural desires toward young girls. You might caution your neighbors about that," Rebecca advised him. "If they come back, make sure your daughter is well hidden."

"I guess we'll have to be extra careful," said the sodbuster. "Thanks for the information. And thanks again for savin' our lives."

Rebecca and Lone Wolf shook hands with the hard-bitten couple and headed for their ponies. Not too much had changed in five years, Rebecca reflected. People's lives on the frontier were still hard and filled with danger. And Tulley was still a bastard.

She mounted up and started after him.

SEVEN

The close call with Jake Tulley spurred Rebecca onward. She helped Lone Wolf scan the trail for signs of the fleeing gang. Broken twigs, fresh horse droppings, bent blades of grass, all told them in which direction Tulley traveled.

"They've got an hour's lead on us," announced Lone Wolf. He'd dismounted to inspect some horse manure. Now he stepped into the saddle.

"Will we find them before dark?"

"Not likely."

"Where do you think they're heading?"

He clucked to his pony and reined the skittish mount back into a trot. "I reckon they've got themselves a campsite somewhere out here. If we keep trackin' we'll run into it sooner or later."

She nodded and rode on ahead. The freedom to ride wherever she wanted, without an escort or a husband, was a heady experience. The conversation with the farm family about Tulley's gang had struck a chord. She gripped the reins tightly as unbidden images of her first days with the

Oglala flooded her mind . . .

. . . After being given to the Oglala, Rebecca and her mother had ridden north for four days with the warriors, to a hill outside their camp. Rebecca remembered the dozens of teepees, their vent flaps opened like giant wings to admit light and air.

With an ear-splitting chorus of war cries, the painted Oglala braves raced like the wind toward the village in the valley.

The older warrior, whom she had decided was the leader, with whom Rebecca rode, urged his spirited horse into a full gallop. She held onto the brave's waist tightly and glanced at the sudden activity in the fast-approaching Indian camp.

She spotted dozens of swarthy squaws, carrying naked babies on their hips, swarms of squealing, bare-butt children racing toward the edge of camp to greet the returning war party and packs of short-haired dogs barking shrilly at all the sudden commotion.

The hurtling warriors raced past brightly-painted buffalo-hide teepees and into the large center area of the wide, concentric circles of lodges. Rebecca shivered with anxiety and glanced at the giggling children and laughing squaws who studied her with wide-eyed interest. Clouds of throat-clogging dust rose in the middle of the noisy camp and almost obliterated the shouting celebrants.

After pounding around the camp for several minutes, shouting their accomplishments, the painted warriors reined in their snorting ponies and began to greet their loved ones. Rebecca's sinewy captor reined in his pony before a spectacularly large, highly painted lodge and, with a firm tug, sent her flying to the ground. She landed heavily in a tangle of arms and legs. A moment later, her wide-eyed mother, shaken emotionally to the point of near collapse, was tossed equally callously beside her.

Still on their knees, mother and daughter clung together in mutual support. Rebecca, her own blue cotton dress sweat-stained and dusty, noticed that her mother's calico frock had been torn in several places. The rents had happened during the frequent rapes the older woman had been subjected to. Rebecca's ears still rang with her mother's pitiful cries for mercy. Hannah Caldwell's face was pale and vacant under her newly acquired sunburn.

Without warning, dozens of chanting squaws and laughing children closed in around them. They jeered at the two fallen white captives and several reached out to pluck at their clothing. Soon the entire camp gathered around them.

"Mother, what is going to happen?"

"Don't ask, child. So far they have spared you, though I don't know why. It's all . . . all like the last time." The momentary intelligence left Hannah's eyes and she began to mutter again.

Several boys dashed into the center of the circle and pulled Rebecca's flowing black hair. The other Indians laughed and chattered even louder. Rebecca winced with pain and huddled next to her unbalanced mother.

At a shouted command, the tormentors parted to admit the middle-aged warrior who had carried Rebecca here. He now wore a buckskin shirt under his bone-breastplate and had added leggings.

Rebecca still knelt on the ground, her trembling mother in her arms. Suddenly she saw the crowd part again to allow a slender, teenaged girl into the middle. Rebecca saw the chief point at the two captives and speak briefly to the girl in Lakota. Then the long-haired teenager stepped closer to Rebecca.

"My name is Red Shawl," she said in near perfect English. "I am here to act as interpreter. Chief Iron Calf wishes to speak to you." To Rebecca, her voice, speaking their own tongue sounded soft and sweet.

Rebecca blinked with astonishment. "How . . . how is it you speak our language?" she inquired in a low, timid voice. She still clutched her mother. In her present state, she took little satisfaction in having been right about her captor.

"Rebecca," snapped her mother, returned to reality for a moment. "It is some kind of trick. Do not speak with this girl."

"It is no trick," Red Shawl returned. "I am the only member of the band who speaks the whiteman's tongue well enough to talk with you. I lived for two years at Fort Robinson, where my father was an army scout. That is where I learned to speak English."

"What does the chief want to say to us?" asked Rebecca.

"*No!*" gasped her mother.

"Mother, we must," Rebecca tried to reason with her. "At least we will know what is to become of us."

Iron Calf spoke sharply in Lakota. Red Shawl nodded.

"Our chief grows impatient," she warned. "You must listen to him now."

Iron Calf spoke rapidly in the Lakota tongue. When he finished the gathered tribesmen howled with delight. Red Shawl turned and faced Rebecca and her mother.

"Iron Calf say that the war party against the white men was a great success. It was big medicine for all the warriors who fought with courage."

Iron Calf spoke again for several seconds.

To Rebecca's confusion, only the squaws cheered him this time. The men stood silent, impassive.

"Iron Calf also say," continued Red Shawl, "that his strong warriors have captured many horses and many gifts for the women of our band."

For a third time, the chief spoke loudly to his people. When he finished, Rebecca heard what sounded like an angry murmur ripple among the women.

When Red Shawl turned to face her this time, she

noticed a flicker of anxiety cross the teenager's face, clouding her eyes. Red Shawl fidgeted with the fringe on her dress and avoided looking directly at Rebecca.

"This time Iron Calf say . . . that the two white women will be kept with the band forever. The young half-blood will be a slave who will work with the women until she proves herself worthy to be a daughter of the Oglala. The golden-haired woman will . . . will serve the chief's three wives and dwell in a small lodge beside his second teepee."

Rebecca's hands went to her mouth. Beside her, Hannah Caldwell recoiled as though slapped. A haunted expression replaced the horror and revulsion that had clouded her features for the past four days.

"Oh . . . no . . . not that. Please . . . not . . . *that!*" she wailed a moment before she fell into a faint.

Rebecca caught her mother before she slumped to the hard-packed earth. In a flash of insight, Rebecca came to realize how old her mother had become. At thirty, Hannah Caldwell already had streaks of gray in her blonde hair, her hands had become rough and red and her face lined. The prairie, never kind to women, had taken its toll. With it, too, the scarlet imprint of her abuse at the hand of the Sioux. It had been a warrior of Bent Elk's Oglala, Rebecca knew from her mother's embarrassed recounting. But which one. Did he still live in this band of Iron Calf's? A sudden commotion rose among the women, calling Rebecca back to the present.

With her unconscious mother resting in her slender arms, Rebecca glanced up to see a squat, middle-aged squaw with craggy facial features and black braids burst through the outer ring of the people. The buckskin-clad squaw staggered into the center of the circle. She stopped in front of Iron Calf and began to berate the chief in a high-pitched, angry voice.

"What's the matter?" Rebecca asked Red Shawl.

"That is Rattling Blanket, Chief Iron Calf's number one

wife. She is accusing him of being selfish by bringing a white women into his teepee."

The idea astounded Rebecca. "She's jealous of my mother?" Red Shawl nodded. "But why?"

"She is very angry, too," the young interpreter added.

It was then that Rebecca noticed the knife in Rattling Blanket's hand. Without warning, she discovered how angry.

Shouting a final epithet at the chief, Rattling Blanket turned toward Rebecca's mother. Her bitter brown eyes glowed like two burning coals. She strode briskly to where the captives sat. Rebecca's heart pounded as the craggy-faced woman approached, her knife upraised. Then she lunged toward Hannah Caldwell.

"Look out!" cried Red Shawl.

"No!" Rebecca shrieked.

She dove toward Rattling Blanket's feet with a certainty of death. As her mother fell back to the ground, Rebecca exerted her last vestiges of strength to prevent the awful murder. Her brazen act caught the chief's number one wife completely by surprise.

Rebecca caught the charging squaw's left ankle and pulled her feet out from under her. The startled Oglala woman fell heavily on her face in a small cloud of dust. The circle of Indians erupted with laughter.

"*Hau! Hau!*" Chief Iron Calf, laughing harder than anyone, shouted words of approval and stepped quickly to where Rattling Blanket struggled to get to her feet. He wrenched the blade from his angry wife's hand.

Rattling Blanket began to pummel Iron Calf with blows to his bone breastplate. The amused chief held his wife at arm's length and motioned for a couple of the camp's watchmen, the *akicita*, to take her away. The policemen hauled Rattling Blanket toward a slightly smaller teepee, situated beside the tall, ornately decorated one.

Iron Calf muttered something to Red Shawl and then

shouted at the nearby people, who cheered. Almost at once the gathering dispersed and Red Shawl turned to Rebecca.

"Iron Calf is going to give away the prizes he captured on the warpath. He has instructed several of the camp's widows to take you in the morning and put you to work."

All the tension of the day's horrible events seemed to boil up inside of Rebecca. Hot tears welled in her eyes, but she fought them down. A streak of stubborn rebelliousness blossomed in her mind and she set her will to resist every indignity that these savages might heap upon her.

"Yes," Red Shawl went on. "And I'm afraid the work will be quite hard. You will get all the dirty jobs that the other women do not want."

"I feel like I've entered another world," Rebecca pronounced coldly.

Hannah Caldwell moaned and began to come around.

"What about my mother?"

"Iron Calf say that golden-haired woman is to be brought to his second teepee. There she will serve every need of his other two wives, Blue Bear Girl and Red Shirt Woman."

"Rebecca . . .?" her mother asked in a tremulous voice.

"I'm here, Mother."

She saw her mother's blue eyes focus on Red Shawl. Suddenly, as though the young interpreter's lean face pierced her clouded memory, Hannah's face slackened in defeated horror.

"She . . . said . . . I was going to be a slave to the chief's wives? Oh, no. After what happened to me years ago, I . . . can't bear that. I can't! I won't!" Hannah broke down and started to sob.

Her shoulders heaved as she buried her sunburnt face in her daughter's shoulder. Rebecca's eyes filled with sympathetic tears, though her breast heaved with the fires of rebellion. She sat in the middle of the dusty Oglala camp stroking her mother's fading, honey-blonde hair. Gently, with Red Shawl's aid, the *akicita* separated the two hopeless women, taking each to her determined fate.

The next morning, Red Shawl appeared and spoke harshly to an old woman who pounded Rebecca's slender back with a willow switch. She had dropped a hot stone in such a manner it split the buffalo paunch cauldron suspended on a wooden tripod. All the contents had spilled out and the sharp-voiced widow belabored the white captive about it. With the punishment ceased, Red Shawl took Rebecca aside.

"Chief Iron Calf has decided to give Oglala names to you and your mother," the girl announced. "Your mother will be known as Golden Hair. And you, because you are half Oglala from birth, though still part white, will be called Whiterobe Girl. *Śinaskawin*," she repeated in Lakota.

Astonished at this turn, Rebecca's mouth gaped. "B-but we're not Indians," she cried, resistance flaring. "We're Caldwells and we're white women! Can't you understand?"

Her words touched indifferent ears.

"Never!" Rebecca flared. "I am not an Indian. I am not!"

Red Shawl touched her shoulder. "Here comes your mother. It is time for the announcement of your naming to be made."

Rebecca looked up and received another jolt. She watched her glassy-eyed mother being led to the middle of the camp by several squaws. She saw that her ashen-faced parent had retreated into a state of total withdrawal.

"No! Stop this . . . this farce!" she shouted, then leaped toward her imprisoned mother.

A large hand cuffed her on the side of the head.

Shaking off the stinging blow, she watched her trancelike mother shuffle to where Chief Iron Calf stood with the camp crier. Two of the women to whom she had been assigned hustled Rebecca forward also.

Iron Calf lighted a ceremonial pipe, blew puffs to the east, the south, west and north, into the sky and to the ground below. Then he passed it to another stern-looking warrior and raised both hands above his head.

"This is a happy day in our camp." Red Shawl translated his words as he spoke in a high, sing-song voice. "There will be feasting tonight. The Great Spirit has brought us two women who, by rights, belong in this band. It is fitting, then, that they be given names. In honor of this, to the old widow, Sings-While-She-Walks, I give one fine pony. To the leader of the Raven-owners Society, who was my strong right arm on the raid, I give three ponies. To all the Oglala in this band, I give meat and sweet berries. Let the captives come forth."

Hard hands gripped Rebecca's arms and she was propelled forward, alongside her mother. "These women shall be known for all time as Golden Hair and Whiterobe Girl," the chief decreed.

"No!" Rebecca shouted. "I am not an Indian! I never will be!" Hot tears scalded Rebecca's cheeks. The finality of this pronouncement filled her with a sudden horror that overwhelmed her resolve. She clasped her mother to her breast.

"Oh, Mother, Mother, why don't you resist this, help me fight it. I . . . am . . . not . . . an . . . Indian!"

The *akicita* separated them and Rebecca looked into blank, unregistering eyes. Hannah Caldwell had made the final retreat from an unbearable reality into the swirling convolutions of her tormented mind. Rebecca watched the entranced woman being led away and her heart seemed to stop.

Trapped between the white and red worlds, her identity threatened, a far worse blow struck her. She felt she had lost her mother forever . . .

. . . Rebecca sat trembling atop her pony. She was only dimly aware that she had reined in.

"Are you all right?" Lone Wolf inquired with concern. "You look kinda pale."

"I'll be fine in . . . in a minute."

"Rememberin' again, huh?"

She nodded. "I don't think I'll ever forget what happened to me."

"That's good."

Rebecca glanced sharply at her shaven-head companion. "Good?"

"It'll keep you after Tulley an' the rest when the goin' gets tough. I got a feelin' you'll be runnin' into some big guns before you're through."

Rebecca smiled and sighed. "I'll be all right," she insisted, her mind now free, for the moment, of the ugly memories. "How's the tracking going?"

"We still have us a clear trail to follow. A wagon an' three riders joined up a coupla' miles back. Don't know if it was the gang or not. Not for sure yet."

"I only wish we were not riding into Oglala country."

Lone Wolf clucked sympathetically. "I don't blame you. We'll be coming up on the buffalo hunting grounds soon. That oughtta bring back some memories."

"Yes . . . unfortunately. I only hope it doesn't bring along any Oglala braves."

They cantered across the open, rolling prairie, a familiar land where Rebecca had lived, hunted and wanted to escape. A wild, free land that mocked her even while she had taken part in numerous hunts . . .

. . . "Have you ever seen so many buffalo, *Śinaskawin?*" asked Red Shawl, Rebecca's only friend. Rebecca had turned fifteen and it was her first buffalo hunt. It had happened four years ago, yet it seemed like yesterday.

"Never in my life," Rebecca replied truthfully.

The ambling herd of bison stretched across the lush summertime prairie for as far as she could see. The snorting beasts grazed in the wavering grass and wallowed in dusty hollows worn into the Dakota sod. Despite her continued resistance to accepting the band as her people, the Oglala side of Rebecca thrilled at the sight.

"What happens next?" Rebecca inquired, genuinely taken by the excitement of the hunt.

Red Shawl could hardly control her enthusiasm as she spoke. "First, the warriors will make the surround, closing off the herd's escape. Then, after they've killed the number the hunting chief has decreed, it is our turn to run into the grass and butcher the fallen animals."

"All of them?"

Red Shawl nodded quickly.

"There will be dozens. Maybe even hundreds."

"I know," replied Red Shawl. "Sometimes we spend days out with the herd."

Rebecca peered through the shimmering late summer heat and watched two columns of fast-riding braves attack the suddenly panic-stricken buffalo. She knew it was dangerous to ride into the middle of a herd, though that's what the Oglala braves now did.

She watched with awe as the hunters burst into the milling beasts and worked with daring efficiency until about a hundred frantic creatures became trapped in a tight circle of ready bows and lances.

Then, with seeming disregard for their personal safety, a few of the bravest hunters plunged their wild-eyed ponies deep into the thrashing swarm of frightened buffalo, their short, razor-sharp lances piercing the big furry prey behind the last ribs in order to collapse the big animals' lungs. Involuntarily, Rebecca gasped as a crazed buffalo turned and slashed a prancing Oglala mount. The startled rider hung onto his wounded pony rather than risk being pounded into jelly under heavy hoofs. Other Oglala hunters sat atop their experienced buffalo ponies and shot arrow after arrow into the massed herd. One of them, Rebecca noticed, was a youth, not yet made a warrior, by the name of Four Horns. Of late, she had noticed him watching her closely. Unbidden, and to her dismay, she breathed a prayer for his safety.

"Soon it will be our turn!" cried Red Shawl, drawing Rebecca from her private thoughts.

"How do you know?"

"See," said the slender sixteen-year-old girl. She pointed a brown finger at the bleating buffalo. "Our men are finishing off the wounded animals."

Rebecca heard the deep-throated death bellows of the bleeding buffalo rise into the sweltering, dust-clouded air. She felt sorry for the dying creatures, but she knew, too, that the buffalo meant survival for the Oglala.

"Now!" shouted Red Shawl.

"What? Why?"

"Look, Standing Bear, the hunt chief, is calling for the women."

"What will I do?"

"Oh, hurry. You will learn when you get there."

Soon dozens of women, their hands full of knives, sprinted toward the fallen animals. Now, Rebecca knew, came long hours of hard work as the women dressed and butchered the fallen carcasses, while boys too young to join the hunt made bundles of the meat, wrapped them in hides and loaded them on horse-drawn travois.

"Of course, you will get the dirty work—squeezing out the intestines," Red Shawl had told her. Caught in the frenzy of the work, that didn't seem to matter to Rebecca for now.

For the rest of the day, and into the cool, summer night, Rebecca and the chattering women all around her sliced and slashed the buffalo into pieces. Then she gathered the animal's intestines, separated heart, lungs, liver and kidneys from the rest and squeezed empty the long, fat coils of intestine. Nothing was ever wasted. Even the brains and other internal organs were used in curing the hides. Meanwhile, small, skinny boys, clad only in old, ragged loincloths or entirely naked, lugged huge strips of bloody meat back to camp to be dried for winter. Every part of the buffalo, not consumed as food, was put to some other practical use. Horns, bones, hoofs, became household items. The hides, both with and without the thick downy fur, had many uses. Even the stomach lining of an unborn calf that Rebecca suddenly encountered in the belly of its mother, would be employed as a bag for harvesting wild berries.

"Look at you," Red Shawl laughed. "You've covered with blood. Around them the other women joined in the merriment.

Rebecca glanced at her clothes and winced. "Ach! You're right. And I smell. I can't wait for a bath." In a year's time, Rebecca had cast off her white aversion to frequent bathing and looked forward, as her sole comfort and release from unrelenting toil, to the daily bath.

The front of her short, buckskin dress had become soaked with glistening buffalo blood, dark red-brown like the rich soil. Her hands and arms were stained the same color with slimy gore. Even her sweaty face had become speckled with carmine. Yes, the bath was what she needed. Any break in the monotonous daily routine of life in the Oglala camp was a luxury to be savored . . .

. . . A sudden thunderclap cut into Rebecca's thoughts. She looked up and noticed that the sky had become totally overcast, the fat, black bellies of rainclouds hanging low toward the earth. Huge drops of rain began to splatter on the ground.

"That's the end of our trackin' for a while," Lone Wolf observed. The big white Indian reined in his pony and scanned the countryside.

Lightning flashed and crackled from gigantic towers of dark clouds and the air tingled with ozone. The downpour intensified, drawing the horizon in on them to a range of only a few feet. Water fell in lashing gray sheets, bounding upward where it struck the hard-packed prairie soil. In brief seconds, both travelers became soaked to the skin. Their ponies twitched their skin and rolled whitened eyes in nervous reaction to the steady boom of thunder and shied from each brilliant streak of electrical fury.

Water dripped from the white woman's hat Rebecca wore and she tore it from her head, letting the howling wind take it away. Somehow she felt better for doing it. A constant line of drips streamed from the tip of Lone Wolf's nose and he squinted his eyes against the tearing fury of the maelstrom.

"We have to find shelter for the night," he announced, stating the obvious.

Rebecca looked around her. "We're still in Oglala country," she cautioned.

"Yeah, and with both of us bein' a tad bit unpopular with our red brothers we better find a good place to hole up 'till this storm passes."

"There are some caves nearby, I remember," Rebecca offered over the raging tumult.

"Good. Are they dry during storms? Some of those setups carry underground rivers."

"I . . . I think they are fine. First, let's find them."

A fifteen minute search located a small, rock-strewn hillside. While Lone Wolf tethered the horses, Rebecca entered the nearest cave. She found it tight and dry and quickly built a fire. She resented the storm's interference, which forced them to spend a night so close to her former captors. While the heavens unleashed their agony on her, it seemed time closed in. The Sioux might find them in the morning, or Tulley might make good a clean escape.

And she wanted in the most consuming way to track down Bitter Creek Jake and his gang . . . and kill them all.

EIGHT

Rebecca squatted next to the crackling fire and listened to the storm rage outside. They had both changed into fresh clothing, Lone Wolf to a fringed buckskin hunting shirt and leggings, she to her soft, beaded leather dress that extended to mid-calf. How good it felt, she reveled, then cast a guilty glance at the sodden white woman's clothes lying near the back of the cave. Flashes of lightning streaked the nighttime sky. Lone Wolf had shot a rabbit that had sought shelter from the rain and now they enjoyed the fresh meat for their supper. The cave felt warm and dry.

"Hummm," Rebecca murmured. "This tastes good."

"Hard travelin' makes you hungry."

"Don't I know. Yet it seems like we've been tracking Tulley for months. I can't believe how hungry I am."

"I'll save some rabbit for your breakfast."

She looked up. "You sound like you're not going to be here for breakfast."

"This storm will have caused the gang to hole up, too.

They can't be far from us now." He glanced out the cave entrance to confirm his next words. "The rain's lettin' up. Most of the gang's sign will have been wiped out, so I want to push on tonight while there's still a chance to catch up. I'll be back first thing in the morning."

"Don't the horses need a rest? They've been pushed awfully hard," Rebecca observed.

"Planned to scout afoot. Speakin' of the horses, you noticed how well they're travelin' since we started grainin' 'em?"

"You're right, they are," Rebecca returned brightly. "In Iron Calf's camp I thought I only imagined that white men's horses had more stamina."

"No. They do. Indian ponies eat only grass. Not much bottom to 'em. Well . . ." Lone Wolf stood as he spoke. "Best be goin'."

"Be careful." Rebecca scanned the cave's shadowy interior. She didn't look forward to spending the night alone. Not in Oglala country. A thunderclap exploded nearby.

"There's plenty of Arbuckles left," she told Lone Wolf. "I'll have a pot of coffee ready when you get back."

Lone Wolf chuckled. "I'll need it if I run into Tulley's bunch."

"Save Tulley for me," Rebecca cautioned.

"He's all yours," Lone Wolf agreed.

He grabbed his weapons and strode briskly past the tethered horses outside the cave. Rebecca watched him go, not envying his long, wet journey.

She finished her supper and listened to the patter of the rain for a while. The flickering firelight brought immediate images of Iron Calf's village. Of other nights with the flames patterning writhing shadows on the thinly scraped, cured hides that formed the walls of the small lodge where she slept with her addled mother. Had her days there been so entirely terrible? Iron Calf's wives had quickly donated the hides for the tent. Bad or not, she definitely did not want to return to that way of life. Mockingly, her mind called her "White Squaw," and she realized that she really didn't want to go back to being a white woman either. Not one sullied by life with the Sioux. What, then? her conscience taunted. Finally she tossed another log on the fire, laid back on a makeshift bed of buffalo grass and drifted off to sleep.

Immediately her nightmares began. Jake Tulley, Chief Iron Calf, her mother's butchered body, mutilated corpses, and a hundred other vivid images paraded through her restive mind. She tossed and turned throughout the long night. Finally she awakened at dawn to the chirping and twittering of birds, crickets and animals.

Birds . . . crickets . . . animals? No!

Rebecca shot upright and listened again.

Her experienced ears knew the animal-like signals of a stalking Oglala war party when they heard them. She pressed her back against the cold stone wall of the cave and studied the brightening underbrush in front of her.

After a long moment, she saw tell-tale movements in the bushes. No doubt about it, she thought. A war party was approaching the cave. The sharp whinny of her tethered pony punctuated her thoughts.

Rebecca studied the surrounding terrain and began to make plans for an escape. She spotted a rocky ridge about a hundred yards away. If she left the cave now her surprise exit would give her a head start.

Gathering her feet under her, she dashed from the cave.

Immediately a war cry ripped the morning peace.

As she raced for the rocky ridge, Rebecca heard the babble of angry voices speaking Lakota. Her stomach tightened with fear. Glancing over her shoulder as she ran, her breath escaping from her lips in wheezing gasps, she saw several mounted Oglala warriors in determined pursuit.

I'm not going back to the Sioux, she told herself

resolutely. I must escape.

With a determination born of necessity, she pumped her slender, shapely legs even faster as she raced toward the boulder-strewn rise.

Reaching the gentle slope leading to the ridge, she dropped behind an enormous boulder. She sucked fresh morning air into her hungry lungs. Even though an early chill hung on the air, her slender body had become saturated with perspiration. Her long black hair clung to her face.

Several strident war cries jangled on her nerves.

She caught her breath and looked up quickly, her blue eyes fixed on the half dozen Oglala warriors who galloped toward the boulder.

Turning sharply, Rebecca pushed away from the big rock and began to climb. She scanned the terrain above her, intent on locating a place to make a stand. She figured her only chance lay in reaching a small copse of scraggly junipers near the top of the hill.

Slipping and sliding on the loose gravel that covered the side of the slope, Rebecca grimaced with pain as cruel stones bit into the flesh on her knees and clawing underbrush clutched at her legs. The morning breeze whipped little clouds of dust up into her throat and nose, causing her to gag. Behind her she heard the drumming of hoofbeats as the Oglala closed the gap.

Finally she reached the top of the rocky ridge and stopped to check the progress of the warriors. Her slender legs trembled from exertion and her lungs felt about to burst. Glancing back toward the cave, she saw the galloping braves riding up the slope, only fifty yards behind her. Her earlier fear changed to rising anger.

Rebecca turned and dashed for the safety of the wooded copse fifty yards away. Halfway to the junipers, her rubbery legs buckled. She sprawled on the rock-strewn ground. Noseclogging dust showered her face. New resolve flooded her body with a reserve of strength.

Her fingers plucked at her belt pouch while she shot to her feet again. Damn, she would have to get a holster for it, she thought while the Smith and Wessen came free in her grip. Summoning all her energy, she renewed her dash toward the junipers.

An instant later she heard a triumphant whoop, right on her heels.

Rebecca glanced over her shoulder and saw a charging Oglala brave bearing down on her. The warrior's hawk-nosed face was aglow with anticipation. Suddenly his expression changed to one of consternation when Rebecca slowed her pace and spun in a small flurry of dust.

"Nooo!" she shouted her defiance and swung up her .38 revolver, steadied in a two-hand grip, and rapidly squeezed the trigger. The Little Russian spat a long tongue of fire. Once, then again. The exultant war cry changed to a yelp of startled pain.

A red-and-black figure-eight appeared, like a new nipple, on the left side of the Oglala warrior's breast, seeping thin trickles of blood. His heart burst into fragments and his body leaped backward over the churning hindquarters of his war pony, to land with a solid, meaty plop on the hard ground.

Instantly Rebecca began her dash for the defensive position she had selected among the evergreens. The little, palmated needles seemed to grow enormously as she neared her goal. A quick glance behind showed the dead brave's companions whipping their mounts in pursuit. With a final burst of effort Rebecca lurched in among the trees. Sudden fire exploded up her left leg when she twisted her ankle on a hidden squirrel hole. For a moment she went to her knees.

Five screaming warriors thundered into the copse and jostled to form a circle around her. She raised her Smith and Wesson and fired again.

One Oglala grunted when the 148 grain .38 bullet

smashed into his shoulder, causing him to drop the lance in his right hand. Rebecca squeezed the trigger once more when he jumped his pony closer, toward her. The slug gouged flesh and hair from the side of his head, partly severing one braid. The warrior fell from his pony, unconscious and bleeding.

Suddenly, before Rebecca could react, one of the mounted braves looped a rawhide lariat over her head. He cinched it tightly around her arms and chest. She struggled futilely against the taut rope in an attempt to bring her gun into play. Another brave reached down and yanked the .38 from her numb fingers.

"What are you going to do?" she stammered in Lakota.

"We are taking you home for punishment. You have taken the lives of your own people. For that you will die."

One brave dismounted to tend the wounded man.

With a sudden chorus of shrill war cries, the other four naked Sioux warriors dug their heels into the flanks of their ponies. They hurtled toward the open prairie beyond the cave. Realizing that she would have to run at full speed or be jerked off her feet and dragged, Rebecca pumped her already exhausted legs and ran behind the Oglala.

When they reached the small cave and her tethered pony, Rebecca cried out and fell head-first onto the ground. She held onto the taut rope. Without a backward glance, the brave continued to drag her toward the grassland like a haltered steer.

A split second later, Lone Wolf leaped from a nearby tree. He smashed into the warrior who held the other end of the lariat. The startled brave flew off his mount and landed in a cloud of dust. He released the rope an instant before he fell.

Rebecca stopped abruptly. Her teeth gritted on a mouthful of dirt. She glanced up and saw Lone Wolf sitting astride the fallen warrior's pony. He had a notched arrow ready to be released. Immediately Rebecca loosened the braided leather loop and scrambled toward the fallen man's weapons.

He had an old Colt's Dragoon pistol, rusty and uncared-for, which she doubted would fire safely. She abandoned that, took his knife and the Winchester carbine he had carried in the crook of his right elbow. She turned about and raised the brass stud-decorated stock to her cheek.

One warrior had already gone down, she observed. The feathered end of one of Lone Wolf's arrows protruded from his chest. The deeply tanned young white man released another shaft and it bit into flesh in the thigh of a second Oglala. Then the buckhorn sights of the Winchester in Rebecca's hands settled on the wide expanse of white quill breastplate on the brave who had taken her revolver. Her finger twitched.

Shards of porcupine quill flew like shrapnel when the .44-40 slug punched through the breastplate and struck the Oglala in the sternum. Bits of his own ribcage ripped lung tissue and the big slug shocked his heart to stillness.

Swiftly levering another cartridge into the chamber, Rebecca looked for a new target. From behind her she heard the familiar sharp bark of the *Ihoka,* or Badger, Warrior Society, and a moment later the air-warbling zip of an arrow going overhead.

The Badger pitched over his pony's head and came to a skidding stop at Rebecca's feet, downed by one of Lone Wolf's shafts, which broke off in the fall. Rebecca stepped astraddle of the corpse and swung the Winchester toward the wounded brave, who had recovered consciousness.

A sharp crack from the .44-40 sent a slung winging toward the warrior. It smacked into the side of his head and unhinged his jaw, then angled upward, pulping brain tissue and spraying blood from his nose, mouth and ears. He went slack and lay about his pony's neck, in an awkward, mortal embrace.

Quickly Rebecca looked around for more of the enemy,

only to discover there were none.

Lone Wolf dismounted and walked over to her. "Is that pot of coffee ready?" he inquired with a sober face.

In spite of her harrowing escape from recapture, Rebecca's lips twitched into a small smile, which widened, then broke apart in a rich rumble of laughter. "Hoo! Hoo, boy! I thought I was going back," she exclaimed, her voice cracking. "If you want coffee, you'll have to make it yourself. The Arbuckles is in my trail bag." Rebecca followed him to the cave.

There she slumped against the cool stone wall and tried to catch her breath. Everything had happened so fast. The realization of how close she'd actually come to being returned to the Oglala hardened her resolve. The warriors' promise of punishment acted as a spur.

Her ordeal placed her forever beyond the pale, the way the whites saw it. The killing of Oglala warriors expelled her also from the band that had been her home. It left her entirely on her own. And she liked it.

Lone Wolf had the water boiling and the heady aroma of cooking coffee filled the cave when Rebecca left to retrieve her Smith and Wesson. To judge from events so far, she would need it in the future.

The decorated Winchester would also be quite a prize and she hoped the downed Oglala carried a good supply of ammunition. Searching the dead warriors proved more productive than Rebecca had hoped. This party must have hit a hide hunter's camp, for one brave had been carrying a big .50-120-800 Sharps rifle, complete with a tang peepsight, saddle case, bullet mold and Lyman tong tool for reloading the big cartridges. His gear also yielded primers, powder, lead bars and fifty loaded rounds. The hunter must have been taken unaware and the warrior definitely had not returned to his band since the coup, Rebecca reckoned.

Now, with a more respectable arsenal, she really felt ready to take on Tulley and his men.

NINE

Her composure restored, Rebecca and Lone Wolf disposed of the dead Oglala, gathered their gear and started out. Early morning sunlight glinted off puddles accumulated from the night's storm. A huge crow, perched in the junipers, called raucously at their retreating forms.

"I picked up the Tulley gang's sign last night," Lone Wolf told her. "We're getting closer."

They trotted across a wide stretch of grassy, rain-wet prairie. Black clouds, with long, sweeping gray trains of summer rain scudded across the distant sky. Rebecca grew somber as the weather. The encounter with the Sioux had made her realize how treacherous her quest could be.

"And?" she returned.

"They are still headin' north, all right."

"When do you think we will find them?"

"Sometime this afternoon. If nothin' comes along to interrupt. I don't think they suspect anyone is on their trail. Maybe later I'll sneak on ahead again."

She glanced sharply at him. "I want them this time."

Lone Wolf nodded. "You handle Tulley's crew like you did those Oglala an' the Devil's gonna have a busy day."

She felt a warm glow radiating from her chest at this casual praise and growing acceptance of her prowess. "Iron Calf taugh me to shoot a rifle and how to use a bow. Then, later, Four Horns improved my skills and showed me many ways to fight—with knife, tomahawk and bare hands. I can track nearly as well as you," she added proudly. "I am ready for my war with Tulley."

"Let's stretch 'em out, then." Lone Wolf gigged his mount and hid the grin from her. A light of admiration glowed in his blue eyes.

As they urged their spirited ponies into a fast canter across the rolling prairie, Rebecca's mind began to focus on the tussle with the Sioux back at the cave. She thought how close she had been to returning to the Oglala camp. As the miles sped under her pony's hoofs, her mind quickly recalled her days with the Sioux and all the pain and heartbreak she had endured. It was like living in another world . . .

. . . The first weeks of Rebecca's captivity with the Oglala had been absolute hell. She slept and ate outdoors among flea-infested dogs in all sorts of inclement weather. Her many physically demanding jobs as a slave for the other women left her exhausted at the end of each day. Beatings with willow branches also took their toll. Days and weeks rolled past, until finally, after several months, the slender captive was tired, underweight and in need of medical care.

Through all her suffering Rebecca remained resolute. She refused to become an Indian and accept the way of the Oglala. All it would have taken to live in the relative comfort of her mother's small teepee was for her to tell Iron Calf that she was ready to accept her Oglala name. But the emaciated, dir-covered settler girl stubbornly refused to give in.

Rebecca's mother remained in a trance-like state. So far as Rebecca knew, her mother hadn't uttered a word since she'd been pressed into service for Iron Calf's wives. When mother and daughter did meet while preparing hides or picking berries, Rebecca failed to get any kind of verbal response from her glassy-eyed mother. Hannah Caldwell passed a speechless existence among the chief's wives, relieving them of many of their daily chores.

Several times during these first months, Red Shawl approached Rebecca and tried to get her to accept the chief's offer.

"It's better than living like a dog," Red Shawl observed.

"I am not an Indian!" Rebecca replied defiantly.

"Have it your own way. But soon it will be cold. Then see how you like sleeping with the dogs."

After four months, Rebecca came to resemble an animal even more than the dogs. She ate scraps of food from a wooden bowl and snarled and snapped at the beasts if they came close while she fed. She remained tied to a heavy log when she wasn't working and relieved herself in the dirt like the dogs. Her blue cotton dress had gone to tatters and smelled worse than the animals. She wore ankle hobbles all day long to prevent an escape attempt. And some of her many cuts and bruises from the daily beatings she received had deeply festered. She felt weak, sick and completely demoralized.

Yet she refused to become an Indian.

"I'll never be an Indian!" she shouted out in frustration and rebellion one early Fall night. Then she buried her head in her calloused hands and bawled like a baby.

Long after the first snows fell, Rebecca finally succumbed and agreed to become Whiterobe Girl. Her blue lips and trembling limbs forced her to it. Although constantly tired, she realized she had put on muscle during her degredation. By accepting adoption as Iron Calf's daughter and gaining freedom of the camp, she figured she could find a way to escape. She even relented to learning the Lakota language.

During Rebecca's adoption ceremony, her mother experienced one of her rare, lucid moments. She drew her daughter aside and in cracked, hoarsely whispered English, told her, "Whatever happens, you . . . must not . . . let Iron Calf consider you as a wife. You must not!"

Soon, Rebecca began to take part in looting raids on wagon trains. On one such occasion she spotted a tiny derringer sticking out from the vest pocket of a dead pioneer's suit. A further examination of the dead man's bloodied clothes revealed a dozen .32 caliber cartridges, which Rebecca immediately hid in her knee-high leggings.

The gun was a Ried's Knuckleduster, .32 caliber pocket pistol. It had no barrel, but fired instead from its five chambers. It lacked a trigger, too, and was set off by pulling back on the tiny hammer. A finger loop, instead of a grip, allowed the top-heavy piece to double as a bludgeon. Satisfied that at least she had some firepower to help her escape, Rebecca smiled and stuck the derringer in her bosom.

On the same raid, she stopped near a wagon that was being torn apart by half a dozen squealing Oglala women. She suddenly spotted a thick family Bible that had been discarded by the squaws.

"Come on, Whiterobe Girl, there is plenty of *wasicun* cooking pots in here!" cried one of the swarthy, smooth-faced women from inside the looted conestoga.

"Yes! And sugar!" yelled another excitedly.

"I've found something here," she replied, stepping over to the leather-bound Holy Bible.

"That's nothing but the whiteman's spotted leaves."

"*Sinaskawin*, the good stuff is in here," Red Shawl admonished.

"*Hecitu welo*. That is true," Rebecca evaded, remaining with her new-found treasure.

She knelt and rescued the family Bible from an avalanche of discarded furniture and leather trunks. She sat on the cool grass with the Book on her knees and opened it to its title page. Hand-written in a neat scroll script was the complete family history of the folks who'd been riding in the looted wagon. With growing sadness Rebecca began to read the names aloud.

"James Elliott Sanders, born 1827 . . ."

"Sarah Anne Thornbrough Sanders, born 1831 . . ."

"Adam Thornbrough Sanders, born 1849 . . . died 1850."

"Alice Marie Sanders, born 1852 . . ."

Hot tears began to roll down Rebecca's face. Her hands started to tremble so the words blurred. Her fierce longing for the simple pleasures and conventions of the white man's civilization overwhelmed her. She ached for the laughing camaraderie of other young people at church and at school, of continuity and solidity in life. Her mind started to focus on what it must be like back in Jury Wells where her mother had taken her so many times in the past . . .

Suddenly the Holy Bible flew from her hands. Rebecca sucked in her breath and looked up defiantly.

Chief Iron Calf hovered over her, the Bible grasped in his big right hand and a scowl etched on his hawk-nosed face.

"Is this my daughter?" he snapped in consternation. His lips curled scornfully. "I should have known Whiterobe Girl could never be other than a half-white!" He shook the sacred book under her nose. "These are white man's words," he sneered. "The same as they use to rob us of our land and our honor with their false treaties."

Iron Calf turned toward a crackling fire in one of the wagons. With all his might he hurled the heavy family Bible into the hungry flames.

Rebecca watched the leather-bound tome crinkle in the yellow blaze. She glanced at the bloody destruction all around her. She gritted her teeth and quickly touched the derringer through her elkskin dress.

"Some day," she said softly. "Some day I'll escape . . ."

. . . Lone Wolf touched Rebecca's arm and snapped her back to the present. She blinked several times and focused on his smiling face.

"Why don't you rest here," he suggested. Lone Wolf indicated a stand of tall cottonwoods with trunks so vast a man could not reach around them.

"Are you going on ahead?" she asked.

He nodded. "I think we're close to the gang. If we're not careful we might lose our advantage of surprise. I'll be right back."

"Like the last time, huh?"

The white warrior grinned. "You know I would do anything for a cup of your coffee."

Rebecca led her snorting pony into the cool shade of the trees and watched Lone Wolf ride away. She sat on the ground and let her mind wander once again. Memories of her Oglala years came floating to the surface . . .

. . . One of Rebecca's saddest experiences was the death of her baby. She had given birth six months after her marriage to Four Horns, who had become a warrior. It had been an easy pregnancy.

When her labor pains began in earnest, she was taken by her friend, Red Shawl, to a squat brush lodge, separate from the others. There she lay upon a bed of fresh pine boughs and was told to take hold of wooden stakes that had been driven into the ground.

"When the pains come, strain against the stakes," Red Shawl advised her.

For the next hour, Rebecca did as instructed, while her friend constantly wiped at a skein of perspiration that formed on the laboring girl's face. Then Rebecca shrieked and cried out in agony.

"The pains are great! Oooh, it hurts sooo!"

"Quickly, grab the stakes tightly and push with all your might," Red Shawl urged. She signaled through the closed door flap for the midwife.

Within minutes the baby was born.

"My baby," breathed Rebecca. "My own." Her pretty face glistened with new perspiration and a radiant glow.

"Yes . . . and he's a beauty."

"It's . . . it's a boy?"

Red Shawl chuckled. "Yes, and the way he's kicking and screaming I think he's ready to go buffalo hunting with his father." She held up the crying infant.

"Our son!" exulted Rebecca. She gawked at the shriveled, red-face child. Red Shawl cleaned the baby with sweet prairie grass that had been soaked in warm water, wiped him completely with buffalo grease, wrapped him in soft otterskin robes and placed him beside Rebecca, who lay on her back atop some blankets.

"Hello, baby," Rebecca murmured in English.

Holding her newborn child in her arms for the first time, her eyes filled with tears of sorrow when she realized her glassy-eyed mother had no idea of what had taken place.

"Oh, Mother," sobbed Rebecca. "I am so happy and . . . and you can't share in it."

She hugged her newborn son. Tears continued to stream down her lovely face. "I'd like to name the baby Jeremiah, in honor of his great-grandpa, but I don't think Four Horns would understand."

"Maybe it is better that way," Red Shawl admonished, her conviction springing from an aversion to white men.

The baby was finally named *Cetan*, Little Falcon.

When her son was two months old, a Crow war party attacked the Oglala camp. Rebecca knew all about the fierce hatred between the Dakota and the Crow. She knew, too, that the savage Crow usually killed all their enemies without taking prisoners.

"Little Falcon!" gasped Rebecca, clutching her son to her breast. "And Mother!"

Crouched on the ground, Rebecca gathered her jumbled thoughts. She decided to race toward the spot behind Iron Calf's teepee where she'd buried the Knuckleduster so long ago for safekeeping. At least she'd have some protection for the three of them against the murderous Crow.

Throughout the camp, the Oglala had been jolted from the deep sleep of pre-dawn and boiled out of their lodges to engage the enemy. Men and women both clutched weapons, many naked and still flushed with slumber or lovemaking. They yelled defiance at the attackers and the few firearms in camp erupted in a ragged fusillade. Little Falcon clutched at his mother's hair and howled in mingled fright and discomfort.

Racing into action, Rebecca sprinted toward the flat field behind the chief's painted teepee. All around she saw the burning lodges of the Oglala.

Horror clutched her heart when she saw Red Shawl shoving Hannah Caldwell from her flaming small lodge. She turned and raced toward the blazing teepee.

"Mother!" she cried, praying the shock of the attack would restore Hannah's reason.

She grabbed her gagging mother and hauled her away from the conflagration. Her eyes widened when she saw hungry yellow flames consuming the lodge's buffalo hide covering.

"Red Shawl!" shouted Rebecca. Then she glimpsed her slender friend inside the teepee. She had saved Hannah, but still crawled toward the small, round entrance hole, clutching a bag of Hannah's few, precious possessions.

"I'm coming," yelled Red Shawl. "I . . . had to . . ."

To Rebecca's growing horror, Red Shawl's words cut off when the entire flaming structure fell to the ground in a fiery heap. A shower of sparks leaped into the air and thick greasy black smoke billowed into the sky.

Rebecca tried several times to get close to the burning lodge. Each time she was repelled by the intense heat from the crackling yellow flames. She fell to her knees beside her soot-covered mother and burst into tears.

"My only friend is dead!" she cried in English.

All around her the frantic battle raged on.

Sobbing with frustration, Rebecca abandoned her efforts. She dragged her mind-numbed mother along, again determined to reach her secreted weapon. Charging Crow warriors intervened.

Snorting war ponies danced with mincing steps and dust-shrouded the bronze, naked-chested men astride them. Rebecca spun on one heel and pulled her mother after her. Hannah Caldwell stumbled dumbly along. An arrow hissed past Rebecca's ear and struck an unburned lodge a few strides away. She hurried in that direction.

Inside the illusory cover of the conical hide lodge, she found what she had hoped for. A boy's hunting bow rested on its rack to one side of the central firepit. To her surprise, she found the child's weapon difficult to string. Good, she thought. It would be strong enough to kill a man.

She picked up her son from the dirt floor and popped him into a nearby cradle board, which she put in place on her back. The lodge, she knew, would not be a safe place for him. Then she slung a quiver of arrows from her left shoulder, so that it dangled awkwardly under her arm. Selecting a shaft, she nocked it and stepped to the entrance hole.

Her disordered mother huddled at her feet as she swiftly brought up the bow. She had no lack of targets. A Crow jerked his pony to a dust-showering halt directly in front of her and looked down with amused contempt.

His sneer got wiped from his lips when the flare-based hunting point buried deeply in his flat, muscular abdomen. He swayed atop his mount and opened his mouth to scream.

Instead, he vomited a great gout of blood and slid from his war horse's back, kicked spasmodically for a few seconds and died. Rebecca didn't waste time watching the spectacle. Another arrow came to hand and she drew the hunting bow to full reach. With a ghostly whirr, the shaft sped outward.

It lodged itself in another Crow warrior's thigh. He yelped once and turned toward her, his old Spencer rifle aimed at her chest. Then a stone war club smashed in the side of his head. Wielded by a young Oglala, one of the *akicita,* it caved in skull bone and pulped brain tissue.

The Crow fell dead and the young "policeman" turned toward Rebecca with a friendly wave. "Good shooting, *Šinaskawin!"*

Off to her left, near the pony herd, she saw the Oglala men grouping for a counterattack. For a moment her heart swelled with pride. Her husband, Four Horns, would be among them. At the time of their marriage, he had been proclaimed a warrior. He had been initiated into the Raven-owner's Society at the birth of their son. She had little time for patriotic thoughts. Two more Crow braves pounded through the confusion of the camp, directly toward her.

One came from the right, the other from the left. She chose to confront the nearer first, turning to the right. Her fingers fumbled with an arrow, removing it at last from its clumsy position and fitting the notched end to the string.

Her aim hurried by the delay, the shaft buzzed off to strike the charging pony in the chest. The animal squealed in wounded frenzy and went to its knees, catapulting its rider over its head. The young Crow struck on the top of his head and a loud crack sounded when his neck broke. The mortally wounded beast thrashed in the dust, its cries blending with those of wounded and dying humans. A sudden, solid blow to her back sent Rebecca sprawling in the dirt.

She felt as though her spine had cracked. Her chin struck the hard-packed earth of the longterm encampment and blackness swarmed over her conscious mind.

The impact had wrenched the lance from the young Crow's hand. He rode past it with no thought for its loss. After all, it had served its purpose. Behind him it swayed in the breeze, impaled in the tiny, writhing form on Rebecca's back.

Iron Calf led his warriors well. Those who could had caught up war ponies and they led the charge across the wide camp, driving the enemy before them. When two senior warriors of the Raven-owners Society fell, Four Horns leaped forward to shout encouragement to his fellow *Kagi Yuha*.

"*Hu ihpeya wicayapo!*" he shouted, calling for total defeat of the enemy in the most insulting terms, implying the Crow warriors would be forced to submit to sodomy in their overthrow. The blood ran hot in his veins and he burned in the lust for battle.

Four Horns felt the hammer-fisted blow to his chest an instant before he saw the muzzle bloom of the .52 caliber Spencer repeater in the hands of the Crow war leader. His body seemed to float off the ground and he had no sensation of pain when his back contacted the hard dirt. A red haze misted his eyes and slowly faded to black while the sounds of battle drew away from him into an eternal silence.

"*Cetan! Śinaskawin!* My son! My wife!" he thought in a last flash of consciousness.

Then, suddenly, the fighting ended. Only a diminishing swirl of dust and scattered Crow war cries remained of the attacking force. The counterattack had driven the hated *Kagi* from the village. Flames from burning lodges crackled loudly in the silence.

"*Haun-nn . . . haun-nn,*" a dying man cried.

"*A-i-i-i! A-i-i-i!* Hiye haya!" the grieving women began to chant while they searched among the dead for loved ones.

The words, when they came to her, sounded alien at first. Slowly Rebecca made sense of them and located herself in the Oglala camp. The battle! Had the Crow won? Had the warriors driven them off? Terrible memories came back to her. She groaned and tried to rise, feeling still the unwieldly weight at her back and a dull pain near her left shoulder blade. Her vision cleared as Blue Bear Girl staggered toward her, anguish plain on the chubby Sioux girl's face.

"Wha . . . what has happened?" Rebecca croaked out.

"*A-i-i-i, Šinaskawin!* Four Horns is killed in battle and you are a widow. Oh! Oh, how unfortunate." Blue Bear Girl extended a knife toward Rebecca, haft first.

"Help me," Rebecca pleaded. "Please help me up."

Blue Bear Girl's eyes widened in horror then and she bit her lower lip to suppress a cry of anguish. For a moment she sheathed her flencing knife and grasped the shaft of the lance that protruded from Rebecca's cradle board. Tears ran from Blue Bear Girl's eyes when she wrenched the wicked point from the tiny, lifeless body. Rebecca saw the blood dripping from the flint blade and realized with ghastly certainty what it meant.

"*Micinkši!* My son! My son!" she wailed, already grieving in the sure knowledge of her awful loss.

A fresh gush of tears flowed down Blue Bear Girl's cheeks and she blubbered her sorrowful reply. "He . . . he . . . is . . . dead, too. Oh, oh, most sorrow-laden woman!" Again she drew her knife and thrust it toward Rebecca.

"What? What is this for?"

"You must show your grief, Whiterobe Girl. Cut your hair, slash your arms to mourn your dead. It is the custom."

A howl of anguish burst from Rebecca's lips. She clutched herself and rocked on her knees. Then came the realization that it could be worse, her tragedy complete. "My mother?" she asked through trembling lips.

Blue Bear Girl tossed her head and turned a nervous glance back over her shoulder. "Golden Hair is much taken by *nagi napeyapi*. Where she has gone, none can reach her. Nor will she come back."

"Dead, too!" Rebecca wailed, unfamiliar with the Lakota term for deep psychic shock.

"No. But her conscious spirit no longer dwells in her body. She is as a hollow vessel. Big medicine now and much to be revered. But you have lost your man and your son. Come, take the knife. Slash your arms and grieve as is seemly."

Revulsion swept over Rebecca at the thought of self-mutilation. She looked wildly about and saw many squaws gashing their arms, the blood running in bright red ribbons. Many young, unmarried girls did likewise, and some children. Several of the mourners pressed in on her, their expressions a mixture of anguish and threat. Her hand trembled when she reached for the offered blade.

"How do I do this? Is there anything I should say?"

"Nothing in words. Only let your grief flow with your blood."

Hesitantly Rebecca reached up for a long braid. She grasped it and began to saw through with the knife. "*Hau-hau!*" the women exclaimed in approval.

Suddenly the enormity of her loss swept over Rebecca. She was a widow, without a protector, without rights to his property, without even a lodge to shelter in, as the curling wisps of smoke from nearby told her. And her son, the pride of her youth and hope of her future. Dead also. An anguished screech burst deep in her throat and rose to a savage howl of enormous agony. Seemingly of its own volition, the knife flashed and a thin red line appeared on her forearm.

The lips of the wound turned back and blood began to flow. Another cut. There! And there! Heart aching, body numb to the pain she inflicted, Rebecca gave full vent to her torment. In that one brief moment she felt more one with the Oglala than ever before or after. Ah, God, how she grieved.

Iron Calf, though seriously wounded, recovered enough by that evening to summon Rebecca to his lodge.

"*Sinaskawin*, you are a widow now. Without a husband you have no protector, no provider and fire has destroyed your only possession, the lodge. You are young. You must take a new man soon."

"No! I cannot! I . . . I loved Four Horns. There is no other for me."

"Hear me. In a sacred manner I speak. It is the way of the Dakota. You can not waste your life in mourning. Without a man you have only your food bowl, the few things you saved from the fire. What will you do in the Moons of Frozen Water and of Deep Snow? How will you survive?"

"I do not wish to survive," Rebecca returned vehemently.

"Such talk is foolish. Go and think upon what I have said. There are more days and you will see the wisdom of a new man. Go now, my daughter."

Outside the lodge Rebecca's mother came to her, supported by her old enemy, Rattling Blanket. "Do what Iron Calf urges you, Rebecca," Hannah Caldwell begged with the last earthly shred of her reason. "He only wants what is best for you."

"How can that be?" Rebecca snapped scornfully, wretched in her misery.

"Why, don't you know? Couldn't you tell?" Hannah asked, her face transported for the moment to youthfulness. Shyly she patted at a stray strand of hair. "Iron Calf is truly your father. He is the young warrior who had his way with me nearly seventeen long years ago."

"No, Mother! Oh, no!" Rebecca hugged her mother to her, seeking a denial, only to watch the last weak glow of lucidity fade from Hannah Caldwell's eyes.

Days turned to weeks and the weeks passed into months. Despite her mother's startling revelation, Rebecca resisted the pressure toward taking a new man. Many asked, for she was considered a rare beauty to the men of the Oglala camp. In spite of secret help from Blue Bear Girl and the sympathy of all the camp, her self-imposed isolation caused her station in life to slowly degrade into a state worse than when she had been a slave. She hunted for herself and her deranged mother. Hunger haunted her at times, along with debilitating grief for her loss. She grew thin, dirty and unkempt. Her single deerhide dress fell to rags. Still she turned aside all offers of marriage.

Snow came early. Yet Rebecca's will remained unshaken.

Then, in the Moon of Popping Branches—February—she contracted a wracking cold, which rapidly turned to a raging fever. On the point of death, she was taken into Iron Calf's lodge. Little hope for her recovery was held by the medicine man, for her will to live burned low. Gradually she strengthened. The fever left her and at last her eyes opened on a new day.

The first sight of her swimming eyes was the aged, leathery face of Broken Wing, a camp bachelor of some fifty-five summers. Only a few white nubs of teeth showed when he parted his lips in a comforting smile.

"*Šinaskawin*, I will take you into my lodge," he announced in a raspy voice.

Rebellion flared once more in Rebecca's breast. Her long illness quickly sapped her resolve and she lay back, her face averted.

"I will take care of you and provide for you," continued Broken Wing. "My needs are simple and my teepee is always warm."

Rebecca's swirling mind mulled over the proposition, too weakened to find suitable objections. The prospect didn't look too good.

Broken Wing, she had been told, had chosen a solitary

life. In his puberty vision, as a boy of twelve, he had reached for the browstrap, instead of the bow string, when offered by *Ptesanwin*, Buffalo-cow Woman, the spiritual messenger of the Great Spirit. He had, for a time, become a Contrary. What use would a man who let other men use him in the manner of a squaw have for a woman around his lodge? she wondered. Then she recalled other stories about Broken Wing, camp gossip repeated with relish by the women at their work.

He was said to have as healthy a desire for women as any man and an enormous cock that split like a stone wedge. Images of the detailed vignettes repelled her, yet she somehow felt excited by them. Could they be true? Hesitantly she asked a timid question.

"And what . . . what do you want in return?"

"In return?" Broken Wing queried, feigning shock and a little genuine hurt. "Why, I only want to take care of a beautiful woman and have her smile at me."

Emboldened, Rebecca chuckled before replying. "Yes, but what is your price?"

A shy smile cracked Broken Wing's leathery face. "Well, after all these years," he began, "I have a . . . a great sexual appetite."

Laughter filled Iron Calf's lodge. Rebecca turned her head to the skin wall and closed her eyes. She might have guessed. The Oglala, indeed all the Sioux she had encountered, loved an off-color joke. In his youth, Broken Wing might have been a Contrary, but now he had every intention of making up for lost time. She sighed.

"Yes, Broken Wing. I will come to live in your lodge. You will not find me . . . find me, ah, lacking in my own appetite. And I will make you fine moccasins, beautiful loincloths and supple war shirts."

"Good. It is good. I like you now, *Śinaskawin*. With a few beatings you will make a good wife."

Two days later, Rebecca rose on shaky legs, rolled her

robes, a gift from Iron Calf, shouldered them, along with an iron kettle and cooking utensils, provided by Blue Bear Girl, and walked to Broken Wing's lodge.

Life with Broken Wing turned out to be living hell for the first few months. True to his word, he administered frequent beatings with willow switches and, on one occasion, a braided horse tail-hair quirt. Rebecca's stubborn will and hot temper flashed, though she bit her lip and submitted.

Broken Wing provided more than ample food. Also many skins that she must process, cure and make into clothing. Her teeth ached constantly from chewing shaved deerhide, rabbit and buffalo skins. She also learned, and often, that he had not been exaggerating his sexual prowess.

On the night after her full health returned, he took her for the first time. By the flickering light of the low-burning fire he shyly undressed her, like a nervous bridegroom. Her honey-tan flesh glistened and he twisted and trembled in excitement. Behind the flap of his loincloth, Rebecca saw the persistent swelling of his maleness. Then he removed his single garment.

Rebecca's eyes widened at sight of the largest penis she had ever encountered. Its length reached nearly two handspans of a big man and she could not close her fingers around the thick base, though she tried with an eagerness that surprised her new husband.

Slowly she worked her way up toward the dark purple tip, stroking, squeezing, teasing him to such a quivering height of expectation that she thought he would explode all over her before they had even joined in the delights of coupling. When he seemed unable to endure more, she arched her back, stood on tiptoe and plunged the monstrous phallus deep within her wet and palpitating mound.

Excruciating pain seemed to split her asunder, yet she

drove herself against Broken Wing, hips grinding, undulating, ingesting more and more of that vibrant fleshly shaft until their pelvic bones clashed and they merged one body into another.

"Aaaah! Oooh, Broken Wing! Aaaaaah, how I have missed this!" she cried wantonly.

The old man marveled. He had never engaged in the battle of love standing upright before. A surge of incredible passion boiled up and he began to thrust at her silken purse, boring deeply within, sliding out in a languid, tantalizing manner that charged his whole being with incredible jolts of pure pleasure. So powerful were the stimulating sensations that he soon burst open, spilling his flaming seed within the pink-walled channel he had so violently possessed.

They fell in a heap on the piled buffalo robes.

For a year and a half, Rebecca endured torments by day, ranging from indifferent cuffs and verbal abuse to brutal whippings with willow switches. At night she felt herself transported to ethereal, heart-piercing bliss by the continual antics of her lover. He taught her to take him in her mouth and she grew practiced at it.

"*Ceazin,*" he would purr. "*Ceazin.*" And Rebecca would cover the swollen, purple-red glans of his enormous penis with her lips, her tongue describing tingling spirals over its surface. The more and deeper she took him into her questing throat, the more she began to like it.

By the time spring, 1875 came, she had tamed old Broken Wing's lust. The beatings and carnal demands had both started to moderate. Small doses of sex several times a week seemed to satisfy the wizened old timer.

At the end of May, early one morning after Rebecca returned to camp from a berry picking trip into the bushes, the camp's ponies began to nicker. She stopped short. A moment later she noticed that the village's many short-haired dogs had also become restive.

"What is it?" she wondered aloud.

"*Šinaskawin!*" snapped Broken Wing. "Bring me some of those berries."

"Wait. Don't you hear it?"

Broken Wing shuffled over to where Rebecca stood with the buffalo paunch full of freshly picked choke-cherries.

"Give me those," he demanded. He snatched the bag from her hands. "What good are you? I wonder why I took you into my lodge."

In that instant she heard the whistle of an arrow.

It made a meaty smack when it struck Broken Wing's back.

"*Haun-nn, haun-nn,*" the old man's death cry quavered.

"Raiders!" Rebecca shouted. She looked at the quivering, feathered shaft in the old warrior's back. "It's another attack!"

Her warning spread rapidly. Soon the Oglala camp came alive with anxious shouts and war cries.

"The Crow!" "*Kangi! Kangi!*"

"Get your weapons!"

"Boys to the pony herd!"

Rebecca stepped over Broken Wing's bleeding corpse and checked her immediate surroundings. A quick backward glance said her only farewell to the hated husband-adored lover, then she dashed toward the grassy area behind old Iron Calf's lodge and her buried Knuckleduster. This time, she thought, she was on her own. Now she'd really need the gun.

She glanced at the camp's perimeter and saw about a hundred Crow warriors, stuffed ravens braided into their long, high-crested black hair, leaping into the Oglala village. They gripped war hatchets and heavy stone clubs in their hands. Behind them, a line of shaven-pate Strong Hearts sat their ponies and fired arrows into camp.

"Not again!" muttered Rebecca as she ran. "Not this time."

She reached the spot in the ground where she had buried the deerskin sack containing her derringer. Arrows, bullets and powder smoke filled the air everywhere, along with the warriors' shouts and the screams of wounded and dying. She dropped to her knees and quickly scratched at the black Dakota soil.

"Oh, damn!" she cried in frustration when a fingernail broke. She drew her flencing knife and continued to gouge at the stubborn earth.

Within seconds, Rebecca tore the deerskin bag from its hiding place. She began to fish for the tiny gun she'd taken from the dead settler. Grasping the barrelless revolver with her right hand, she clutched the extra cartridges in her left. Rebecca rose to her feet and shoved the weapon out in front of her. Not thirty feet away, a Crow warrior ran toward Iron Calf's lodge with a flaming brand to torch the hide-covered tent.

She had never test-fired the little Knuckleduster, so her first shot went wild. She pulled back on the hammer and let go. A .32 slug smacked meatily into the warrior's right thigh. Again she eared back the hammer and released it as he turned toward her. The bullet entered his stomach and he doubled over. She turned to run to safety.

And crashed into the broad chest of a massive Crow warrior.

"Oh!" she blurted, then arced the loaded derringer upward, toward the shaven-headed Strong Heart's face. She began to pull back the hammer.

In a flash of movement, the big Crow brave whipped out with his left hand and knocked the derringer from her grasp. The diminutive weapon sailed into the nearby grass. Rebecca winced at the pain and glanced at the tall, buckskin-clad enemy.

The warrior blocking her path wore the crested roach of a Strong Heart, an unusual style among the Crow. Stranger still, the narrow ridge of hair down the middle of his shaven pate was blond. She looked closely into his piercing blue eyes.

Blue eyes? she wondered.

Rebecca quickly remembered the tales she'd heard each winter about a blond-headed, blue-eyed Crow warrior, a member of the fierce Strong Heart Society. His name was Lone Wolf. He was considered to be one of the best fighters among the Crow. Legend made him out to be taller than any two normal warriors and stronger than four. It was said he could ride, track, rope, kill and hunt better than almost anybody but a Dakota. Now it appeared she'd run into him at the worst possible time.

"Do you speak English?" inquired the blond warrior, surprise coloring his words.

Rebecca stiffened. "Get away from me!" she shouted in the same language.

"How is it that you speak the white man's tongue?" he questioned.

Rebecca stared at him, eyes ablaze with defiance.

The blue-eyed Crow lowered his war hatchet and smiled at her. "Are you a captive of the Oglalas? Is that why you're here in their camp?" He made as though to touch her.

Rebecca took a quick step backward and nodded hesitantly. "Yes . . . I was taken along with my mother, five years ago. A-are you going to kill me?"

He laughed. "No. Why should I?"

"I thought for a moment you were the Crow brave called Lone Wolf."

"I am Lone Wolf. But why does that mean I would kill you?"

"You are a legend among my . . . ah, among the Oglala. But . . ." she trailed off in confusion.

"I have been Lone Wolf for the past ten years," he explained. "I was Brett Baylor, Nebraska homesteader, before that. But that was so long ago I nearly forget what it was like."

"You mean . . . you're a captive, too?"

He nodded. "In a way, yes. And to tell the truth, I haven't had this much English spoken to me for nearly nine years. So you'll have to go a might slow for a while. What is your name for a start?"

"Rebecca Caldwell." All around them the Oglala fought the invading Crow in the teepee-dotted camp. War cries and death screams filled the fragrant spring air.

"Then that explains your blue eyes and blond hair," Rebecca said, thinking aloud.

"You're one of the few white captives I've come across."

"Haven't you ever tried to escape?"

Lone Wolf shook his head, resignedly. "Only once, nine years ago," he told her, displaying a mutilated left ear. "This is what I got for my troubles."

"That's horrible!"

He shrugged it off. "What about you? Have you tried to escape from the Sioux?"

"The right chance has never come. But I'm ready now. That's why I hid a gun."

Lone Wolf took Rebecca by the arm. He led her behind a screen of low, lodge-pole pines. "Tell me quickly what happened to you," he said, eager to hear a white person speak. "I haven't had anybody to talk with in all the years with the *Absaroka.*"

Rapidly she told him about her cowardly uncles, the Bitter Creek Jake Tulley gang, her mother's fate at the hands of the Oglala tribe and her own life with the Sioux. At the end, she felt drained and Lone Wolf shook his head sympathetically.

"You've had it rough."

She nodded morosely. "I'm ready to leave."

"Why don't you?"

She looked up, hope born in her eyes. "Now? During the battle?"

"That's what you planned, isn't it?"

"But . . . but I'm your captive," Rebecca returned.

Lone Wolf bit his lower lip before speaking. "I can't tell you all my story now," he began. "Though I'll say that the Crow killed my eighteen year old bride."

"I'm sorry," Rebecca offered sincerely.

"I've more or less put that tragedy out of my life . . . until now, that is. I owe the Crow no loyalty."

"What does that have to do with escaping?"

He smiled. "I've always carried a plan of escape in my mind, looking for the right opportunity to employ it. This seems like a better chance than most."

"Do you mean it?" Rebecca implored, her excitement growing.

"Yes. Only I'm not plannin' on headin' back to the white man's world. I've been an Indian for too long."

"But you could change back again."

"Not sure I want to," he replied. "I'm no Indian and I ain't really a white man. I'm . . . somewhere in between."

"What about your family? Or your wife's family? I'm sure they'd be willing to help you adjust."

"No!" he snapped.

His violent reaction stunned her. "But, why? What's the matter with that?"

Lone Wolf looked at her, a sad loneliness in his cerulean eyes. "I hold myself responsible for my wife's death. Hell, if I'd protected her a little better at our homestead, then maybe Mary Anne would be alive today. And . . . our son. I wouldn't know how to face her relatives now."

Rebecca let his words hang for a moment. The tumult of battle washed over them, urging instant flight.

"Well, *I'm* ready to escape," she decided aloud.

She watched as his imposing, confident posture returned. "And I'll go with you."

"What about my mother?"

"We'll get her, too."

Lone Wolf reached down and scooped up Rebecca's tiny

137

derringer. He examined it curiously before handing it back to her. "You may need this."

"Thank you. What . . . what should I call you?"

A thin-lipped smile split his rugged features. "I ain't been called Brett for ten years. Call me Lone Wolf, it's what I am."

Rebecca laughed and suddenly felt better. "All right, Lone Wolf, so long as you don't call me *Sinaskawin*. I'm tired of being Whiterobe Girl of the Oglala."

"That's a deal."

"Look out!" Rebecca suddenly cried, pointing toward the Oglala camp.

Lone Wolf turned and both of them watched a scowling Crow war chief ride toward them. The approaching leader was broad of shoulder, with a hideously scarred face. He had several red hands painted on his broad chest and a large, glossy-feathered raven bobbed in his cresseted hair.

"That's Scar-on-Face," Lone Wolf told her. "He's war leader on this raid. I suppose he's coming to ask what the hell I'm doin' talkin' to a beautiful Oglala girl instead of takin' her scalp."

"What are you going to do?"

"Tell him we're leavin' Indian country."

"But . . .?"

Lone Wolf gave her a grim smile. "Leave him to me."

Swiftly the muscle-bulging Crow chief rode up to Lone Wolf. He glared at Rebecca. Without warning, Lone Wolf struck out with his war hatchet and sliced Scar-on-Face's skull in two. The huge warrior swayed in the saddle and blood spurted high into the air.

Rebecca stared blankly, sickened but unable to look away.

"He knows we're leavin' now," Lone Wolf announced. He reached for Rebecca's arm, hurrying from the scene. "We have to find your mother. Where is she?"

"In that teepee over there. The little one," she told him, pointing.

"We'll get her and you'll be gone from here forever."

His words were like a fresh breeze after a thunderstorm.

Together they walked into the raging battle in the Oglala camp. Rebecca led Lone Wolf toward the small lodge where her mother still lived out her vacant days. Suddenly she stopped, eyes widening in horror.

"What's the matter?"

"It's my mother," Rebecca wailed, pointing a trembling finger at a huddled form on the ground.

Hannah Caldwell lay in a pool of blood near Iron Calf's lodge, her throat slashed from ear to ear, forehead caved in by a war club. Her glassy eyes stared unseeing at the crystal blue sky. A wide smile creased Hannah's age-scamed face. It gave the appearance of contentment, as though she had finally found peace.

"Mother, oh, Mother!" Rebecca grieved.

Lone Wolf reached out and stopped her impulsive rush toward the dead woman. "We must leave."

"But my mother . . ."

"Let's go . . . or there won't be any going," Lone Wolf told her, eyes on the swirling conflict that still raged.

Rebecca broke from his grasp and rushed to her mother's side. Ignoring the ugly wounds and growing pool of blood on the ground, she knelt quickly and kissed her mother on the cheek.

"Good-bye, Mother. Now, you, too, are free," she said softly.

"Let's go, now!" Lone Wolf urged.

Rebecca stood quickly, glanced one final time at her fallen mother, then turned her back on the Oglala village that had been, for better or worse, her home for five years.

They took a couple of war ponies and dashed into the forest.

Later in the day, after hearing the details of the Tulley gang's deal with the Sioux years ago, Lone Wolf offered his own story and pledged his help to Rebecca in getting her revenge. His offer surprised her.

"You mean you are willing to go after the men who gave me away? Why would you want to do that now that you have your freedom?"

Lone Wolf moved closer to her and looked deeply into her eyes. "Like I told you when I spoke of my past, you remind me of my wife. Perhaps, just perhaps, I can redeem myself in my own eyes by helping you find your revenge. If you let me help, maybe I can put to good use all the skills I learned from the Crow. After all, two *Indians* stalking them are better than one."

Rebecca looked away, her eyes misting.

"But . . . We'll travel as friends, not lovers," Lone Wolf offered hesitantly. "I honor the memory of my wife . . . and . . . I have taken a vow. It's not important that you know what that is now. Only, trust me, I *want* to help."

Rebecca smiled and reached impulsively for his hand.

"Thank you for your kind words," she said in a tone of near-dismissal. She looked at him again. "And I accept your offer."

Suddenly Rebecca had no qualms about looking for her uncles and the Jake Tulley gang. She felt a surge of confidence wash into her breast.

She would never be afraid again . . .

. . . Rebecca returned to the present with a start. Her mental excursion into her recent past had left her feeling wrung out. The haunting memories had not been purged, though some of the more painful ghosts had been laid to rest. She rose quickly and looked at the surrounding prairie. For a fleeting instant, she half expected to see another war party.

Satisified she was alone with her pony, she sat again and waited for Lone Wolf to return with news about the Tulley gang.

After all, she had lots of scores to settle.

TEN

Lone Wolf hadn't been inside a whorehouse since his Civil War days. So when the Tulley gang's tracks led him to the Silver Wing Saloon, perched incongruously twenty miles from nowhere on the prairie and ten miles from where he had left Rebecca, he hesitated before deciding upon his next course of action.

He tethered his pony to a stunted tree in a nearby wash and studied the bawdyhouse's layout. He hunkered in the buffalo grass at the lip of the small draw as though scouting another tribe's campsite. The large, two-story pleasure palace had been exiled from distant Jury Wells and sat alone in the middle of the prairie. Still, it attracted a large clientele. Lone Wolf knew from past encounters with renegade whites, while still a Crow warrior, that the Silver Wing was a hangout for drifters, killers and badmen in general.

The perfect sort of place to attract the Tulley gang.

Lone Wolf decided to investigate the unsavory joint. First he needed a way to get in.

He scanned the clapboard building and the packed corral beside it. Within a minute he had observed two rifle-toting sentries patrolling the grounds. An embryotic plot formed in his brain.

While still fleshing out his plan, Lone Wolf padded silently toward one of the unsuspecting guards. Adrenalin began to pump through his veins. A smile cracked his leathery face. As he sneaked up to within twenty yards of a tall, sleepy-eyed sentry, he suddenly knew the reason he couldn't become a white man again—he loved the freedom of the prairie, the excitement of the hunt, the animal-like satisfaction he felt after a kill. He enjoyed being an Indian, without accepting their cultural restrictions. In short, he was comfortable as a white warrior, a man with no race, yet a man of the world in the truest sense.

He came to within ten feet of the drowsy guard. Still his presence had remained undetected. The other man patrolled the opposite side of the big house of ill-repute.

Piano music tinkled inside the cantina. Men laughed and a shrill squeal came from one of the soiled doves.

Lone Wolf waited until the tall guard left his post. He leaned his Winchester against the corral rail, opened his fly and began to relieve himself. Instantly Lone Wolf stepped briskly from hiding, came up behind the sentry and felled him with a quick rabbit punch.

It took Lone Wolf only seconds to drag the unconscious man into the low barn, strip off his clothes and put them on over his buckskins. The garments fit poorly, but would serve. He especially needed the man's hat to hide the blond ridge of hair down the middle of his shaven head. He left the guard in his longjohns, retrieved the hat from outside and started for the bawdyhouse.

He had barely begun when he heard the front door of the cantina open. Loud piano music and boisterous laughter reached his ears. Trying to act as much like a white man as he could, the transformed Crow warrior strode toward the open door and stepped into the den of iniquity.

Immediately, several whores accosted him.

"Why, hello, handsome," a thin painted blonde purred.

"Come right in, lover," added a plump redhead.

A bold brunette, wearing only a scrap of clothing, swivelhipped up to him and hooked her arm in his. "I'm yours for the evening, darling," she announced, giving her sisters a hard glare. "Wanna drink?"

Lone Wolf blinked several times to acclimate his eyes to the dimness inside. Smoke and the stench of rotgut whiskey burned his nostrils. He felt awkward being with so many whites again.

He quickly scanned the crowded interior and noticed a dozen or so gunmen drinking at the polished mahogany bar, several card tables full of enthusiastic poker players and at least a score of painted ladies hovering around the entire scene. A wide-eyed black piano player pounded the keyboard on a raised platform at the rear of the main room. An ornate crystal chandelier hung over the center of the saloon. A heavy cloud of tobacco smoke was suspended over the heads of the customers. His nostrils wrinkled at the sour, unwashed odor of white men.

"How 'bout that drink, tall and handsome?" asked the brunette. She pulled him from the clutches of her fellow whores. "Buy me a drink, what say?"

He stumbled toward a table in the corner of the cantina and glanced at the stubbled faces all around him. He was hoping to find at least some of the Tulley gang. The problem remained, he didn't know what any of them looked like.

The brunette pushed him into a chair. "There, now, isn't that better?"

Lone Wolf glanced at the long-haired girl as though noticing her for the first time. His casual look turned to a concentrated stare when he observed her large, swelling breasts, their mounded tops protruding from the open decolletage of the hand-span waisted costume she wore. Its sea-green color matched her eyes.

"Wha-at?" he asked, distracted.

"How 'bout a drink?" the soiled dove repeated snappishly.

He nodded, eyes fixed on her heaving bosom.

Impatiently, the whore grabbed a bottle from a nearby table. She poured into two used glasses sitting before them.

"Ain't never seen you in here before," she observed, recorking the bottle. "But you're sure a cute one."

Mechanically Lone Wolf sipped his drink, strangling slightly on its harsh, unfamiliar taste. He debated whether to involve the girl in his search for Tulley's men. His feeling of awkwardness at being suddenly thrust among so many whites had started to wear off. To his shame and amazement, he felt his manhood swelling in response to her animal presence. Angrily he thrust aside his momentary flare of lust. He was about to probe the brunette for information when an especially loud piece of conversation from a nearby table caught his attention. He perked up immediately.

"Hey, Virgil," called a gruff voice. "Looks like you got your hands full!"

"Two at a time. That's how I like 'em."

A pair of soiled doves giggled.

Lone Wolf turned slowly in his chair. The name Virgil had struck a chord. Was it Rebecca's uncle, the one who rode with Tulley?

"Noisy, ain't he?" the brunette observed. "You can even hear him over that damn piano music."

"Who is he?"

Lone Wolf watched the short, pudgy man with a girl on each arm. Virgil sat several tables away, surrounded by four gunhawks.

"That's Virgil Caldwell," the bawd replied. "He's one of our regulars. Most of the girls like him 'cause he's pretty

loose with his money and he likes to do the wildest things."
She ran the pink tip of her tongue over her upper lip in a
suggestive manner.

"Kinda loose with his tongue, too."

The whore laughed. "Hey, that's funny." She changed
abruptly. "But don't let him hear nothin' like that. He
hangs out with a rough crowd."

"So do I."

The chippie reached over and touched his hand.

As she did, Lone Wolf saw Virgil Caldwell rise shakily
and wobble toward the narrow staircase on the other side of
the room.

"See you boys back at camp," he called to the gunmen. "I
got me a couple of hot pistols right here and a bottle full of
good whiskey. I'm hankerin' to see which gets used up
first."

"I'll tell Tulley all about it," yelled one hardcase.

"You do that," Virgil responded amid the other men's
laughter.

Lone Wolf stiffened. His good fortune surprised him.
He'd stumbled upon some of Tulley's boys, fresh from their
failed attack on the settler's house back on the trail. Better,
he had not drawn any suspicion to himself by asking
questions.

"Hey, wouldn't old Jake love to be in my boots right
now?" Virgil crowed as he lurched toward the first landing.

The gunmen laughed again, while Virgil unsteadily
mounted the stairs.

Lone Wolf felt a hand on his crotch.

He turned sharply and looked into the whore's washed-
out green eyes. "Wanna join 'em upstairs?" she asked,
nodding toward the staircase. "Can't beat my price."

"Where's that lead to?"

"To fun and games, honey, fun and games. Seriously, the
bird cages are up there. My room's among 'em." The
brunette began to massage his cock, which, despite his strict

self-discipline and his vow, rebelliously began to stiffen.

Lone Wolf stood suddenly, nearly upsetting the wobbly table. "Come on, let's go," he croaked. He grabbed her hand and kept his eyes on Virgil, who was still negotiating the stairs.

"My God!" yelped the whore. "When you get ready, you do get ready."

As Lone Wolf picked his way across the smoky room and reached the staircase, Virgil and his two giggling doxies disappeared somewhere on the second floor.

"How many rooms up there?" Lone Wolf demanded.

"Five bird cages and one suite."

"A suite?"

"Yeah. For special customers. You know, big spenders?"

"Like Virgil?"

She nodded. "He's always got money."

As they mounted the creaking stairs, Lone Wolf began to think of a plan. He'd entered the badman's haven without any major problems, now he would have to make good use of his time. He decided to interrogate Virgil. And it wouldn't be difficult. He'd learned some persuasive questioning techniques from the Crow. Smiling, he followed the brunette whore.

The second story corridor had three doors on the left and two on the right. Several smoky kerosene lamps bathed the hallway in a subdued amber light. The soiled dove led Lone Wolf to one of the rooms on the left.

"Where's the suite?" he inquired.

"Across the hall from us. Can't you hear Virgil's voice?"

A booming shout and crackling laughter escaped from the suite.

The hooker dragged Lone Wolf into the tiny room and shut the door. The closet-sized cubicle contained a tired bed, a single hard-backed chair and a small commode with a chipped white porcelain wash basin and pitcher. A candle in a wooden holder flickered alongside them.

By the time Lone Wolf turned around to face the well-used drab, she had taken off her skimpy clothes. He scanned her naked body, noticing the purple bruises on her legs, probably left by some over-eager customer. Her breasts were small and slightly sagging, her stomach flat, showing stretch marks. Her pubic glistened in the sparse light. Artificial desire leaped from her washed out eyes.

"Well, do you like what ya see?"

"Lovely," Lone Wolf replied dryly.

Then he stepped forward and removed his hat. His shaven head reflected the candlelight and his narrow ridge of hair stood erect on his shiny pate.

He watched her eyes expand and roll wildly.

"You're . . . you're an Injun!" She started to scream, but Lone Wolf moved faster.

He covered her mouth with one big hand and rapped her gently, though soundly, with the pommel of his hunting knife. Her eyes rolled up in their sockets and she fell senseless to the bed.

Without wasting a second, Lone Wolf tore off the guard's clothes, revealing his buckskins. He gripped his hunting knife, listened for sounds from the corridor and stepped from the dingy crib. He shut the door softly.

Lone Wolf pressed up against the suite's door. He heard soft female voices and a low, masculine moan. Wrapping his hand around the white ceramic knob, he slowly opened the latch and eased the partition away from the jamb. After a moment's pause he slipped into the suite.

The dimly-lit apartment consisted of two rooms, partially partitioned by a folding screen. A small window opened onto the corral. Virgil and his pair of naked playmates occupied the bedroom on the other side of the screen. Lone Wolf padded across the outer chamber, his knife leading the way.

He heard the voices more clearly.

"Oh, sweetheart," Virgil groaned. "Don't stop."

A soiled dove giggled. "You like that, don'tcha? When Beth does that?"

"It's heaven, honey. Now you get on top of me . . . like that . . . so's you can lick it when it comes outta her."

Lone Wolf grabbed the dressing screen and tossed it aside.

The whores screamed. Virgil tried vainly to sit up.

"What have we here?" Lone Wolf drawled. "If it ain't Virgil Caldwell himself."

Virgil pushed the girls aside and struggled to a sitting position. He tried to look intimidating in spite of his nakedness and semi-drunken state. The two bare whores covered their breasts in a surprising display of modesty. Virgil started to go for his revolver, lying on the floor.

Lone Wolf kicked the gun away.

"Who are you?" demanded Rebecca's uncle. He flicked a quick glance at Lone Wolf's blond ridge of hair.

"He's an Injun, can't you see?" a whore injected.

"I'm a feller who needs some information."

"What kinda information?"

"About Jake Tulley."

The whores huddled together on the bed. "Tell him what he wants to know, Virgil. He scares me," Beth wailed.

Lone Wolf watched Virgil's florid face contort with indecision. His red-rimmed eyes flitted to the Colt on the far side of the room.

Then voices rose from the hallway.

"He's in the suite!" shouted the brunette. She had obviously recovered from the tap on the jaw. "He's an Injun. Got his head shaved and everything."

"An' the bastard stole my clothes!" bellowed the guard from outside.

Suddenly the suite's door swung open. Three gun-toting hardcases poured into the room. They spotted Lone Wolf and began to raise their six-shooters.

"Don't! You'll hit me, you idiots!" Virgil bellowed.

Lone Wolf kicked out the room's kerosene lamp, then ducked low.

Six-guns belched fire and lead. The explosions reverberated painfully in the confines of the darkened room. Lone Wolf charged in below the flashes, knife swinging at the gunmen. He knocked them down like saplings in the path of a buffalo stampede. One man yelled out painfully.

"He cut me! He cut me."

"Where'd he go?" a voice demanded.

"Jesus!" cried Virgil.

"Get a light!"

"Don't shoot, it's me."

Leaving the shouting and confusion behind, Lone Wolf raced toward the stairs. He leaped down them three at a time until he reached the saloon floor. His sudden appearnce took everyone by surprise. One gunman, noticing his Indian hairstyle, began to draw his weapon.

Lone Wolf upset the card table onto the gunman. He threw his knife into the arm of a second.

Whores screamed. Outlaws swore. Card players ducked, cursing as their chips flew.

Suddenly an arm wrapped around Lone Wolf's throat and threatened to cut off his air supply. A quick elbow to the gut of the man behind him took care of that problem. He raced toward the front door.

Virgil, still stark naked, appeared at the top of the stairs. "Stop that renegade bastard. I wanna know who in hell he is."

A guard burst in from outside.

Lone Wolf ducked aside and slugged the man low in the stomach. A loud grunt accompanied the gunslinger's involuntary bow. A quick, two-handed rabbit punch to the back of the hardcase's neck drove him, buck-teeth first, to the rough wooden planks of the small porch. Lone Wolf glanced up and saw several tough-looking hombres headed that way from the corral.

He spun on one moccasined foot and leaped back inside. He jerked the glass-paned door closed behind him. Boots clumped on the stoop outside and a shot blasted shards of one window into the room. Lone Wolf ran across the saloon, catching his former pursuers by surprise with the tactic.

He jumped onto the bar, kicked a short-barreled scattergun from the barkeep's hands and glanced up at the crystal chandelier. With a mighty leap he grabbed onto the ornate rim and swung back and forth.

Several gunmen started to draw a bead on him with their six-guns. He quickly gained momentum and swung onto the top of the stairs, knocking Virgil Caldwell to the carpeted floor in the process.

"Son of a bitch!" roared Virgil.

Lone Wolf rushed past the naked whores and ran into the suite. He stepped over to the room's only window and kicked out the grimy glass. He started to climb to freedom when he heard a metallic click at the door.

He turned and spotted the brunette.

"You punched me, you bastard!" she accused.

"You're not going to let that spoil our relationship, are you?" he returned. She menaced with her tiny pistol. "Now, don't do anything foolish," he cautioned. His eyes went to the .41 rim-fire derringer she aimed at his head. "I'm sure we can work somethin' out."

"You're an Injun! A lousy Injun. Why didn't you tell me when you came in here?"

His eyes spotted Virgil's gun a few feet away on the floor.

A second later, two gunhawks appeared behind the whore. Each brandished his six-gun. Virgil poked his head between them from the corridor.

"There's the bastard," Rebecca's uncle yelled.

Lone Wolf seized a slim opportunity.

Without warning he tore the mattress from the bed and

150

flung it toward the gunmen. The brunette shrieked with surprise. Reflexively, the pistoleros fired.

Lone Wolf had already dived to the floor. He grabbed Virgil's Colt and came up blazing. One of the two toughs cried with pain and Virgil ducked out of the doorway.

The brunette struggled under the mattress.

Lone Wolf turned toward the window, poked the Colt under his knife belt and stepped through the broken pane. He looked back and saw the other tough trying to line up on him. He quickly threw two more rounds toward the man, then replaced Virgil's Colt in his waistband. He grasped the bottom of the sash with both hands and lowered himself to full length. He held on for a moment before dropping to the ground. He sprinted toward the draw beyond the corral.

Lone Wolf swung into the saddle and heeled his pony's sides. He had lost his knife and failed to discover the exact location of the Tulley gang's hideout. Yet he had good news for Rebecca.

Her Uncle Virgil was close at hand and Lone Wolf had his gun.

ELEVEN

Insects buzzed lazily in the grass and the sun had swung far over the meridian by the time Lone Wolf returned. Rebecca greeted him warmly, glad to see he had come back unharmed. He gave her a quick summary of his adventures, then they began to ride on.

"Where are we headed?" he asked.

"Like you told me, Uncle Virgil probably headed north after leaving that bordello. He'll join Tulley and that wagon."

"Let's follow," Lone Wolf agreed.

As the lengthening late afternoon shadows cast long streaks across the Dakota prairie, Rebecca and Lone Wolf slapped the flanks of their Indian ponies and galloped northward. Half an hour before the orange sun dropped behind the western horizon, Rebecca heard the distant report of a high-powered rifle. She pulled back on her reins. Lone Wolf had also heard it and braked his horse in a shower of torn sod.

"I didn't know any white men hunted in these parts,"

Rebecca opined. She peered through the gathering dusk at the desolate prairie.

"Aren't supposed to," Lone Wolf responded dryly. He strained his sensitive ears for other sounds of activity that would identify the hunters. "But I know of some men who seem compelled to ignore the Red Cloud treaty of '66 that closed the Dakotas to whites. They go off in the Hills prospectin' for gold, since Yella Hair surveyed it two years back. Some even jump the line from down this way and take hides off the herds."

"They're risking their hair if the Sioux find them."

"No doubt. But I've never known a white man who could resist the lure of gold. Even if they make it the hard way by skinnin' out buffs. Rotten bastards!" he exclaimed with vehemence. "They move on with the railroad and kill all the prime critters they can shoot at. For the past three winters the band of *Absaroka* I traveled with came near to starvation what with the depleted herds."

"Thought you were anxious to stop playing Indian," Rebecca teased.

"I am. Only in this, right is on the side of the tribes."

"If these are only illegal hunters, I suppose we can afford to forget about them and leave them to the Sioux."

"Out here," he returned, "you can't really forget about anything that might kill you. We'd best be ridin' over and see who they are."

Another shot echoed in the stillness.

"Seems like it's headed over those ridges," Rebecca judged. She pointed toward some grassy sand hills.

Within a few minutes they reined in their horses on the crest of a rock-encrusted ridge, overlooking a vast stretch of the grassy prairie. Rebecca controlled her spirited mount and gazed at the spectacle in front of her.

"My goodness!" she exclaimed, eyes bright with excitement. "I haven't seen so many buffalo since I went hunting with the Oglala."

"Yeah, they stretch way off to the north. Must be ten thousand animals, and this just the lead edge."

Rebecca let her eyes take in the massive brown layer of grazing buffalo that blanketed the prairie for a vast distance.

Another loud shot ripped through the air.

At the front of the herd, a big bull fell on the grassy plain.

"There," Lone Wolf said, pointing to a spot on the far edge of the herd. "Did you see the puff of white smoke from that last shot?"

She nodded. "Looks like half a dozen hunters," she estimated squinting through the early dusk fuzziness.

"Damn!" he swore. "White men huntin' buffalo here means the end of the great herds for sure. Hell, it won't be long before the Territory's crawlin' with dudes with itchy trigger fingers lookin' for a trophy to take back East."

"I see what you mean about not thinking like a white man any more." Rebecca sighed. "Well, we won't find my uncles or Tulley sitting around here." She tore away her gaze from the big buffalo herd.

Nudging her pony in its flanks, she turned the horse and headed off in their original direction. Beyond the herd lay the Black Hills.

Perhaps, before they reached there, she'd get more revenge.

Running Snake had succeeded the old medicine man of Iron Calf's band. Elk Hand had lived too long. By the time Running Snake had taken the buffalo horn headdress of the band's medicine chief, he had long passed his prime. Deep age lines and gullies of wrinkles seamed his face and streaks of gray filled his once-lustrous black braids. The fires of his sacred vision that told of driving the hated whites from their land had been banked into smoldering resentment. Part of it remained focused on the *wasicun*, though most of it he aimed at Elk Hand, until that worthy departed life in his sleep one night. For a while, then, Running Snake had no place to direct his malice.

When Jake Tulley came into his life, that had changed. Tulley offered an opportunity to revenge the honor of the Oglala on the whites. He brought whiskey and rifles and ammunition. Yes, Running Snake gloated, now the *wasicun* would once more taste the bitter bile of fear when the Oglala rode down on them. And the first whites to die, he promised, would be Tulley and his gang. Running Snake had arranged the initial meeting between Iron Calf and the renegade white outlaw. After that, the medicine chief conducted all negotiations. He did it that way to protect his power. Even so, he didn't like the contact with whites. They smelled bad.

Thinking of that, Running Snake shifted restively on the large, flat rock where he sat waiting Tulley's men. A message had come that more of the arms and whiskey waited him. He rode from the Oglala encampment, bringing only two trusted warriors with him. Wisely, Running Snake had decided at the outset to keep even knowledge of the liquor and weapons from the majority of warriors until the right time came for an uprising. Were they to have access to these things too soon, the disastrous effects of whiskey might bring on a premature attack on white settlements and alert the enemy. He paused in his reflections and glanced at the sun. The renegade *wasicun* were late.

Sits-on-Hands, one of his confidants, slipped down one steep side of the ravine chosen for the meeting. "The rolling wood approaches," he announced tersely.

Waste!" Running Snake grunted. Yes, it was good. He needed the supplies they brought to be successful in his bid to become the first medicine *leader* since the Grandfather Times—in those days before the white men.

Jingling harness chain and the clatter of running gear

155

reached Running Snake's ears and dust billowed above the lip of the ravine. He watched, unsmiling, while a four-up team of mules drew the wagon to the convex mound of a cave-in that provided access to the defile. Ponderously, with much rocking and cursing, the white driver negotiated the unstable descent, turned to his left and drew the team to a stop a dozen yards from where the medicine chief and his men waited.

"*Heyo*, Running Snake. I have brought the rifles," a pinched-faced, ferret-eyed man called from the wagon box.

"That is good."

"Do you have the gold?" His smallpox-scarred cheeks writhed with greed.

How foolish these whites are, Running Snake thought contemptuously, to lust after the yellow metal. A man cannot eat it, it is too soft to make arrow points. What's more, it was hard work to obtain it and came dangerously close to offending the Spirits to rip open the breast of the sacred Black Hills to find it. He sighed and patted a beaded leather pouch at his side.

"Yes. I have it here."

"Fine, fine." The weasel's muzzle writhed again. "You gonna haul all this stuff on ponies?"

"That is my problem, is it not?" Never one to leave something to chance, Running Snake had already prepared a caché hole in the wall of the ravine less than a half mile from where they stood. He glowered at the two white men, relishing their unease.

"Uh, yeah. I suppose it is. Now, let me weigh that gold and we'll help ya unload."

In twenty minutes the transaction had been completed. The empty wagon rattled off into the distance. Running Snake turned to his followers.

"Let us go quickly. Sits-on-Hands, you stay to guard the rest while we take the whiskey to the caché." He smiled inwardly to himself, exulting in the moment. With the previous loads brought by Tulley and his men, they would presently have enough.

"Soon," he spoke his thought aloud, "the whites will all die! This shall be Oglala land once more!"

Rebecca reined in and held up her hand. Beside her, Lone Wolf brought his pony around in a tight circle, the animal snorting in disagreement to the halt.

"What's the matter?"

"Listen."

Lone Wolf caught a faint clatter. "Sounds like a wagon comin' our way."

Rebecca and Lone Wolf had ridden for a little over an hour, until the gathering dusk began to obliterate the terrain. They'd reached a spot in the winding, indistinct track about ten miles from the buffalo herd.

"That's what I figured. Now, the Dakota don't use wagons and this is their land. So I reckon whoever is on that wagon is up to no good. Anyone out here is up to no good."

"Including us?"

"Of course," Rebecca returned, her eyes twinkling with mischief. "In which case I think we should arrange to get a look at who is coming without being seen ourselves."

"Good idea. There's a draw over to the right. Should be deep enough to hide the horses and still give us a view."

Together, they eased their mounts off the narrow trace and through the tall buffalo grass to a deeply eroded gulley. In the distance, the wagon noise grew more distinct while they dismounted and urged their suddenly skittish ponies down the steep bank.

"What if it's that wagon of Tulley's we've been following?"

A cold smile lifted the corners of Rebecca's mouth. "Then we give them a nasty surprise."

Three minutes passed and the wagon came into sight over a rolling swell in the undulating prairie. Four mules, a buckboard with improvised wagon bows. Two men on the spring-mounted seat. Slowly it approached, ambling along as though the occupants didn't realize they rode through Indian country. Or had no fear on that account, Rebecca amended her thinking. She recalled Lone Wolf's earlier speculation that Tulley might be trading with the Oglala. For what? Her years with Iron Calf's band gave her only too good an idea. Guns, whiskey, who knew what else, all would be welcomed in the lodges of the Oglala. Her lips formed a grim line as her fury mounted.

In another minute, the wagon pulled abreast of their hiding spot. Lone Wolf put a hand on her forearm and whispered in her ear.

"I've seen that one. The driver. He was at that bawdyhouse where I ran into Virgil."

"What are they doing out here?"

"Whatever it is, they've already done it. That wagon's empty. Now what?"

"Why, we ride out and have a friendly chat."

"Have you lost your senses? Those men are heavily armed."

"So are we." She patted the buttstock of the Winchester they had taken from the Oglala braves who attacked at the cave. "Since we liberated this from my Oglala cousins."

Rebecca's eyebrows suddenly darted upward and she sucked air in through parted lips, formed into a startled "Oh." Had she actually identified herself with those men she hated so?

"Now they're your cousins," Lone Wolf chided gently. "I thought you wanted nothing more to do with the Cut-throat People." He had used the common plains term for the Sioux, which caused Rebecca to bridle even more.

"That's not kind. And besides, we are losing our opportunity to learn where Tulley and his gang are."

"You're right. That trail we've been following is not all that clear. But, perhaps I should maneuver around and we can come at them from two directions."

"They would hear you. Unless we could create some sort of diversion," she speculated.

Lone Wolf chuckled. "The sudden appearance of a good lookin' woman out here in the middle of nowhere would be diversion enough, I'm thinkin'."

"You have a dirty mind."

"And you have a lovely body. Remember, I saw it . . . all of it." Before she could respond, Lone Wolf gathered his reins, swung into the crude wooden, blanket-covered Crow saddle and walked his pony off in the direction taken by the wagon.

Rebecca bit off the sharp retort she had planned and rode up out of the gulley. She dug her heels into her mount's ribs and trotted toward the retreating wagon. A powerful surge of emotion rose in her. Once again revenge lay within her grasp. Her hand dipped to the beaded pouch and opened it. Carefully she arranged the .38 for the fastest possible draw.

Twenty feet from the buckboard she clearly saw the men. Their backs to her, the rattle of the wagon and rumble of wheels had masked the noise of her approach. She gigged her pony again and moved up alongside the wagon at a fast lope.

"Hello there!" she called cheerily.

"Whoa! Whoa, damn ya!" the pinched-faced driver yelled at his team, startled by the sound of a feminine voice. "What th' hell?"

His companion observed the newcomer with considerably less consternation. A nice looker, he approved. Good legs, an' lots of 'em. His eyes rose higher, marking her costume. A niggling worry came alive in his mind. An Injun woman. Could be a trap. But she spoke English. "Be gawdamned! A white squaw!" she spoke aloud.

Rebecca ignored. "I seem to have gotten lost," she rambled on, her eyes fixed on the driver.

"What you lookin' for, ma'am?"

"My name's Rebecca Caldwell, and I'm looking for my uncles."

"Hummm," the driver murmured in caution. He'd heard of Tulley's offer of five hundred for a squaw. Looked like he had it right in front of him. "M'name's Harvey Crowell. Ain't no homesteaders out this way. Why you lookin' for these uncles out here?"

Rebecca shrugged. "I thought I was still in Nebraska. Are you heading anywhere in particular? Maybe you can give me directions back to a town or a farmstead?"

"Now that we might manage," Harvey's companion allowed. He lifted a gunnysack-covered bottle from the floorboards and uncorked it. After a long pull he offered it toward Rebecca. "Care for a swig?"

"No, thank you." *Where was Lone Wolf?* her worried mind questioned. "I really am anxious to locate my uncles. Their names are Ezekial and Virgil Caldwell."

A calculating glow came to Harvey's eyes. He'd recognized the name Caldwell all right and he had been wise to show no sign. This had to be the squaw Tulley wanted.

"Your uncles, eh?" he drawled.

"That's right. It's been a long time since I've seen them. I've got something for them."

Harvey took the bottle from his companion and poured a long draught down his scrawny throat. His ferret eyes glittered with greed. "Well, this is your lucky day. Happens I know both of 'em. But the only niece them boys got was killed by the Sioux about five years back. Least, that's what they say. So, sweet-thing, you better come up with a better story than that. What are you doing out here?"

"Oh, I do have a better story, Mr. Crowell." Her flinty eyes bored into his weasel face.

"Then speak up, damnit!"

Rebecca smiled, then reached into her belt pouch and

160

whipped out the .38 Smith and Wesson. The black hole in the muzzle centered between Harvey's close-set eyes. "If you don't tell me where to find those low-life uncles of mine, I'm going to blow your goddamned brains out," Rebecca told him evenly.

Harvey's jaw dropped in astonishment. Beside him, Skip Tamblin swung the barrel of his short Winchester carbine toward her full, high-breasted chest.

A heavy boom sounded a fraction of a second after Skip flew backward against the seat rest, a howl of agony on his lips. His right arm hung at an odd angle, the shoulder joint smashed to ruin by the big .50 caliber Sharps slug fired by Lone Wolf.

"Oh, Jesus!" Harvey blurted. The small six-shooter had never left its target, nor had the girl blinked at the shot.

"Now, Mr. Crowell, where are Ezekial and Virgil?"

"Uh . . . ah, they ain't nowhere around here. Honest."

A derisive snort of laughter preceded Rebecca's words. "You don't know the meaning of the word. Where are they?"

"It's true, I swear. They ought to be clear an' hell gone back to Nebraski by now."

"What about Tulley? Surely you know Bitter Creek Jake Tulley?"

"Never met the gent," Harvey replied sullenly, licking nervous lips.

Lone Wolf rode up to the side of the buckboard, the Sharps pointed randomly at the two outlaws. "I think he's lying."

"So do I." Rebecca turned a cold, murderous smile on Crowell. "I also think we're going to have the truth out of him. One way . . . or another."

Harvey paled. His eyes grew round and he switched a disconcerted glance from Rebecca to Lone Wolf and back again.

"A white Injun and a white squaw. It don't make sense,"

Skip moaned, one hand clutching his wound.

"It don't have to make sense to you," Rebecca snapped. "All that's keeping you alive is my need for answers." She reached to the woman's flencing knife she wore at her waist and drew it.

"Do you know how the Sioux determine if a man is lying?" she inquired of Harvey.

"N-no. An' I don't think I want to learn."

"You're going to. It's really simple," she went on, extending the knife toward Harvey Crowell, edge upward. "They make a person bite down on a knife blade. If it don't cut him, he's truthful. If it does, they finish the job by slitting his throat. Think you can pass the test, Mr. Crowell?"

Rebecca watched his eyes saucer with fear. "Y-you gotta be crazy!" he shrieked at her.

She pressed the wickedly sharp knife closer. "Bite it, Mr. Crowell. Bite it good and hard."

"Nooo!" Harvey moaned, his voice rising in an effeminate wail. Suddenly he bolted from the buckboard, running before his feet hit the ground. The speed of his escape caught Rebecca by surprise. Not for long, though.

Harvey Crowell had made about twenty yards across the buffalo grass when Rebecca swung her Little Russian into line with the center of his back.

"Stop right there!" she shouted.

Crowell kept running.

Rebecca's lips tightened and her finger squeezed the hair-fine trigger of the full-cocked weapon.

Her first shot tugged at the fleshy roll of fat on Crowell's left side. It staggered him, though he soon regained his speed and direction. The second round from the Smith and Wesson took him squarely in the spine, at the small of his back. He arched backward in a graceful swan-dive and plowed face-first into the dirt.

"You fuckin' killed him!" Skip Tamblin gasped.

"And you're next," Rebecca grimly told him. "Now, where are my uncles and where is Tulley and his gang?"

"H-Harvey was tellin' you the truth. Zeke an' Virgil an' Jake was supposed to meet someone important at a place outside'a Buffalo Gap. Most of the boys is strung out between here an' there, layin' low. Somethin' big is comin' up, but I don't know what. Harvey an' me just delivered a load of whiskey an' rifles to a redstick name o' Runnin' Snake. We was supposed to get back inside Nebraska at quick time. That was Jake's orders."

"Running Snake!" Rebecca turned to Lone Wolf. "That's Iron Calf's medicine chief. Apparently that raid your Crows made a month ago has weakened the old man's power over his band. Running Snake has always been ambitious. Now he's riding high. How many rifles?" she threw at Tamblin.

"Two dozen. Winchester repeaters an' Sharps fifties."

"Who is Tulley and my uncles meeting?"

"I d-don't know. Jake . . . he don't tell us much."

"Somewhere near Buffalo Gap? In Nebraska?"

"Yes. That's it. We was all to jine up in the town later on."

Rebecca's demeanor changed. "Your frankness has bought you your life, my friend. Were I you, I think I would change occupations. Get out of the Territory. Leave the whole area and start over someplace else. California, maybe? Or Arizona?"

Sudden relief numbed Skip's mind and he replied as though in a dream. "Yeah. Yeah. That's what I'll do."

"Whatever, don't go back to Tulley. If you do, next time we will kill you. To insure your change of heart, I think we should make your progress a bit more difficult." She spoke to Lone Wolf. "Cut those mules loose and bring them along with us."

"Y-you're not leavin' me out here without a mount, are you?"

Rebecca's sarcasm stung him. "You are very perceptive.

You'll walk out of here, without that carbine and only one canteen of water."

"You can't! This is Injun country. I . . . I'll die out here."

Bleached skeletons seemed to dance in Rebecca's icy gaze. "I wouldn't be surprised."

TWELVE

"At least we know what my uncles have been up to. And Running Snake's disappearances from camp over the past months are explained." She poked a stick in the campfire, over which Lone Wolf cooked a skewer of four plump prairie grouse.

"I've got a feelin' those fellers told the truth about Tulley an' them goin' to Buffalo Gap," returned Lone Wolf. He squinted into the darkness.

"I guess it's up to me to find out," Rebecca offered.

"Feel up to it?"

She shrugged. "Four days ago was the first time in five years I set foot in a white man's town. Suppose I'll have to get used to shops and women with parasols."

Lone Wolf chuckled. "You handled yourself rather nicely with Harvey and his friend. I don't think you'll have any trouble."

Rebecca sighed and her mouth suddenly watered at the delicious odor of the roasting birds. "Am I *right*, Lone Wolf?"

"You mean about huntin' those bastards down?"

"No. Yes. Well," she evaded even longer, "what I mean is am I right about not wanting to return to the white world? Even as a little girl I heard the remarks people made about women who had been captives of the Indians. They . . . weren't kind. And neither were the ways people treated them. I don't want to be a white woman. It's not that I'm afraid, it's that I can't be. I've been married—if you can call it that—and the mother of a child. I lived with the Oglala. I really did *live* the life of any woman in the camp. It . . . changed me. Yes . . ." she paused, shuddered. "Yet, I don't want to go back. I loved Four Horns. When he died, a part of me died, too." Her face clouded. "There are . . . no more happy memories with Iron Calf's band."

"Then what do you want to do?"

"Get revenge!" she spat, eyes flaming with determination.

"Remember, don't let your anger keep you from thinkin' clearly. These killers ain't just cowpokes. If you can't find your uncles or some of the Tulley gang in Buffalo Gap, then get out and I'll help you 'til we find them."

She smiled. "Thanks."

Taking a deep breath, she reached for the grilled bird Lone Wolf offered her. She took a bite, smacked her lips.

"This is delicious."

"Be better with some salt."

"Salt! We went without it so often in Iron Calf's camp I've almost forgotten how good it is."

Two days later, Rebecca parted from her companion and swung her mount's nose in the direction of Buffalo Gap. A weathered, hand-painted sign announced that the small Nebraska community lay two miles beyond a long swell in the endless grass of the plains. Once more dressed as a white woman, in the corduroy riding habit, she trotted her pony along the well-worn road. She felt distinctly uncomfortable. Not alone from apprehension about what would find in

166

Buffalo Gap. She didn't like the strictures and oppressive warmth of the clothing she wore. Actually, Rebecca admitted, she really did prefer the roomy, comfortable dresses of the Oglala.

Loping along the sunny prairie road toward Buffalo Gap, she noticed a large bonfire alongside the trail a quarter mile ahead. She saw a large group of laughing townspeople gathered around the roaring blaze, sandwiches in their hands and smiles on their faces. Many of them wore costumes or clothing of red, white and blue. Bunting fluttered in the pre-noon breeze and many children waved small American flags. The Fourth of July!

Strange, but she had not thought of the holiday in five long years. Firecrackers burst with bright flashes and pungent puffs of smoke and the youngsters squealed in delight. Loath to stop for anything, yet too far along to turn back, she kept riding and tried to shade her face with the awkward, floppy hat that she had perched on her head.

Suddenly, with the sounds of the celebration rising toward her, Rebecca felt terribly alone.

Rebecca trotted past the partying throng, uncomfortably aware of their probing gazes as she rode by. Once she had passed the fire and the people around it, she sighed with relief. Then she heard the drumming of hoofs.

"Wait!" cried an approaching rider.

Her body tightened, prepared for anything. She turned to look.

"Stop, please," shouted the mounted stranger.

Stifling an urge to dig her heels into the ribs of her pony and race toward Buffalo Gap, Rebecca reined in her mount and waited in the sunlight. Who could be calling her? And why?

She reached for her .38.

The shouting rider reined in his sorrel. He was about twenty or so, with wire-rimmed glasses, neatly-trimmed brown hair and tender eyes. Rebecca relaxed and removed her hand from the hidden Smith and Wesson.

"Boy, I thought you weren't going to stop," panted the hard-breathing young man.

"Who are you?"

"That's what I've come to ask you, ma'am," he returned. He removed his wide-brimmed Stetson. "I mean, I saw you ride past the fire back there and thought I recognized you."

She stiffened. "You . . . you must be mistaken. I've only recently come to these parts."

She watched the bespectacled young man lean forward on the back of his sorrel mare. He peered intently at her half-hidden face.

"Rebecca!" he declared suddenly. "I knew it was you!"

A twinge of anxiety pinched her stomach. "I beg your pardon?"

"Rebecca Caldwell. I can't believe it."

She stared icily at him.

"Don't you recognize me? It's Sam, Sammy, Wade, your former neighbor. Don't you remember the day me an' a couple of my friends caught you skinny dippin' at the ol' Caldwell swimmin' hole?"

Rebecca smiled sheepisly at the recollection. "Sam Wade," she said. "My, you've grown up."

He winced, not far enough removed from the tyranny of adults who used that phrase on all children. "And so have you, Rebecca," he returned. "But you're still as beautiful as ever."

"Like down at the swimming hole?" Then she paused, uncertain how to continue.

Sam Wade blushed. "W-where have you been?"

There came the question she'd been dreading.

"Everybody thought you'd been killed by Indians. I mean, with your Grandpa Jeremiah bein' found dead and everything and Sioux arrows stuck in the house."

"I . . . I went away for a while," she evaded. "Now I'm back," she added without offering any further details. "Are you living in Buffalo Gap?" She wanted to change the subject.

Sam nodded. "Well, after your grandpa was killed and the Indian troubles worsened, my family and me moved into Buffalo Gap. I'm stock clerk at the general store there. Maw, bless her soul, passed on three years ago. My father runs the telegraph office. Anyway, why don't you join our Fourth of July picnic?"

Rebecca felt a strange twinge of nostalgia when Sam mentioned picnics. She knew her years with the Oglala had robbed her of the good times she might have had while growing up in the white man's civilization.

"And you recognized me as I rode past?" she returned, bypassing the invitation.

"Almost immediately," he responded. "I've had a crush on you for years. I think you knew that before I caught you at the swimming hole."

"Yes," Rebecca replied. "I knew it, Sam." She felt flushed.

"So," Sam went on, brightening, "it was only natural that I came after you. I've missed you, Rebecca."

Suddenly she had an urge to tell Sam everything. She felt like revealing what sort of hell she'd gone through with the Sioux. After all, she needed somebody to help her in Buffalo Gap. Sam Wade seemed the logical choice. Then she felt a stab of caution.

What if he was in cahoots with Tulley? She dismissed the thought at once. Besides, she had to trust someone.

"Sam," began Rebecca, her quavering voice strangely full of emotion, "I have a story to tell you. It's about where I've been the past five years."

His brow winkled. "I don't understand."

"Let's ride into town slowly," she suggested. "I'll tell you a story like none you ever heard before."

Then, while the two former neighbors trotted slowly along the sun-bright road into Buffalo Gap, Rebecca told Sam Wade nearly everything that had happened to her from the moment the Indians attacked the Caldwell farm to the day Lone Wolf appeared. She explained her business-like relationship with Lone Wolf, and told him about her plans for revenge. She did not tell him about Four Horns or old Broken Wing.

When she finished, Rebecca noticed they had reached the outskirts of town. The pretty nineteen-year-old reined in her pony and looked at Sam. She felt like an enormous weight had been removed from her shoulders.

"Rebecca," Sam began softly. His eyes were full of tenderness. "I'm nearly speechless. Of course, I felt bad about what happened to you. And I want to help you become a white woman again." He reached out and squeezed her hand. His sympathy prevented him from seeing her reaction to his last sentence.

"Also," he went on, "I'll ask around town. Somebody must know something about Tulley and his gang."

Rebecca smiled at him. "Thanks, Sam. You're good for me."

"In fact," offered the young shop clerk, "I'll even take you home for dinner. My father and my two sisters would love to have you."

"B-but, Sam, it's been five years since I've been around white folks much. I won't know how to act. I'll just make a big fool of myself!"

Sam smiled indulgently and nudged their horses. "Nonsense," he pronounced. "You're the type of woman who'll never make a fool out of herself. Besides, if you're stalkin' Jake Tulley and his boys, you might as well get used to bein' a white woman again."

She knew Sam meant well. "All right," Rebecca allowed reluctantly. "One thing, though. Please don't mention to anybody about . . . about my years with the Oglala. No sense in advertising it."

Sam Wade nodded. He knew well the treatment such women often got. "Agreed. Now, let's head into town. I'm sure my sisters can find somethin' delicious for a guest to eat."

The roast chicken dinner at the Wade's small, clapboard home along Buffalo Gap's dusty main street reminded Rebecca of the wonderful feasts her mother used to prepare. Even Sam's father, Henry Wade, made her think of Jeremiah Caldwell; long, lean and bearded.

The food was delicious, the atmosphere warm and the conversation convivial. Even Rebecca's skill with knife and fork nearly reached her former competence. All during the meal, she couldn't help glancing at Sam. She noticed her childhood friend was actually quite handsome despite his wire-rim spectacles and his bookish manner. She felt a sudden twinge of desire in her loins and quickly stifled it.

"So," Henry Wade remarked after dinner. "You've been away for a while, eh, Rebecca?"

While Sam's jovial father lit a fat after-dinner cigar, she glanced quickly at Sam. He smiled warmly and winked at her as though to tell her everything was going smoothly.

"Yes," she replied. "I was visiting relatives in Ohio. After my mother and my grandfather were killed by the Sioux, I needed to get away for a while. But I really missed the Nebraska prairie. I simply had to get back." Although unrehearsed, Rebecca found concocting the myths to account for her missing years to be easy and a pleasant game. The Oglala loved games, she recalled unbidden, especially when they involved playing a trick on someone.

"And how are things in Ohio?"

"Just fine, sir."

Rebecca heard Henry Wade chuckle through a blue-white cloud of cigar smoke. "I'm glad you're alive, Rebecca. Old Jeremiah was a good man. I'm happy at least one of the Caldwell women survived that Indian attack."

After an hour of small talk, Rebecca followed Sam into a small back bedroom. He placed a flickering kerosene lamp on a wobbly night stand and gestured toward a wide double bed.

"You can sleep here," he told her.

She took a deep breath. "How did I do?"

"Fine." He reached out and touched her hand. "You'll be all right. You're a white woman again, and none the wiser."

"Thank you, Sam. I really appreciate all you've done tonight. I needed a friend about now. I'm glad you came into my life."

Sam stepped closer and placed a gentle kiss on her forehead. "I'm glad to be of some help," he murmured softly.

Her spine tingled at the touch of his kiss.

"If you need me, I'll be sleeping on the other side of the door in the living room. There's a wash basin next to the night stand."

After Sam shut the slab door behind him, Rebecca smiled and touched the downy mattress. Five years had passed since she had slept in a real bed. Suddenly realizing how weary she was, she peeled off her tight-fitting corduroy riding habit and slipped naked under the covers.

Cool sheets! She closed her eyes and sighed.

Her pleasure seemed short-lived, for after she turned off the kerosene lamp, she tossed and turned atop the fluffy mattress. Her mind's eyes flashed vivid images of her uncles, smiling Jake Tulley doffing his bowler hat, her murdered mother lying in a pool of blood and howling warriors telling her it was time to come back to camp with them.

She sat up in bed and screamed. Her pretty face streamed with perspiration.

Sam burst into the room. "What's the matter?"

"Oh, Sam . . ." she cried. She reached out for him.

He stepped over to the bed and cradled her head against his stomach. He stroked her long, lustrous hair. Rebecca felt the warmth of his body on her face.

"Nightmares, huh?"

She nodded and drew back so she could look at his face.

172

Her eyes flitted from his serious expression to his hairy chest and the skimpy summer-weight, knee-length underdrawers he wore. Rebecca reached out, intoxicated by his nearness, and slipped her hand inside the drawstring waist-band of his shorts. Her long tapered fingers wrapped around his growing penis. He gasped while his cock began to swell in her hand as she felt her own juices starting to flow.

"Rebecca?" he asked, attracted, yet repelled by her forward behavior.

"I need you, Sam. It's the way I've learned and I can't stop myself. Her heart began to beat faster. "Please understand. Stay with me tonight. Make love to me, please!"

She began to rapidly stroke his swollen manhood.

Sam could not believe his good fortune. Entranced, he pressed her face close to his aching organ. Her lips nibbled playfully at the bare skin on his belly. "Yes, Becky. It will be all right for us," he promised. He forced himself away from her erotic massage and closed the door.

After throwing back the bed covers, Rebecca revealed her golden-skinned body to an amazed and excited Sam Wade. She watched Sam step out of his white cotton drawers. He stood naked beside her. She quickly scanned his lean body. Each curve and bulge excited her. She wondered how it would be making love with a man who had hair on his chest.

"Come to me," she breathed huskily.

Sam quickly made room for himself on the creaking double bed. Rebecca sucked in her breath when the warm flesh of his legs touched her thighs. She felt her desire mounting. Her cleft swelled and burst open like a passion flower.

"Oh, Sam, I dreamed about something like this for so long. Now I'm glad it's with you."

"Me, too," he replied, a blissful smile curling his lips.

While Rebecca closed her eyes, groaned and lay back on the mattress, Sam began to smother her tingling body with sensuous kisses. He began at her throat and worked his way across her breasts, where he sucked gently on her hardened nipples. Slowly he moved down her body, expertly arousing her most sensitive places.

His tongue circled her navel and sent a shiver through her heated body. Slowly he worked lower while she trembled in anticipation and spread wide her legs. Then his questing lips found her puffed mound and nibbled at the sparse pubic thatch a second before descending to the final goal.

"Oh, God!" Rebecca gasped. "That's it. That's sooo good. Don't stop!"

He didn't and continued to use his tongue to bring her to the peaks of pleasure. All the while, Rebecca languidly stroked his thick, up-curved penis with one hand while the other eagerly squeezed and molded the pulsing sack of his scrotum.

Finally, Rebecca removed his head from her fully aroused loins and guided his shaft between her trembling thighs.

"You're so nice to me, Sam. So very nice," she murmured. She thrilled to the demanding pressure of his silky shaft.

Gently, he moved his throbbing manhood, rubbing against her enflamed flesh and sending her into more writhing fits atop the bed.

"Now!" she pleaded. "Fill me, Sam!"

Sam drove his hardened mass deep inside her flowing passage and began a long, rhythmic motion that denied all past sensations. Oh, how she loved it. So dearly loved it! Long minutes passed, blended into half an hour and still Sam strove to bring her to greater peaks of ecstacy. Rebecca responded, driving her wildly stimulated pelvis against his.

"Oh, Becky, Becky!" he moaned.

"Yes . . . yes . . . yes, lover. More . . . more . . . now, now, now!"

Within seconds, then, he exploded, filling her with a flood of his hot passion. Finally the moaning shopkeeper and the inflamed white squaw collapsed together in a sated tangle.

Rebecca closed her eyes and sighed.

Somehow, the ugly nightmares had all faded into memory.

THIRTEEN

After a long night of good loving and sated rest, Rebecca and Sam met Lone Wolf outside of town. A glorious prairie sunrise of pale pinks and powder blues brightened the vast plains that spread around them.

"You seem well rested," Lone Wolf remarked.

"Things went well in town," Rebecca replied, a new softness in her voice.

Lone Wolf turned a hard stare on Sam. "Who is your friend?"

Rebecca made the introductions and concluded. "Sam's been getting some information for me about Jake Tulley. And about my uncles."

"How did you happen to come across such news?" Lone Wolf inquired suspiciously. His blond ridge of hair glistened in the early morning sunshine.

Rebecca noticed their mutual antagonism and that Sam seemed reluctant to talk about the gang with Lone Wolf. "It's all right, Sam," she urged, smiling. "He's one of the 'good' Indians."

"Well," began the bespectacled shopkeeper, though he still avoided eye contact with Lone Wolf, "a couple of my friends in Buffalo Gap heard somethin' about the Bitter Creek Jake Tulley gang tradin' whiskey with the Sioux."

"What else?" Lone Wolf pressed.

"Apparently Rebecca's uncles have been workin' for the gang ever since . . . ah, ever since that day when they gave her to the Oglalas."

Lone Wolf threw a curious glance at Rebecca. "It's all right," she soothed. "Sam knows quite a bit about me."

"And where is the gang located?"

"They seem to hang out in Jury Wells. It's about eighteen miles from here. Seems Tulley, himself, was in Buffalo Gap only two days ago. He's gone now, though. Rebecca's uncles seem to have made a regular home for themselves in Jury Wells."

"So Sam and I are going to Jury Wells," Rebecca added.

"That makes three of us," Lone Wolf put in. He turned the head of his war pony. "Why don't you two ride along the main road. I'll keep off to the side in case somethin' happens."

"What could happen?" Sam asked in innocence.

"Anything," Rebecca quickly interjected. "If you knew Tulley like we do, Sam, you'd know." She glanced at the white warrior. "We'll see you outside of Jury Wells."

Lone Wolf nodded and trotted away.

She saw Sam swallow hard. "Do you trust that Injun?"

"With my life."

Rebecca heeled her pony into motion and Sam followed. As the two former neighbors cantered along the dusty road toward Jury Wells, Rebecca told Sam about Lone Wolf's tragic past. Also of his aid in helping her escape.

"No wonder you trust him," he responded, impressed.

"He's helped me so much already," Rebecca summed up. She caught Sam's inquiring look. "And, no, we don't sleep together."

"Oh," he replied, smiling.

"He wouldn't," she added, a mischievous twinkle in her eye. With a sudden laugh, she slapped her pony on its rump and loped toward Jury Wells.

Half an hour from Jury Wells, Rebecca glanced at the side of the road and tried to spot Lone Wolf in the underbrush. There. She saw him instantly, like any proper Oglala woman. She turned away and continued to ride, her desire for vengeance building again with each mile.

"We're almost there," Sam told her.

"Good. We'll be in time for lunch," Rebecca replied. She glanced up at the midday sun. "Maybe I'll find Uncle Ezekial in Jury Wells' best restaurant. He always did like to put on fancy clothes and eat out."

Without warning, two drifters burst from the cover of some nearby bushes. The outlaws edged up to Rebecca and Sam before they had time to react.

"Oh, Christ!" Sam stammered. "Do what they tell you, Rebecca."

Like hell, she thought.

"Hold it right there!" snapped a lean, scruffy road agent. He gripped a four-and-three-quarter-inch Peacemaker, leveled at the young couple.

"One move and you're both dead," snarled his plump, long-haired companion.

"We haven't any money," Sam protested.

"We'll see about that. Now get down off them horses."

Sam complied right away. Rebecca hesitated.

"Now!" roared the lean bandit.

"Hell, Ben," enthused the plump outlaw, "this here filly's got some spirit! Ol' Jake'll be tickled to death to hear about us takin' her."

Jake! Rebecca's pulse quickened.

"You boys wouldn't happen to be talking about Jake Tulley, would you?" she inquired meekly. She dismounted and stood beside Sam.

"Don't be foolish," Sam whispered.

"Shut up, you," growled the plump outlaw. He smashed his revolver on the side of Sam's head. The bespectacled shopkeeper cried out and wobbled slightly.

"You know Jake, do ya, Missy?" demanded the lean bandit.

She nodded. "I met him a while back."

"Then we'll tell Jake we met ya," the gunman said through a guffaw. "But it's too bad you ain't gonna see him for yourself. I got me a better idea of what to do with you."

"Like what?" Rebecca demanded coolly.

Ben studied her closely. "I'm bettin' you're that squaw he wants, all decked out like a white woman. He's put five hundred dollars on your head . . . and all we gotta bring him is your head."

"Yeah. But first let's strip her and see what she looks like," his chubby companion suggested.

"Why not? Tulley won't complain if that part's a little used."

Before she realized what was happening, Ben reached out and began to unbutton her tight-fitting blouse. A sour whiskey breath came from his thin, cruel lips.

"No!" Sam yelled, leaping at the bandit.

"Get back, shopkeeper," snarled the plump killer. He lashed out with his pistol once again and struck Sam in the face. A tooth splintered and blood flowed from his mashed nose.

Sam fell to the ground like a sack of potatoes.

In a blur, Smith and Wesson justice appeared in Rebecca's hand. A quick shot belched from the muzzle, though it went wide of its mark. The slug gouged flesh and shaggy hair from the right side of the road agent's head. Ben's chin jerked skyward and a thin spray of blood misted the air. His eyes rolled in their sockets. His knees sagged and he fell to the road.

"What the hell?" his pudgy companion blurted.

Before he gathered his thoughts and brought his .44 into play, Rebecca swung her Little Russian toward him and squeezed through the double-action trigger. A .38 caliber bullet tore into the outlaw's wide-eyed face. The impact knocked him backward against the rump of his prancing horse.

"Rebecca, look out!" Sam found voice to shout.

Lanky Ben had regained his senses enough to try bringing his six-gun into play. The ugly muzzle pointed at the white squaw's belly.

With a burst of speed, Rebecca whipped the Smith toward the wavering gunman. She extended her arm full length and tightened her finger on the trigger.

A loud report sounded across the fields.

The bandit's head snapped back in a shower of blood and his eyebrows flashed out of existence in the hell-fire of the muzzle blast, only a foot from his face. His heavy body sagged sideways and he toppled to the dark, rich soil.

"Je-sus Christ!" Sam breathed, awestruck. "Where did you learn to shoot like that?"

"You'd be surprised what you can do when vengeance is pushing you on." Rebecca swung atop her restive paint. A warm rush of self-confidence washed through her chest as she glanced at the corpses on the ground.

"So Tulley's put a price on my head," she observed.

"Yeah," Sam speculated. "And every two-bit gunhand in the country will try to collect it."

"I don't think these two were part of his gang," Rebecca observed.

"What makes you think so?"

"They were too slow. Amateurs compared to Tulley's men." She looked back at the bodies.

And, yeah, she thought, I *can* take care of myself.

The last time Rebecca had been in Jury Wells she was thirteen years old and attended a church-sponsored quilting bee with her mother. Now, six years later, she trotted beside Sam down the largest of Jury Wells' three mud-clogged streets. She studied the high-fronted shops; the local saloon with its share of regulars hanging around the door like vultures, the small, but comfortable hotel, and the tiny church on the edge of town, with a hand-lettered sign announcing a box supper and prayer meeting on Saturday.

Rebecca edged her pony among buckboards and saddle horses belonging to farmers from the surrounding area. Although the women and farm hands around town went about their business without so much as casting a glance at her, she felt as though all eyes were upon her.

"Let's get a couple of rooms in the hotel," Sam suggested. He tethered his horse.

"I don't have any money," she protested. She tied the pony's reins to the rail. "Besides, how long will we be here? This town makes me nervous."

"Be strong," he told her. "Just like you were back on the road. And don't worry, I have money enough for both of us."

"Out there was different. I haven't been in too many towns during the past five years."

"The rooms might come in handy. It could take a while to find your uncles."

Rebecca turned her gaze along the boardwalk and suddenly sucked in her breath. Deeply seated anger caused a vein to throb in both temples.

Sam put a hand gently on her arm. "What's wrong?"

"I just saw Uncle Ezekial." She pointed toward the nearby general store on the same side of the street. Her gesture indicated a lean, bony man with shaggy brown hair. The gaunt, neatly-dressed man had deep-set eyes and a bushy moustache. He was talking to a couple of hardcases.

"That's him." Her simmering anger began to boil over. Her voice hardened. "That's the uncle who helped translate the Sioux language so Jake Tulley could give my mother and me away."

180

"What about your Uncle Virgil?"

"He's probably somewhere nearby."

Uncle Ezekial looked at them.

"He's comin' this way," Sam observed.

Ezekial Caldwell turned on his heel and began to head the two gunhands down the wooden sidewalk to where Rebecca and Sam stood in front of the hotel.

Rebecca's instincts said to run. Her heart said, kill.

Instead, she remained outwardly calm, though raging inside, while the uncle who'd abandoned her made his way toward her.

"What are you going to do?" Sam asked anxiously.

"I . . . I don't know."

Uncle Ezekial drew nearer. "Good day, Miss," he said, tipping his dusty, wide-brimmed hat. His eyes flickered over her, admiring, undressing her with ravenous hunger. Then he walked briskly past and didn't look back.

Relief sagged Rebecca's jaw.

"He didn't even recognize me."

Sam chuckled. "Five years is a long time. You've become a woman. You're not the little wide-eyed child he remembers."

With the tension relieved, Ezekial's close scrutiny inspired her. "I've got a plan," she announced suddenly. "Let's get those rooms and talk it over. I have a feeling that Uncle Ezekial is a sucker for young women from out of town."

Fifteen minutes later, after pacing back and forth like a caged lioness on the creaking, warped floorboards in Sam's hotel room, Rebecca stopped and smiled.

"Well, what do you think?"

Sam removed his wire-rimmed glasses and cleaned them with his handkerchief. "It's dangerous. But I like the plan," he allowed.

She applauded like a little girl. "I knew you would," she enthused. "With this Decency League you told me about running all the soiled doves out of town, I figure Ezekial will fall head over heels for any young girl passing through."

The scheme was simple, yet potentially dangerous. Sam was to approach her uncle and tell him that Rebecca was his sister's friend, and that he was escorting her to St. Louis. For the right price, Sam would say, he'd arrange a secret meeting between Ezekial and Rebecca at a convenient and romantic spot outside of town. Then, when Uncle Ezekial arrived to claim her, Lone Wolf, Rebecca and Sam would capture him.

"I'll set the meeting up right away," Sam offered.

Rebecca's pulse raced in anticipation.

Later that evening, Rebecca waited outside the big front window of the Jury Wells Hotel. She stood so her face was illuminated by the flickering kerosene lamp inside the building.

Still dressed in the same corduroy riding outfit, she watched the saloon across the street. She waited for Sam to appear on the narrow wooden sidewalk with her Uncle Ezekial. The plan called for Sam to discuss the deal with her uncle and to whet his appetite by showing her from a distance.

Suddenly she spotted trouble.

Trotting down the street, astride a painted Indian pony, her new buckskin-clad frontiersman husband riding ahead of her, came Swift Doe, a young Oglala girl who had left Iron Calf's band for love of a white man.

Rebecca glanced quickly at the saloon. Still no sign of Sam and her uncle. A sudden word of recognition by Swift Doe might ruin the entire plan. Rebecca turned and ducked into the hotel.

Too late!

"*Śinashawin!*" cried Swift Doe in Lakota.

Rebecca stayed in the lobby and ignored her.

"Whiterobe Girl! It's me, Swift Doe," shouted the Oglala girl, this time in heavily accented English.

Townspeople began to look at the shouting Sioux. Gawkers gathered on both plankwalks.

Rebecca cringed, but tried to make it seem as though she didn't know what in hell the crazy Indian woman out on the street was yelling about. Color spread on her cheeks, betraying her pretense.

Finally the clop-clop of the two horses hoofs faded in the cool evening air. Rebecca ventured out once again, her heart still beating a tune against her ribs. She turned to glance at the saloon while she pushed her long hair away from her eyes. She caught her breath. Uncle Ezekial, Sam and two hard-cases stared at her from across the street. The startled nineteen-year-old straightened the wrinkles in her riding suit and tried to act sexy.

Soon Sam's meeting with Uncle Ezekial broke up and the bookish-looking shopkeeper strode briskly across the muddy street.

"It's all set," he said, smiling.

"Did Ezekial recognize me?"

"Not a bit. But he sure liked what he saw. In fact, he wants a closer look at breakfast tomorrow. I told him to drop by our table in the hotel dining room."

"A close-up? He might recognize me."

"Remember, this was all your idea," Sam said through a chuckle. "If we're goin' to flush the badmen out into the open, it looks like it'll take a close-up peek by your uncle to get the job done."

Rebecca wasn't looking forward to breakfast.

FOURTEEN

As the setting sun cast a spectacular colored light show on darkening clouds, Rebecca and Sam rode out to the edge of town. Before long they found themselves staring into Lone Wolf's icy blue eyes. They told him about the plan and then returned to the hotel by nine-thirty.

Sam stood in the doorway to his second floor room. "Tomorrow you get a little more revenge. How does it feel?"

"Good." Rebecca shrugged off the comment. "Lone Wolf says violence becomes a habit after a while. I only hope I can quit killing when the time comes."

"So far you've handled yourself like a veteran gunfighter. All the same, you are still the sweet, lady-like person underneath. I can understand your desire for vengeance, but I'm positive you'll return to your normal self once the debt is paid."

"Still, I wonder," she sighed out, her eyes clouding.

"About what?"

"I wonder if I can really kill my own flesh and blood when the time comes." She watched Sam's eyebrows shoot up.

"Uncle Ezekial? Hell, what kinda flesh and blood is he? He gave you away to the Sioux, didn't he?"

"Yeah. Yet . . . he's still my mother's brother."

An awkward silence fell between them. At last, Rebecca glanced up and smiled.

"What am I so glum about?" she asked rhetorically. A mischievous glint danced in her blue eyes. "We've got the whole night ahead of us."

She saw a smile tug at the corners of Sam's mouth. His pale blue eyes came to life behind his wire-rimmed glasses.

"Got somethin' special in mind, lady?"

Rebecca reached out and gently massaged his penis through the material of his trousers. His swiftly hardening cock felt like an axe handle.

"Nothing special," she rejoined, her juices beginning to flow.

Rebecca's body tingled with desire as she recalled the previous night's amorous encounter. Maybe it was due to her years in captivity, but suddenly she wanted to make up for lost time in the arms of a gentle, yet strong white man. Her nipples hardened and her velvety purse began to moisten and open its tender folds. Urgently she continued to rub Sam's rock-hard cock.

"I think we'd better go into your room," he suggested in a strained voice. He pointed toward the stairwell where the voices of some hotel guests were getting a bit too close.

Quickly she ushered him into her nearby room and shut the door. "Sam, please! Make me feel like a whole woman again." She began undressing.

He chuckled throatily and began to unbutton his vest. "We're good together, aren't we?" he asked anxiously.

"You're good for me, Sam," she murmured. Her slippery channel ached for the sensuous touch of his tongue.

"Now, Sam!" she cried, stridently, standing naked in the middle of the lamp-lit room.

She erotically ran her long, tapered fingers over her firm,

globular breasts. Gently she flicked the rosy-colored nipples until they grew erect and hard.

"Jesus!" gusted Sam, removing his trousers.

Then, while watching him strip, she let her long fingers drop across her flat belly to her already moist and palpitating mound. They lingered there in the silky folds of flesh, causing her to close her eyes and moan with desire.

"Oh . . . God!" she breathed, her fingers working feverishly inside her pink, sweet passage.

Sam stood completely naked in front of her. His lean body reflected the orange shadows of the flickering kerosene lamp. Rebecca dropped onto her knees and grasped his long, veined penis in her hands. She guided his rod-like shaft to her lips and teased the sensitive tip with gentle nuzzling. Then she moistened the entire length, from its thick base to its tingling tip. Sam groaned and writhed. He'd had some experience in his life, though nothing like the exquisite pleasure that Rebecca could bring to him. She flicked his glans with the tip of her tongue, sending the bookish shopkeeper into new spasms of delight.

"You're the best ever, Rebecca!"

"You're not so bad, yourself," she murmured gently, squeezing his pulsing penis.

Sam took her in his arms and lifted her upright, then began to smother her with kisses. His broad, hairy chest pressed against her breasts and she sucked in her breath. How different it felt from the smooth, hairless skin of Four Horns. She clung to him and returned his kisses with passionate intensity. It was as though his very presence certified her freedom from the Oglala band. And all the joy she felt was but a bonus.

Then Sam led her by the hand to the room's brass bed and placed her gently onto the downy mattress. Her lustrous hair splayed out on the white pillow case. She moaned with anticipation and slowly spread her long, golden legs. Her thrumming secret place opened outward to him like a plethora of pink petals. With a gasp, Sam responded adroitly.

He knelt on the mattress between her thighs, his mouth lowering toward her sparse, glistening bush. His warm, panted breath gave her new shocks of delight.

She gasped and closed her eyes.

Sam pressed his lips against her and his long tongue stabbed deeply between the lacy veils of her treasure chest.

"Ooooh!" Rebecca moaned. She began to writhe on the bed.

Again and again, Sam's dexterous tongue massaged her until she grew delirious with rapture. His tongue explored, probed her innermost regions and flicked thrillingly against her swollen pleasure node. Four Horns had been capable in this marvelous form of union, yet she had never experienced such a delightful sensation until Sam had come into her life.

While he pleasured her in so marvelous a way, she reached up and fondled his balls as though they were marbles in a sack. Frequently her long fingers strayed to his elongated shaft and stroked it gently. Then she slid him atop her and took him in the manner Broken Wing enjoyed most of all.

Her lips closed over his fevered pole, cool and satin-smooth. Her tongue described enchanting spirals on the spongy tip, then curled around the shaft and rode it to its base.

"Oh, Becky!" he cried out. He removed his lips from her quivering mound and thrashed his head from side to side. Then he plunged downward again and resumed his remarkable efforts.

They seemed to burst apart together. Sam's spasms subsided at last, but Rebecca, consumed by her need, would give him no rest.

"Now, Sam!" she gusted out. "I'm ready for you. Fill me like you did before."

Without a wasted motion, his engorged organ still rod-stiff, he reversed himself and hovered over her shapely body for a moment, then came down slowly on her soft contours.

His hairy body touched her tingling flesh and his intoxicating male scent nearly caused her to have another orgasm. She closed her eyes and sucked in her breath as she felt his massive shaft of flesh probe at the portal, then slowly enter her. His long penis seemed to expand as it plunged toward her depths.

Rebecca groaned in delight and gnawed at his shoulder.

Again and again he plunged his throbbing cock into Rebecca's inner-most chamber. The tip of his rod pressed thrillingly against the mouth of her womb. She arched her back to meet his every thrust, enveloping every inch of his incredibly long, hard cock.

A great chorus seemed to be singing paeans of joy in her head. With a tingling start, Rebecca realized that it was her own voice, purring with happiness like a contented pussycat. Shards of bright, colored light exploded in her brain and she increased the energy of her answering thrusts. Her silken flesh glistened with a thin film of perspiration, generated by the power of their endeavors.

"More," she panted out. "More . . . deeper, Sam . . . deeper."

"Oooh, Becky, Becky, I've wanted this for us since I saw you naked at the swimming hole." Sam's powerful thrusts slowed, gentled for a long minute. "You were only twelve and I was fourteen. I went home and flogged myself until my pecker got sore. Oh, how I wanted to touch your beautiful body."

"You are now, Sam. You . . . really . . . are!" Rebecca wailed while her body peaked and marvelous tremors of rich delight rippled through her.

Finally, after rocking in soulful rhythm atop the creaking brass bed for more than an hour, Rebecca arched again and met Sam as he exploded into her.

Trembling, they collapsed onto the bed.

Rebecca tried to catch her breath. Her fully-sated body went limp as a wet dishcloth. Neither of the passion-soaked lovers spoke for several minutes. They remained coupled and enjoyed the delicious post-sexual moments in silence. Finally she spoke softly, her voice slicing through the stillness.

"You were wonderful, Sam." She kissed his forehead gently.

He looked into her eyes. "And you are simply the best."

They remained clasped together like two spoons in a drawer. Rebecca closed her eyes and felt a warm rush of happiness spread through her chest. The Oglala camp seemed as far away as the moon.

The next morning at breakfast, Rebecca sipped some bitter frontier coffee and watched the hotel's front door for her Uncle Ezekial. She wore a blue calico dress and matching sun-bonnet that Sam had purchased for the occasion the evening before.

"What time did he say he'd be here?"

Sam shrugged and forked more ham and eggs into his mouth. "Just said breakfast time."

"Maybe he's a late riser. The sun's been up for an hour."

"Yeah. He could be sound asleep."

She snorted. "Don't see how his conscience would let him sleep."

Sam chuckled. "Relax." He pushed his wire-rimmed spectacles further onto the bridge of his nose. "Let's hope Lone Wolf is ready."

"Now that's one thing you can count on."

Before long the hotel's small dining room filled with early rising guests. Rebecca sipped her second cup of coffee and kept her eyes fixed on the door.

Then she stiffened. "He's coming," she announced in a low whisper. Out the hotel's big front window, she saw Uncle Ezekial and his two gunmen walking briskly from the saloon toward the hotel.

"Good," Sam replied, putting down his fork. "Now maybe we can begin the day's business. I can't wait 'till you finish this vengeance stuff. Then there can be more times like last night," he ended with a wry twinkle in his eyes.

Rebecca arranged the blue sun-bonnet so it covered a good part of her face. "How's this look?"

"Beautiful," Sam returned, rising. "I don't think your uncle will recognize you even close up. But it's a shame to cover such a pretty face."

"Flattery will get you nowhere, sir," she quipped. She straightened her new calico dress and quickly recalled the blue cotton frock she'd worn for months in the Oglala camp while sleeping outdoors with the dogs.

Uncle Ezekial appeared at the doorway. Covertly, Rebecca studied her dead mother's bony brother. His deep-set brown eyes and busy moustache were the same as that day when her life changed forever. His vested suit, purchased with stolen money, was a recent addition to his appearance. Rebecca sat stiffly while partially shading her face with the bonnet. Her anger began to surface once again, and she clenched her fists.

"Let me talk to him," Sam advised.

He left and Rebecca watched the meeting at the doorway. She pretended to sip her coffee while her evil uncle studied her closely.

After several minutes that seemed like hours, Sam returned to the table. Her uncle left the hotel with his gunhawks, a jauntiness about his step.

"Well?" she asked breathlessly.

"Everything's all set," Sam announced, sitting again.

"What did my uncle say?"

"He said, 'There's somethin' mighty familiar about that young woman.' "

"He said *that?*"

"Yeah. Also that it didn't matter, a good piece was a good piece. He's crazy about you. Says he hasn't had a good romp since the church ladies chased Dolly Pringle and her girls out of town. He's giving me twenty bucks for you."

190

She smiled icily.

She had set the trap and the quarry had taken the bait.

Half an hour later, after she had changed into her riding outfit, Rebecca cantered across the prairie with Sam. She glanced overhead at the threatening sky.

"Looks like rain," she shouted.

He nodded. "Great day to spend inside with a bottle of good whiskey."

"Yeah," she replied. "Or a good man." Her mind returned to her uncle's bony face. "But I got me some important business to take care of."

"That's why I brought along my trusty Star." He patted the six-gun strapped to his thigh.

They rode ahead in silence.

Ten minutes later Rebecca turned and looked at Sam. "Did you make sure my uncle was going to meet us at the big fork in the road? That's where Lone Wolf's waiting."

Sam nodded. "Everything's all set," he replied. "Your uncle said he would meet us there at noon."

Rebecca sighed and tried to relax.

She didn't even have a chance to catch her breath.

Without warning, three riders with drawn six-guns burst from the surrounding underbrush. They dashed in front of Rebecca and Sam. Her war-wise Indian pony reared and struck out at one hardcase. He yelled in surprise and promptly reined to one side to avoid the flashing hoofs.

"Control that horse or I'll shoot it out from under you." It was Uncle Ezekial.

Rebecca brought the animal to a standstill and glared at the intruders.

"What are you doin' here?" Sam asked in a thin, frightened voice. "I thought we had agreed to meet at the fork in the road."

Rebecca heard her uncle laugh harshly. "Sonny," he barked in a gruff voice, "I didn't live this long by keepin' my word."

191

Rebecca sat frozen on her pony, watching for an opportunity.

"Now," Ezekial went on. "Let's have a real good look at this beauty you're pimpin' to me."

"Leave her alone," Sam rumbled. "We have a deal."

"Shut up, sonny-boy," Ezekial threatened.

The two gunslingers cocked their Peacemakers and aimed at Sam's face. After glancing fearfully at Rebecca, the bespectacled shopkeeper swallowed hard and didn't move again.

A cool breeze began to swirl dust into the air.

Instantly a whiplash of large raindrops fell from the blackened sky and splattered on the ground. Rebecca smiled sardonically and figured the gloomy setting was perfect for revealing her true identity to her uncle.

"You don't recognize me, do you, Ezekial?" she demanded suddenly in a calm voice.

Uncle Ezekial and the two gunmen looked at her sharply. She saw her uncle's cavernous eyes narrow.

"After all, it's been five years."

Ezekial began to stroke his moustache.

"Five years is a long time. A person can change. Especially if that person has been living with a band of wild Sioux." Her voice hardened. "Isn't that right, *Uncle* Ezekial?"

She watched the blood drain from his bony, cadaverous face.

"Re . . . Rebecca?"

She nodded. "I survived the hell you sent me into, Ezekial. I survived to return and pay you and the others back for what you did to my mother and me."

Rebecca let her words sink in. Then she watched in surprise when her evil uncle's eyes crinkled in amusement.

"*You* . . . gonna pay *me* back?" he asked incredulous. "Now that's the funniest damn thing I've heard in years."

"You got it coming, Ezekial," Rebecca insisted. Her

pent-up anger rose again. "Your sister, Hannah, was killed by Crow raiders. I lost my teenage years to a band of savages. Yeah, you got it coming all right."

Uncle Ezekial stopped laughing and glanced at her. His deep-set brown eyes narrowed. "Now," he began. "Let me tell you something really funny. I'm gonna take your half-breed ass to Jake Tulley. He's offered a five hundred dollar reward for your sweet little body. He can afford it. Ever since we gave you and Hannah to them Oglalas, we've been doin' all right tradin' booze an' rifles to the tribes. Now, ain't that real funny?"

His companions gave a polite chuckle. Rebecca gritted her teeth. "I know all about the reward," she told her uncle. "Tulley will never live to pay it."

With a speed born of recent practice, Rebecca drew the short-barreled .38 from her reticule. The gunhawks siding her uncle had no warning before the Little Russian blasted into the noontime stillness.

The first slug caught the nearest gunman in the point of his left shoulder. He dropped his six-gun and cried out a second before another bullet slammed into his abdomen. Impact and agony drove him from the saddle. His companion wavered a second, then started to swing his Colt away from Sam.

Rebecca shot him high in the chest.

He blinked stupidly and reeled in the saddle. Another slug burnt air beside his head and he dove for safety on the ground. Rebecca wasted another shot on his retreating figure, then turned the muzzle toward her uncle.

Ezekial's eyes rounded with sudden terror. "No!"

His protest got lost in the explosion of powder.

Rebecca's last bullet struck her uncle's left arm, shattering the upper bone. Beside her, Sam had his Star out and fired a shot at the retreating gunslinger.

Instantly Ezekial Caldwell dug his spurs into the side of his horse and galloped like hell past Sam. The shopkeeper turned and fired two wild shots at the fleeing uncle. Unharmed, Ezekial disappeared past the fallen gunmen and into the surrounding tall grass.

"Stay here, Sam," yelled Rebecca. She turned the head of her pony and made ready to give chase. "If you want to help, finish off these two."

Rebecca reloaded her Little Russian, dug her heels into her pony's flanks and took off at a gallop after her uncle. Within a few minutes the trail of fresh blood drops led her to a rocky clearing. There she spotted Uncle Ezekial's riderless horse. The lithe nineteen-year-old slipped off her pony and listened intently.

After a tense second, she heard footsteps behind her.

Rebecca startled to whirl around, her reliable Smith and Wesson at the ready. Then a bright ball of pain exploded in her head and she fell to the ground.

Ezekial Caldwell stood over the fallen girl, clutching a wrist-thick cottonwood branch in his one good hand. He panted from the effort of his escape. Lightning blasted loudly through the air and he bent quickly to finish her off. That's when he heard the pounding approach of unshod hoofs.

Quickly Ezekial abandoned his purpose and ran to his ground-reined horse. With a grunt of pain he swung into the saddle and kicked the animal into a fast trot. Wounded, he didn't want to encounter whoever had ridden after them.

There would be time enough, he reckoned. He knew what Rebecca looked like and she would not escape him next time.

FIFTEEN

"He got away."

Rebecca heard Lone Wolf's words brokenly through her returning consciousness. Her head throbbed and a wave of nausea swept over her. The white Indian squatted in a steady downpour and cradled her head in his lap.

"I didn't trust your uncle. That's why I trailed you all the way from Jury Wells. I'm only sorry I didn't get here in time."

"I'm glad you got here at all. He . . . he made a fool of me. Took me by surprise in the oldest ambush setup of all. He would have killed me if you hadn't come along. Oh, damn, my head hurts."

"You're back to normal, I see," Lone Wolf observed through a chuckle. "He whopped you with a hefty hunk of cottonwood. It could have been worse, caved in your skull, if he hadn't been weakened by a wound. Who shot him?"

"I did."

"Good girl."

"There's two men back on the main road. Sam was supposed to take care of them."

"We'd better go back and give him a hand. You want their scalps?"

"No. I've seen enough of that."

Indeed, Rebecca had seen the worst the Indians had to offer—mutilation of their victims. She'd seen dead enemies with their heads bashed in, stomachs ripped open and genitals sliced off. She'd come across warriors with their brains scooped out, their ears cut off and their eyeballs gouged out. She had become inured to it, but that didn't mean she had to like it.

Soon the rain ended with the same suddenness with which it started, to be replaced by a brilliant afternoon sun. Rebecca, Sam and Lone Wolf swung the two dead men across their horses and began to make plans.

"Where's the next town that Jake Tulley might head to?" she queried Sam.

He shrugged his shoulders. "Well, the Tulley gang's been shootin' the hell outta just about every little outpost from here to Colorado. That limits the choice of hangouts."

"What's the next town along this road?"

"Deer Creek," Sam told her. "It's always been known for outlaw troubles."

"All right," she decided. "We'll take these bodies into Buffalo Gap, then head for Deer Creek."

As before, Lone Wolf stuck to the distant prairie, on a parallel course, while Rebecca and Sam splashed along the rain-soaked mud road toward Deer Creek. Her head still throbbed and occasionally her vision blurred. Uncle Ezekial had certainly clobbered her. Thought of the man who had betrayed her and her mother, then made her look incompetent by so simple a trick set hot bile to boiling in her stomach. When the time came, she vowed, she would not repeat her errors. Ezekial, Virgil, all of them, would die. To that goal, she fervently hoped Jake Tulley would oblige her by being in Deer Creek.

Agreeing with Lone Wolf's offer to look around the prairie for signs of the gang, Rebecca and Sam left the white warrior back on the road and entered Deer Creek in mid-afternoon of the next day. It was a neat little town, about the size of Jury Wells.

Rebecca figured the best way to attract the attention of Jake Tulley and the others, was to announce her arrival by name at a couple of spots around town. Leaving word at the general mercantile and the two saloons, Rebecca and Sam then retired to the cramped dining room of the town's small, but neat hotel. There they waited while sipping coffee.

"I hope you know what you're doing," Sam decried for the dozenth time.

"I don't," she replied honestly. "But I don't know any other way to rouse the curiosity of the Tulley gang than to let them know I'm here. That bounty ought to bring them out of the woodwork. For another thing, when they see Ezekial all shot up they should get all hot and bothered."

Sam sighed. "Let's see what happens."

They didn't have long to wait.

"Miss Caldwell?" asked an elderly gentleman.

Rebecca looked up from her table and saw a roly-poly, gray-haired man standing next to her. "Yes?"

"My name is Orville Styles," the man replied in a pleasant voice. He indicated a tall, elegant, handsome young man beside him. "This is my son, Roger."

The young man bowed slightly.

Rebecca smiled. "What can I do for you?"

"May we sit down for a moment?"

"Be my guests."

While the two strangers pulled up chairs, Rebecca quickly studied them. The plump older man with the jovial face appeared to be a well-to-do farmer. He was dressed in a shiny blue suit, white shirt with black string tie and a wide-brimmed Stetson hat. His expensive, hand-rolled eastern cigars indicated he was a man of some means.

His handsome, debonair son appeared to be in his mid-thirties. Rebecca's gaze lingered for a moment on the good-looking man's lean, muscular body. Like his father, Roger Styles was attired in a neatly-pressed three piece business suit, gray in color, and was impeccably groomed. His long black sideburns, wavy ebony hair and neatly-trimmed handlebar moustache seemed perfect for his warm, intelligent face. Rebecca noticed that Roger Styles' soft blue eyes held no malice and that his warm smile added to the overall impression of congeniality.

She introduced Sam and then waited.

"Now," began Orville Styles, pulling his hard-backed wooden chair closer to the table. "I suppose you wonder why I'm here?"

"It crossed my mind," Rebecca returned dryly. She wondered if the two strangers had any connection with the Tulley gang. If so, why all the niceties?

"Simply put, Miss Caldwell, your late grandaddy and me were as close as two peas in a pod," the gray-haired farmer told her. He puffed on his expensive cigar. "When old Jeremiah died about five years back, I felt as though I'd lost my own brother."

"My father is a farmer, just like your grandfather," added Roger Styles. His blue eyes sparkled as he looked at Rebecca.

She noticed Sam had started to squirm in his seat.

"So," continued Orville Styles, "when I heard just now that you were in town, I had to come and introduce myself. You see, we all thought that both you and young Hannah were killed by the Sioux."

Rebecca swallowed at the mention of the Indians and her mother. "Well, as you can see, Mr. Styles, I'm alive and well."

"And very pretty, I might add," Roger Styles inserted.

Rebecca felt her cheeks flush. Sam scowled.

"The only question I have, Rebecca, is why in tarnation are you looking for that murdering rascal Jake Tulley? That's what they told me in the saloon. Seems to me he'd be a good character to avoid."

She smiled. "Let's just say I have something to give him."

"I told Rebecca to avoid this Tulley fellah," Sam spoke up suddenly. He cast a cold, possessive glance at Roger Styles.

The debonair young man smiled, stroked his handlebar moustache and nodded. "I've not met Mr. Tulley personally, but I've heard he's a ruthless bandit who's well worth staying away from."

"I thank you gentlemen for your concern," Rebecca responded. She was relieved that the Styles were old friends of her grandfather, though in a way she resented their interruption. She was growing a little anxious to finally meet Tulley face to face.

"To show you how concerned I really am," offered dapper Roger Styles, "I'd like to invite you—and your friend—upstairs to my private suite for a snifter of brandy. Perhaps then I can tell you what I know about Bitter Creek Jake Tulley."

"Well . . ." Sam began.

"We'd be delighted, Mr. Styles," Rebecca interrupted. She figured since all her other leads had failed to locate Tulley, perhaps this would come to something.

"Call me Roger."

She smiled and looked into the handsome young businessman's twinkling blue eyes. "All right, Roger," she returned. She noticed that Sam was seething with jealousy.

Orville Styles rose from his chair. "Since you young folks are determined to pass the day talkin' about such a scoundrel as Jake Tulley, I suppose I'll just mosey along to check on my seed grain order."

"Thank you for stopping by," Rebecca told the old man. "I'm sure my grandfather would have appreciated your concern."

The gray-haired man made an almost courtly bow. "I'm just glad to see that you're safe and sound, Rebecca. I was afraid that you'd been killed."

Then the cigar-smoking farmer walked out of the hotel.

Roger Styles rose and pulled back Rebecca's chair. "Shall we?"

Rebecca flushed slightly and smiled. Sam Wade sneered.

On the way to the stairs, Rebecca saw Roger Styles stop behind her to chat with the hotel's cadaverous desk clerk.

"Just ordered some brandy," he explained, catching up.

"Sounds delightful," Rebecca offered. She wondered why such a refined, handsome man would be content living on the wild Nebraska plains.

"Yeah, real nice," Sam nodded sourly.

When they reached the second floor, Rebecca entered Roger Styles' two-room suite directly behind Sam. She noticed at once the elegant furnishings, the big brass bed and the paintings of nude young women on the red-striped papered walls.

"Beautiful," she said appraisingly. "Although I can't say I care for your taste in paintings."

Roger Styles chuckled and remained standing in the doorway. "No, but you can't fault my taste in beautiful women. Like yourself, for instance. Now I betcha you're one helluva good fuck."

Rebecca froze in the middle of the suite. The sudden, harsh words struck her like a Sioux war club.

Sam grew livid. "Now wait just a minute!"

Daftly, Roger Styles stepped aside. Two burly men armed with Bowie knives burst into the suite.

"What is this all about?" Sam demanded.

Rebecca watched Roger Styles nod at the toughs. Then he closed the door and walked to where she stood. The scowling killers took a few steps toward Sam and raised their knives.

"No!" cried Sam. His hands shot up in front of his face in a futile attempt to stop the downward arc of the heavy blades.

One of the killers stepped behind Sam and slapped a big hand over the shouting shopkeeper's mouth. Then the other man plunged his knife again and again into Sam's suddenly exposed mid-section. Blood gouted from the dying man's many wounds like water through a sieve. It sprayed his murderer and the floor of Styles' suite.

Rebecca felt a wave of nausea wash over her. She reached in her reticule for her revolver. Roger Styles clamped a hand on her wrist.

"No, no," he said, smiling. "Mustn't make any noise."

Sam convulsed violently in the big bandit's strong grasp, then slumped dead on the suite's wooden floor.

Rebecca felt her courage waning. The one gentle person, other than Lone Wolf, who'd treated her with some dignity after her escape lay in a pool of blood at her feet.

"Get him outta here," ordered Styles, his debonair manners gone.

The killers dragged Sam Wade's bleeding corpse from the suite and closed the door. Roger Styles removed the Smith and Wesson from Rebecca's bag.

"It isn't nice for little girls to carry guns, you know," Roger chided.

Rebecca struck at him with her nails and leaped away. She felt the bile rising in the back of her throat. She rubbed away the hurt from her wrist where he'd been clamping his hand like a vice. Then she glared at the smiling, nattily-dressed businessman.

"Who are you?" she demanded.

She watched Roger remove his suit jacket. "I'm a friend of Jake Tulley's," he told her. He fixed Rebecca with an icy stare that made her shiver. "I think ol' Jake'll be glad to see you again after all these years."

"You're . . . you're one of the gang?"

Styles unbuttoned his shirt and laughed. "Honey, I *am* the gang. Hell, I had been the brains behind the gang even before Tulley gave you to the Sioux."

Rebecca's head reeled with the sudden revelation.

"And now," the dapper gang leader announced as he continued to undress, "I'm going to make sure Jake Tulley has a chance to even his score with you. You've killed entirely too many of our men, you know."

Rebecca had been in such a state of distress that only now did she become aware of Roger Styles' state of undress. Her big blue eyes fixed on his naked body and the growing penis he fondled affectionately.

"You see, honey," Styles began as he took a couple of steps toward her. His elongated shaft was full grown now. "We've got a profitable little deal going here. First we get the Sioux stirred up with liquor and guns, then the army will run them the hell out of Dakota Territory. While the lout Tulley and his gang kill off the buffalo for the profit in hides, other of my men will be filling claims on the prime parcels of land in the Black Hills.

"I know exactly where they are," he bragged on. "You see, Jake Tulley and I were with Gen'ral Custer two years ago when he surveyed the area. We made copies of all the land plats. But the government back East is goin' soft on the Indians. We have to get them out to be able to control the land. Once that is accomplished, there's an enormous amount of money to be made selling to the flow of settlers that is bound to come. To say nothing of the gold. Oh, my, you should see the gold Custer's men found. In less than two years, Jake and I will be rolling in more treasure than you've ever dreamed of. Speaking of treasures, I've got one right here for you," he concluded, rapidly stroking his throbbing cock.

Rebecca stepped backward and bumped into a padded chair. She stopped short, her retreat cut off. Roger Styles lunged forward and grabbed her.

Rebecca screamed and he slapped her. The stinging blow to her face brought stars to her eyes. Her slender legs buckled.

"And the best part of the whole deal," Styles went on, holding the struggling girl, "is that I get to sample your wares before I send you on to Tulley. This'll be the first time I've ever fucked a girl who's been laid by the redskins." He reached for her clothing.

"No!" she shouted, pushing against his arms.

His superior strength overpowered her. Within seconds the naked outlaw leader had pulled the split-skirt of her corduroy riding habit down around her knees.

"You filthy bastard," she cried.

Styles flung her across the bed in the next room and finished removing her clothes. His thick, powerful fingers twined in the elastic top of her frilly pink bloomers and ripped them apart, revealing her sparsely-thatched mound. A wild gleam lighted his eyes at the sight. He licked suddenly dry lips and jabbed two stiffened fingers into her dry, unyielding cleft. Rebecca tried to twist away while his other hand moved in a blur, masturbating toward an explosive climax.

Suddenly he reached his peak and his hot substance spattered over her bare abdomen. "Aaaah! Aaaah! Oh, baby, that's just the beginning. You're going to be good to me, I know you are," he panted.

Roughly the hard fingers that impaled her left her aching mons. Roger Styles flung himself atop the struggling girl and began to probe with his still-solid penis. Rebecca fought, her mind revolted by this brutal act. Even the Oglala had not raped her. She bit his ear until blood ran and he cried out, more it seemed in ecstasy than pain. Then he reached his goal.

Like a rod of fire-heated iron, Roger's long, slim cock drove into her resisting body. Rebecca cried out again and again as each inch violated her dry, uncooperative passage. Searing waves of pain set her body afire. When will he stop? her mind clamored. When will he ever stop?

Roger grunted and thrust with savage brutality, his face cushioned between her bare breasts. "Loosen up, honey," he complained. "Let go and enjoy it, 'cause you're gonna get a lot more."

At last he stiffened, his back arched away from her passive, defeated figure, legs trembling. "Aaaah! Ooooh, yes-s-s!" he hissed as his euphoria carried him over the threshold. Slowly he withdrew himself.

"There. Now wasn't that nice? I oughtta flip you over and go in your other side, but I'll save that for next time."

Disgust and a black wave of loathing rose in Rebecca's breast. She felt dirty and disgusted. Sam lay dead, she had been defiled in a manner that not even the Oglala had undertaken to do and her plans for revenge lay in ruin.

"Get up," he snarled. Roger pulled on his clothes.

Rebecca glowered at the respectable-looking criminal genius, hating him, hating herself. She caught a glimpse of her Little Russian on the floor in the next room. White-hot fury at the way Styles had treated her coursed through Rebecca's violated body. She pulled up her skirt, clenched her teeth and vowed to get him if it took all her life.

"Don't think none about gettin' back at me," he said, watching her. It was as though he'd been reading her thoughts. "In a little while you and me are goin' to see Jake Tulley."

She felt a stab of anxiety in her gut.

Suddenly the suite's door swung open. Rebecca's jaw sagged when she glanced into the round, smiling face of her pudgy Uncle Virgil.

"You!" she shouted.

Virgil cackled. "It's been a long time, eh, Becky? She a good piece, Roger?" Thirty year old Virgil Caldwell stood in the doorway of Roger's suite staring at his nineteen-year-old niece. His high-pitched, cackling laughter rang in her ears.

"Wasn't nice what you did to Ezekial," he said. "Doc says he won't ever use that arm again."

Rebecca swallowed hard. Her fury made her speechless.

"A couple of the boys who rode in from Jury Wells a few hours ago told about the fellers you an' your shopkeeper friend done in. Well, that clerk paid for his mistake. Now you'll get yours by goin' to Jake."

Rebecca finished buttoning her jacket. Her hands trembled with useless, suppressed rage. She felt sudden beads of perspiration breaking out on her forehead. Thoughts of being scarred for life by Roger Styles' vile sexual assault burned in her brain.

"So you see, Becky," Styles injected. He had completed dressing and looked mild and harmless in his gray suit. "Crime does pay." He and Uncle Virgil guffawed at his witticism.

Rebecca searched for a way out of her predicament. Everything seemed so hopeless.

SIXTEEN

Lone Wolf heard the Oglala warriors coming long before he saw them. His sensitive ears picked up the drumming of hoofs over the thick sod while he paused to scan the horizon from a small cluster of cottonwood trees that had taken root in an old buffalo wallow. He tied his pony out of sight and lay down in the tall grass, hidden from even the most careful observer.

He held his Sharp 50-120-800 buffalo gun in his right hand and four of his precious fifty rounds in the left. A fifth cartridge nestled in the chamber. He thought of himself as a rock, immovable, a part of the terrain, and tried to make himself small. Slowly the thudding of unshod ponies grew closer.

Three minutes went by while he remained motionless, ignoring even the vicious biting flies that settled on his bare back. Then he heard the Sioux talking lightly about their task.

"Ho, brother! It is nice that Running Snake has trusted us to find the white-eyes and lead them to him."

"Yes. He has promised us each a war band of our own when we rise against the whites. Even now I thirst for their blood."

"It will be soon."

When the two Oglala reached a spot within five paces of Lone Wolf, the former Crow warrior rose from concealment, his Sharps at the ready.

The Sioux warriors reined sharply and began to bring up their weapons.

Lone Wolf shot one long-haired brave in the throat. The screaming warrior fell to the ground, choking on his blood, while the wound spewed crimson on the soil. Before Lone Wolf could reload, the other warrior leaped forward over his pony's withers. His war hatchet whistled past Lone Wolf's face. The big white Indian leaped backward, smashed his rifle into the Oglala's chest. He wanted the man alive. For the moment.

He dropped the empty Sharps and drew his war hatchet. The painted Sioux wielded his own flashing steel tomahawk and began to circle.

"Lone Wolf," spoke the warrior.

"Good afternoon, my brother," Lone Wolf replied in Lakota. "It is a good day to die."

The Oglala circled warily and glared at Lone Wolf. The Sioux's glaring eyes, hawk-like nose and high cheekbones gave him a demonic look.

"I heard you were dead," said the Sioux.

"I will never die."

The Sioux laughed. "You will die soon. You are only a white man in Indian's clothing. The Spirits do not protect such men."

"I've done all right so far."

"You haven't fought me yet."

"Lucky for you I haven't. You fight like a squaw."

Lone Wolf watched the warrior's face harden. He knew calling the brave a squaw was the biggest insult possible.

The lean warrior fumed at him.

"What brings the great Lone Wolf to Oglala hunting grounds?" demanded the Oglala. His hand gripped his war hatchet as though it was Lone Wolf's neck.

"I am looking for the white man known as Jake Tulley."

The lean warrior's eyes narrowed slightly. "I am Lame Bear of the Raven-owners Society. I have killed twenty men in battle, most of them *Kangi* whelps like you. Why do you seek Tulley?"

Lone Wolf thought quickly. "I hear that he trades with the Oglala. The whites don't want me in their towns and I can't go back to the Absaroka after killing Scar-on-Face. So, I want to join up with Jake Tulley."

A slight shift in weight from one foot to the other tipped Lone Wolf a fraction of a second before the Oglala Raven-owner feinted to his right, then made a savage forehand slash at the white Indian's chest with his steel hatchet. Lone Wolf jumped out of the way and his tomahawk whistled in.

It opened a six inch line on Lame Bear's right forearm. The Oglala didn't even grunt. "That seems an unlikely story."

"It is true."

The unreality of the conversation seemed not to impress itself on either man. Grimly they continued their stalking.

"We were on our way to find Tulley's men. They bring more guns and whiskey to us."

"Where?"

"The evil whites have a camp near the buffalo herd. They wait there until told where to bring their rolling wood."

"Will you take me there?"

"No."

They stopped circling for a moment. Suddenly Lame Bear lunged at Lone Wolf.

The brave's hatchet tore into Lone Wolf's buckskin shirt, tearing a gash in his left arm. Hot pain sliced all the way to his shoulder. He turned and ducked another swipe.

Lone Wolf stood firm and punched the warrior with a short, hard left.

Stunned, Lame Bear's eyes rolled up in his head and he fell to the ground. Lone Wolf stepped over to him and raised his tomahawk for the kill. He paused a second, then hurtled the blade down, to slice off the top of Lame Bear's skull. He pulled the steel blade free, wiped it clean on the tail of Lame Bear's loincloth. He retrieved his Sharps and the ammunition and strode briskly toward his pony. Tulley was nearby and he wanted to pay him a visit.

An hour later, Lone Wolf crouched low to the ground, draped in the fluffy hide of a coyote he had killed on the way to find Tulley. Stealthily he sneaked through the tall prairie grass toward the grazing herd and Tulley's camp. He hoped to reconnoiter the camp and report back to Rebecca.

Feeling like a stalking Crow warrior once again, he slithered through the buffalo grass a short fifty yards from the grazing herd. He knew buffalo were never spooked by a solitary coyote. No beast in its right mind would challenge a two thousand pound buffalo that could pound it into jelly in an instant. He kept crawling toward the gang's camp, his Sharp tied over his back by his belt, the ammunition gripped in his hand.

Peering through the shimmering waves of heat that rose from the prairie, Lone Wolf counted at least half a dozen men near the large white tent up ahead.

Then he heard hoofbeats from behind. He froze while the drumming grew louder.

A second later, a bullet tore up the sod close beside his head and he heard a furious spate of shots. Somehow the bandit gang had gotten wise to his ruse and now came after him.

Lone Wolf came to his feet. He turned and ran like hell,

while he struggled awkwardly to get the Sharps off his back and into action. Bullets zipped past his head.

The pounding hoof-beats grew louder. The only direction available to him was into the buffalo herd.

Knowing the animals would object to being interrupted while eating, he braced himself for a sudden attack by one of the massive bulls. He hoped to panic some of the herd into attacking the outlaws, too. It was his only chance.

A big bull at the edge of the herd snorted and started to charge. Lone Wolf glanced at Tulley's men and then at the bull. The animal lumbered toward him, only twenty yards away and gaining rapidly. Lone Wolf went into a crouch and prepared to try an old Crow trick he had seen done several times. Though there were few *old* Crow warriors who tried it more than once.

As the gang neared the restive herd, they reined in their horses. The charging buffalo lowered its horns.

Lone Wolf dropped his rifle and flexed his legs and waited until the last possible moment. Then he drove over the bull's lowered horns and onto its back. He grabbed a handful of fur and straddled the big beast, faced backward. The big bull began to twist and turn. The world whirled and jerked crazily around Lone Wolf. His daring act had bought him a momentary respite from the outlaws.

He felt the buffalo's massive bulk beneath him, the loose hide rolling in an effort to dislodge him. Now he was concerned with being able to get safely off when the time came.

After ten wild seconds that had seemed like hours, Lone Wolf glanced around. He saw the bandits had withdrawn some hundred and fifty yards. He also noticed he was close to where had left his pony. The big buffalo came down stiff-legged and Lone Wolf's kidneys ached. Then the monstrous animal reared high on its hind legs, preparatory to throwing itself over backward. Lone Wolf let go of the bull's shaggy coat and leaped far away into the grass. He rolled to a stop and regained his footing.

The buffalo, glad to be rid of the tormentor on its back, snorted, cast about with its great head, weak eyes seeking its enemy, then returned to the herd. Tulley's killers, noticing Lone Wolf's vulnerability once again, whooped and galloped toward him with weapons raised.

Lone Wolf ran to his pony and grabbed up his bow and quiver. His first sizzling shaft struck the lean owlhoot.

He notched another arrow while the first was still in flight. Tulley's men were within thirty yards. Again the feathered shaft found its target in the chest of a charging hardcase. But the gang kept coming at him. They were now only ten yards away.

A slug nicked his buckskins. Another flew past his head.

Finally two men charged to within ten feet of him and hurled themselves from their mounts. The gunmen slammed into Lone Wolf and knocked the wind from his lungs.

He landed heavily on the grass. The bandits dropped beside him. He struggled to his feet and caught a blur of movement out of the corner of his eye. Then a heavy revolver barrel smashed against his skull.

A brilliant burst of light turned to blackness and a shattering pain radiated from the back of his head.

Lone Wolf's legs turned to water as he started to fall. The hard-packed Dakota prairie rose up and smacked him in the face.

He lay unconscious where he fell.

When Lone Wolf recovered, his head felt like it had been caught in a buffalo stampede. Peering through a curtain of pain, he quickly discovered his arms and ankles were lashed to a ten-foot high wooden cross.

The herd grazed a hundred yards to his left and the outlaw camp shimmered in the heat, fifty yards to his right. He even saw his pony tethered near Tulley's white tent.

"He's comin' around, Jake," called a nearby voice.

Lone Wolf focused his eyes on an approaching man with a bowler hat. He recognized Tulley from seeing the gang at the settler's house back on the trail.

"You're the white Injun who killed some of my boys back at the Silver Wing," Tulley growled. The strutting bandit stepped up to the cross and struck Lone Wolf in the side.

A grunt escaped Lone Wolf's lips. "If you'd been there I would've killed you, too," he snarled in reply. He winced as a shaft of pain shot down his neck and into his arms.

Tulley laughed. "Purty brave words for a man about to die. I wanted to finish you off, but our Injun friend here said it was bad medicine to kill a great warrior while he was unconscious." Tulley hooked a thumb toward the squat form of Running Snake.

Good old Indian superstitions, thought Lone Wolf.

"Hell, Jake," said Luke Wellington. The scar-faced gunhawk ambled over to the cross. "He don't look like no great warrior to me."

The assembled badmen guffawed. Tulley continued.

"So I told them Sioux bastards that I'd let you die out on the prairie. Maybe the buffalo'll knock you down and stomp the shit outta ya."

"If the wolves don't get him first," offered Wellington.

"You're very kind," Lone Wolf replied through stretched lips.

"That's me," Tulley returned glibly. He turned and began to walk toward the campsite. "Kind ol' Jake Tulley, right boys?"

"You tell 'em boss!" one hardcase exclaimed through a giggle, and followed Tulley to camp.

Lone Wolf licked his parched lips and tried to think of a way to escape. He watched Tulley walk to his tent. Another shaft of pain from his head wound sliced through his neck.

He wondered which would be worse, buffalo or wolves.

SEVENTEEN

Filing out of Roger Styles' hotel suite and down the stairs, Rebecca controlled a sudden urge to turn around and gouge out her Uncle Virgil's eyes. She was on her way to Jake Tulley—though not the way she wanted it. Hoping Lone Wolf would somehow spot her dilemma, she decided to wait for a more propitious moment to try an escape.

"Remember, one false move an' I'll cut you down with your own little peashooter," warned Styles.

The ride out of Deer Creek alongside Roger Styles, Uncle Virgil and the two killers who'd butchered Sam Wade left Rebecca wondering if she really was on her way to Jake Tulley. These hardened, vicious men might simply rape her a few times and leave her dead on the searing plains.

Rebecca ached. The small band of brigands had made camp an hour before sundown, a mile or so over the line into Dakota Territory by her reckoning. Roger had not even offered her to the other men. He had taken her hand and roughly jerked her to her feet, a wild light of lust in his eyes. She struggled vainly against him while he dragged her tc a shallow creek that flowed through a defile cut in the grassland.

Without a word, he tore off her clothes and pushed her into the water. Then he quickly disrobed and joined her. Her heart ached with memory of her first encounter with Four Horns.

"Oooh, this is going to be good," he cooed to her, his huge phallus rising above the waist-deep water, its swollen head a purple-red serpent's face. Rebecca shrank from him, her hands clawed, ready to strike. "Yeah," Roger moaned. "That's it. Hurt me a little. Scratch my back and kick me in the balls. I love it that way. Make me hurt," he pleaded.

Suddenly Rebecca realized this sorry excuse for a man could not enjoy normal sex. If he didn't rape, he had to have pain to reach fulfillment. A wave of confidence washed over her.

"No. I want to be nice to you. Come here and let me suck that beautiful thing. Oh, please. I want you so much." Rebecca wanted to gag at the distasteful words she forced from her lips, but her elation grew when she saw the effect.

Roger's erection faded and his face clouded. In one clumsy stride he reached her and swung a hairy-backed hand that connected with her cheek. "Bitch!" he shrieked. "You dirty bitch. You spoiled it."

He hit her over and over, until blood ran from her nose and a split lip, yet his manhood remained a flaccid skin sack, dangling between his legs. At last, with a wretched sob, Roger turned from punching her and slogged out of the water. She spent the rest of the night aching, but in peace.

They hit the trail at first light. After hours of endless riding across the sun-drenched prairie, Rebecca and her escort reined in their horses on a rocky ridge. They scanned a huge buffalo herd on the plains below. Suddenly she knew where they had taken her.

"Ain't that purty?" Virgil asked.

"Money on the hoof," remarked Styles, humoring his subordinates.

Rebecca tried to control her temperamental Indian pony. She glanced at the small knot of rifle-toting gunmen off to one side of the herd. Her heartbeat quickened when she realized Bitter Creek Jake Tulley was probably among them.

"About ready to meet your old friend, Jake?" asked Styles. He laughed harshly. "We sent word you were alive. Let's see if Jake has arranged everything for your welcome."

"Hell," Virgil began, giving Rebecca a contemplative, lustful look. "I can still remember that day when we done gave Hannah and Becky here to the Sioux. I'd been hankerin' ta fuck her since she turned eleven an' got some bumps on her chest. But it was them damned redsticks who got to her first."

"Your sister, Hannah, is dead," Rebecca told him flatly.

Virgil merely shrugged his heavy shoulders. "That's part of the game. Hell, wouldn't you do the same thing to save your hide?"

Rebecca's anger boiled up again.

"Come on," Styles commanded. "We're wastin' time."

The cantering group reached the camp within a few minutes. Rebecca reined in her horse as Jake Tulley came walking haughtily over to her. The outlaw leader smiled broadly.

She felt a cold tremor of revulsion sweep through her stomach. She quickly scanned the gang leader's face, pencil-thin moustache, and the black English bowler he had tipped arrogantly at Rebecca and her mother a moment before he left them for the Indians.

"Well, well," Tulley gloated. He walked up to Rebecca's pony and looked up at her. "It's so nice of you to come and visit me after all these years."

His banter struck his men with hilarity. "And I hear you

are interested in givin' me an' my boys a little of what you dished out to the Oglala." His evil gray eyes were aglow with amusement.

The gang members roared with renewed humor.

"You haven't changed any," Rebecca said tightly.

"Oh, hell no. Life's been good to me."

Then, while Tulley turned and strode back to his white Sibley tent, Rebecca dismounted along with Styles and Uncle Virgil. Their henchmen led the horses away.

"Sit down, you slut!" snapped Virgil.

"Don't talk to your pretty little niece that way, Virgil," Roger Styles remarked. He walked toward Tulley's tent. "The little bitch's a pretty good lay. Treat her with respect, ain't that right, honey?"

Virgil cackled. Rebecca sat heavily on the grass. She licked parched lips. Casually she scanned the gang's makeshift campsite for a possible escape route when she spotted Lone Wolf tied to a wooden cross a short distance away.

She knew she had to take action soon.

Noticing only six gunmen in camp, besides Uncle Virgil, Styles and Tulley, Rebecca began to formulate a plan. She needed Lone Wolf's help if she hoped to ever get away from the gang. She would have to free him first.

She rose quickly and sidled over to Roger Styles. He stood by himself, drinking coffee behind the big tent. Her hand touched the perverted gang leader's arm. He turned sharply and looked at her.

"Oh, Roger," she said sweetly, "I'm sorry for the way I acted back at the creek . . . and I'd like to make it up to you."

Styles uttered a bitter laugh. "What in hell are you talkin' about?"

Rebecca grabbed his crotch and began to tightly squeeze his genitals through the material of his pants. She felt his loins tighten.

"You said you liked it to hurt. Am I doing it right now?"

Styles moaned and thrust his swelling penis toward her.

"Honey, you sure know how to get a man real horny."

"How's about you and me goin' to those trees behind camp for a little . . . farewell, huh? I mean, how else can I make it up to you?"

Styles beamed. "You're serious, ain't ya, honey?"

"Of course!" She jerked purposefully on his rigid shaft.

Styles groaned. "Why not? You're a helluva lay when you act right."

They hurried quickly away from the camp. Nobody seemed to notice. The unlikely couple reached some nearby cottonwoods and stopped to face each other. Her anger flared. Vivid images of Styles' brutal rape flashed before her eyes. Other flashes of her life with the Sioux urged her on. Taking a cue from Lone Wolf's trick of striking before the enemy had a chance to set up a defense, Rebecca reared back and kicked the dapper monster in the balls.

"Take that, *honey!*" she snarled.

Styles' soft blue eyes bulged as he sucked in air. The startled outlaw boss doubled over in pain and tumbled to the grass, his hands at his groin.

Rebecca reached down and grabbed his Remington and a long hunting knife. She turned and looked at the distant gang.

Most of them ambled around camp, killing time. They speculated loudly as to how long it would take the white Indian to die. Rebecca saw her opportunity and raced from the trees.

She dashed through the waving buffalo grass toward Lone Wolf. Running faster than she ever had before, she reached him within seconds. As she did, the gang became aware of her actions.

Lone Wolf looked down at her, not quite believing. "Re-Rebecca, how . . . what . . .?"

She reached up with Styles' hunting knife and sliced the rawhide cords that bound him. The big white warrior tumbled to the ground as a bullet whacked into the cross.

"Here come Tulley's killers," Rebecca cried.

Lone Wolf worked to rub circulation back into his arms and studied the terrain. A sickle-shaped ridge split part of the herd off from the rest, wrapped around in a manner that formed a natural channel toward Tulley's camp.

Rebecca's head swiveled from one direction to the other. The buffalo to one side, Tulley's gunhawks on the other.

"How do we get out of here?"

"Do you want to stampede that herd?"

She smiled eagerly. "Toward Tulley and his men? I'd love to. While I'm spooking the herd, you can be going after your pony and weapons."

Lone Wolf grinned. "Smart girl."

He turned and began to run through the tall grass, while Rebecca dashed in the direction of the grazing buffalo.

Within seconds she reached the outer edge of the milling creatures. She began to wave her arms and yell like a frenzied whore. Her scare tactics produced the desired result. First one of the furry beasts snorted and bolted sideways. Then a fat cow bellowed and leaped away from the dimly perceived creature who threatened her. The sentry bulls on that side bellowed in distress and three hundred buffalo exploded in a lightning dash.

Billows of dust choked the air as seven hundred fifty thousand pounds of powerful flesh thundered over the prairie. The leaders struck the crescent rise and swung in the direction of Tulley's camp. The ground beneath Rebecca's feet vibrated to the cataclysmic pounding of the myriad hard hoofs only fifty yards away from her.

With the horrified whinnies of horses strumming her taut nerves, Rebecca turned toward the gang and instantly focused on Bitter Creek Jake. He sawed frantically at the reins of his roan horse and yelled over the din. Already his terrified men fled in every direction.

Except for Virgil. He appeared out of the dust next to Rebecca. "I'm taking you with me," he growled. He grabbed her slender left arm and began to haul her toward the horses.

"Let go of me," she snapped, pulling free.

"You're a danger to me, you half-breed slut!"

"You're a dead man, Virgil," she told him in a deadly shout over the deafening clamor of the stampeding beasts. He started a sneering retort, then froze.

Until then, Virgil had not seen Roger's Remington in her right hand. Now he stared at the black .44 caliber hole in its muzzle. His face washed white and even though he could not hear the hammer ratchet back, he saw the cylinder rotate when Rebecca cocked the heavy pistol.

"Why you bitch!" growled her uncle. The pudgy killer leaped forward.

Rebecca fired the Remington.

A bullet slammed into Virgil's broad, fleshy face. The hot slug exited at the back of his head in a shower of blood and brain matter. Rebecca ignored the gore and stepped back from her dead uncle. He slumped to the prairie.

She looked at the body. "To hell with you, Uncle Virgil," she snarled, meaning every word.

The hurtling buffalo closed in on the camp and beyond it, the horses.

With time running out, Rebecca ran toward the deserted outlaw camp. She saw Roger Styles, still holding his groin, climb onto the back of his horse and race away after the other gang members. Rebecca grabbed up the reins and leaped atop her nervous pony. She dug her heels into its ribs. She peered through the clouds of throat-clogging dust being kicked into the air by the coursing buffalo. Suddenly she spotted Jake Tulley holding onto his bowler hat with one hand and racing to safety.

So close, yet so far.

Gagging on the billowing clouds of dust, Rebecca slapped her painted pony on its rump and pounded after him. The rampaging buffalo herd closed rapidly on them both. She rode with all her skill to keep ahead of the animals.

Rebecca hunkered against the pony's mane for more speed like she'd been taught. She glanced at Jake Tulley a few yards ahead and watched him turn in his saddle. His six-shooter appeared in his hand.

She saw two puffs of white smoke. Then she heard a bullet zip past her head.

Behind Rebecca the charging buffalo blanketed the prairie like a giant, furry Indian robe that threatened to overtake her. She glanced behind and looked into the beady red eyes of the leaders. Head front again, she lifted the heavy Remington and returned Tulley's fire. The unfamiliar revolver bucked in her hand, stinging her palm, and the slug went wide of its mark.

Out of the corner of her eye, Rebecca spotted Lone Wolf straining toward her. His blond ridge of hair blew in the breeze as he rode at an angle across the front of the panicked beasts.

All the while, Rebecca raced after Jake Tulley. Once more she fired, only to see her bullet miss the target.

Inexorably, the buffalo closed in on her.

Lone Wolf appeared from out of the dust. "Follow me!"

"But Tulley," she protested over the noise.

"Forget about him for now. The buffalo are too close."

"I have to get Tulley."

The next instant, the leaders of the herd passed within twenty yards of her. She saw them and reined sharply to the left. An experienced horsewoman, she managed to keep her seat when her foam-flecked pony's chest crashed into Lone Wolf's surging mount.

With a sudden kick to the flanks of his wild-eyed, highly trained Indian pony, Lone Wolf leaped free of Rebecca and gave her vital room.

Rebecca's pony whinnied sharply and stumbled before regaining stride.

"Hold on!" Lone Wolf shouted.

"This way."

Coaxing the most speed possible from their laboring ponies the big white warrior and Rebecca shot across the dusty plain in a widening angle away from the buffalo. They reached cover in some scraggly cottonwood trees a brief moment before the stampeding herd would have pounded them into jelly.

Rampaging buffalo thundered past while the ground shook like an earthquake. The leading edge of the crazed beasts struck the camp. Tulley's big white tent shuddered and came billowing down. The cook, unable to mount in time, shrieked while the furred animals smashed him into a wet pulp. His hideous cries went unheard in the tumult.

Rebecca grabbed Lone Wolf and gasped for air.

"I . . . almost . . . had . . . Tulley," she said through her labored breathing.

"And the buffalo almost had you."

The noise slowly began to subside.

"Uncle Virgil is dead," she told him, her breathing returning to normal. Her heart slowly calmed after her incredibly close call with death.

Lone Wolf nodded. "Are you finished now?"

She looked at her buckskin-clad companion. "I think you know better than that," she said levelly, her voice hardening. "I won't be finished until they're all dead. I owe that much to my mother's memory. And to myself."

The last of the buffalo galloped past and dust began to settle. Rebecca shuddered and stared at the ravaged prairie.

She knew revenge for the horrible years she'd spent in the Oglala camp was the only thing that mattered to her now. Whatever the cost to her personally, she would avenge herself and her mother's savage handling by the Indians. She would make Tulley and the others pay for her wasted years. And now Roger Styles, the man who'd raped her, had been added to her list of targets. Her seething anger caused her to gnash her teeth.

"Let's go," she said tightly.

EIGHTEEN

Two nights later, in Deer Creek, Rebecca stood peering through the gathering dusk at gray-haired Orville Styles. Her grandfather's roly-poly old friend was visibly distraught at hearing about his dapper son's nefarious schemes. Now he was trying to make it up to Rebecca.

"I never had any idea that Roger was mixed up with Tulley and his ilk." He puffed on a hand-rolled cigar. "When I heard about Roger's alliance with Tulley from some hunting buddies who happened to see the buffalo stampede I was astonished. I've decided to disinherit him as my son. Roger had me completely fooled. And . . . and I feel the fool for it."

Rebecca, still dressed in the dead settler woman's corduroy riding habit, smiled weakly. "I believe you, Mr. Styles," she replied. "You son seems to have the ability to trick people with his charm."

"I . . . I want to make it up to you in some way," he offered.

"That's not necessary," she quickly refused. It was her campaign of vengeance and Rebecca wanted to involve as

222

few people as possible.

The memory of Sam Wade made her swallow hard.

"But you must need something," insisted Styles.

Rebecca pursed her lips. "Well, my pony was lamed in the buffalo stampede. And I don't fancy walking after Jake Tulley and his boys."

Orville Styles' face lighted with excitement and he snapped his fingers. "I've got just the animal for you," he declared. "Wait here an' I'll be right back."

Within minutes the gray-haired farmer emerged from the nearby livery stable leading the most beautiful sorrel gelding Rebecca had ever seen.

"His name's Ike and he's the fastest horse on my spread."

"For me?" Rebecca squeaked, astounded. Her blue eyes widened in appreciation of the magnificent animal.

"For your mission of vengeance."

"I . . . I don't know what to say, 'cept, thank you."

"That's words enough. Just ride him in good health," replied the cigar-smoking farmer. Styles helped her up into the fancily-decorated saddle. "And may he help you get what you want."

Rebecca felt the bulk of the big horse beneath her and smiled. "He's beautiful."

"And so are you, Rebecca," said Orville Styles. Then he reached into his pocket. "Now here's something else I want you to have," he said. He pressed one hundred dollars in double-eagles into Rebecca's soft little hand.

"No. I . . . I can't take this."

"Yes you can. As a favor to an old friend of your grandaddy."

"But . . ."

"After livin' with them Oglala for five years, you'll need some money to help you become a white woman again, don't you think?" He winked at her.

For an instant, Rebecca's stomach froze. "You know . . . about me?"

Orville Styles smiled warmly. "Let's just say I suspected as much." The twinkle in his eye increased. "Now here's something else that belongs to you." He handed her a voucher slip, headed, "State of Nebraska."

"What is this?"

"Those low-life scum that hang out with Tulley all have fliers out on 'em. There's eight hundred dollars the sheriff said for me to give you for the ones you done in."

"But . . . then why the money you gave me?"

"Figgered if I didn't get mine in first, you might turn it down. Only one thing I ask. If you catch up with that worthless Roger . . . well . . . just don't tell me what happens."

"Mr. Styles," Rebecca began, tears welling in her eyes.

"Now, you better hit the road before it gets too dark."

"I . . . I really thank you. I haven't met too many kind people in the past few years."

Styles reached up and patted her hand. "Good luck," he said. "And take care of Ike."

"I will," she promised. She wiped away a vagrant tear. "And I'll be fine, too. Back in the Oglala camp my mother told me to be strong. I can do that now. And, I'm not going to give up 'till I avenge us both."

"May God go with you," Styles murmured.

Rebecca turned the head of her big horse and trotted out of town. On the outskirts of Deer Creek she saw Lone Wolf sitting astride his painted pony. The tall white warrior's blond ridge of hair ruffled slightly in the breeze. Reining in Ike before she reached Lone Wolf, Rebecca turned on her creaking, unfamiliar saddle and waved goodbye to the distant, lonely figure of Orville Styles.

Then she trotted onto the darkening prairie.

She still had some scores to settle.